"Readers will fervently hope that Anderson has more novels in her because this one is a winner."

– Kirkus Reviews (starred review)

RUNNING from MOLOKA`I

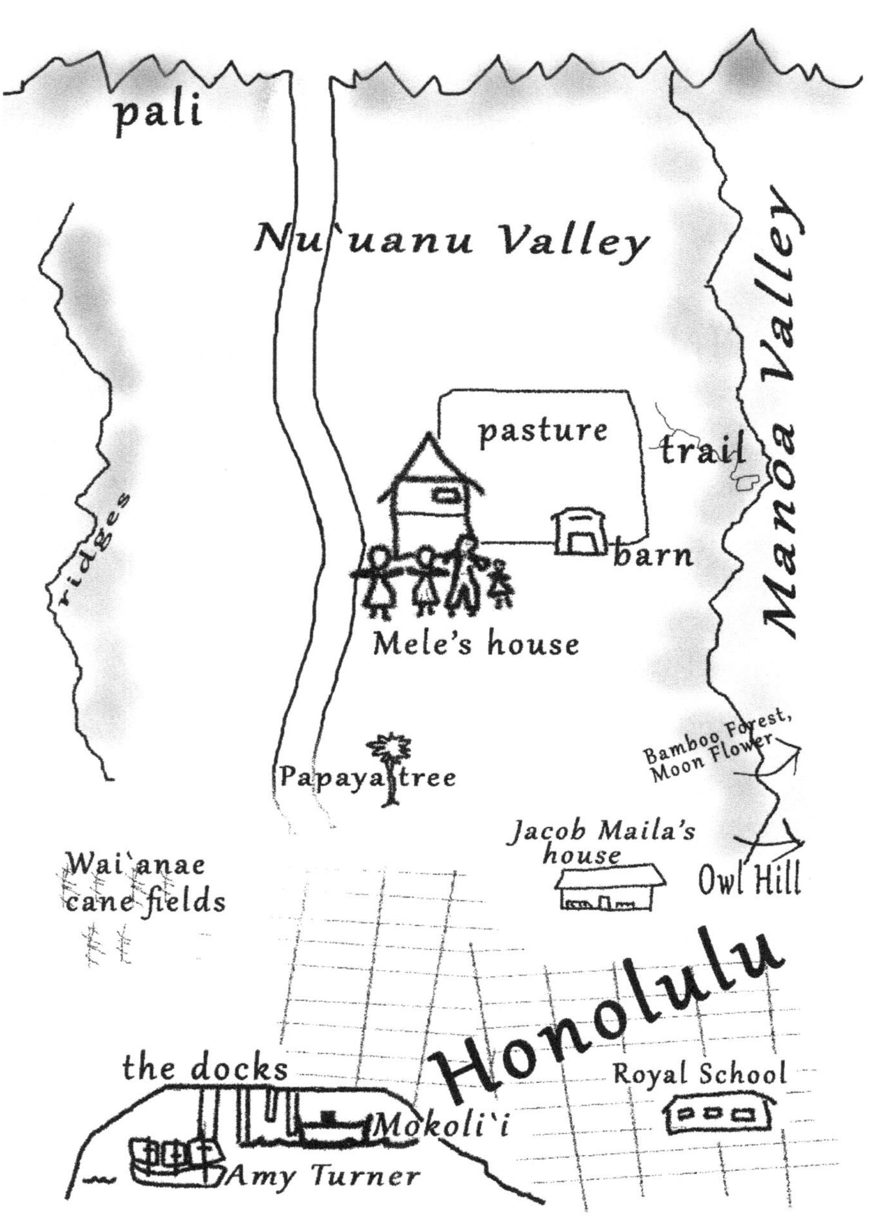
pali
Nu`uanu Valley
Manoa Valley
pasture
trail
barn
ridges
Mele's house
Papaya tree
Bamboo Forest,
Moon Flower
Jacob Maila's
house
Owl Hill
Wai`anae
cane fields
Honolulu
the docks
Royal School
Mokoli`i
Amy Turner

RUNNING from MOLOKA`I

Jill P. Anderson

RUNNING FROM MOLOKA`I

Running from Moloka`i is a work of historical fiction. Numerous characters are actual historical figures, and numerous events are actual historical events. They are represented here to the best of the author's ability given available research. Other characters are fictionalized; any resemblance to actual persons, living or dead, is coincidental. Some story events are based on non-specific events known to have occurred in this historical time.

All photos of historical figures are in public domain.

Cover art: "Tunnels of Moonlight" by Jenifer Prince, Maui, Hawaii
www.jeniferprince.com

Cover and book Design: Love Song Graphics

ISBN 978-1-7354906-0-1

Library of Congress Number:
2020911944

Anderson, Jill P.
Running from Moloka`i
Includes bibliographical and supplemental references
ISBN 978-1-7354906-0-1 (softcover)
ISBN 978-1-7354906-1-8 (ebook)
1. Historical fiction 2. Hawaiian history 3. Leprosy 4. Hansen's Disease 5. Moloka`i 6. Exile 7. Deadly diseases 8. Kalaupapa

Printed in the United States of America, First Edition 2020
Love Song Graphics, Gig Harbor, WA
For permissions: www.jill-anderson.com

Dedicated to
Bernard Punikai`a

whose childhood was stolen by a small mark on his cheek.
Thank you for trusting me and for giving your
blessing to this book.

ACKNOWLEDGEMENTS

My sincere thanks and gratitude to those who helped and supported me in bringing this to the light of day. "I could not have done it without you," seems trite, but when I say it to Kathy Williams, it is absolutely true. My appreciation to Kathy Saideman for your keen eye in developmental editing and again to Kathy Williams for your sharp line editing. To my beta readers—Jim Lawry, Bill Wolf, Bill Brown, Lanihuli Freidenburg, and Bob Julyan—thank you so much for slogging through a far from polished version and for your suggestions. To Jane McPhetres Johnson for proofreading, thank you. Also to Lanihuli Freidenburg—I admire your fluency in Hawaiian and so appreciate your gentle guidance and help with the language. Mahalo!

My appreciation also to the generosity of librarians and curators at Univ. of Hawaii – Manoa, Bishop Museum, Punahoa School, the Hawaii State Archives, and the Hawaiian Historical Society.

CONTENTS

PROLOGUE

I was a barefoot girl with a Hawaiian mama and a white papa, longing for a moment that would define me. I wanted a shiny moment, like when the firebrand is tossed over the cliff and lights up the night sky!

Instead, I was sent a kona wind.

So was Keahi, the boy I loved.

When this happens, you board up your house and hold your breath. The dancing pili grass is hardly affected by such a gale. But a tree, half-uprooted and already hanging over a cliff? It will never be the same. How can the wind know how desperately the tree clings to the only soil it has ever known? The wind merely yanks the tree away and lets it fall, with no plan for what will happen next.

An island boy named Jacob Maila was my kona wind. I had never met him. He came into my life, tore me from the security of my childhood beliefs, and was gone. It took Jacob Maila and Manu—Manu, who had never touched a piece of silk—to show me that some things could not be fixed by the father I adored. My white, physician father. Mama was right—he was not God. He was only a man standing out in the pasture with the moon lighting up his shirt as he bent over, shaking, after Mimo was taken.

At first, I saw myself as separate from those hidden by their families. After all, they had leprosy while I had the protection of my white blood. But after Jacob Maila, the lines began to blur. Papa, Keahi, me, those hidden by loved ones, those taken—we were all clinging to our own cliffs. Some died, some held their breath, some lived to find redemption.

By the end of that year, I felt as if I had done all of these.

Chapter 1

UNDER THE CHINESE LANTERNS

Honolulu, Hawai`i

When I was a keiki, a little child, I lived in a house that changed colors. Most of the time our house was white, the color of the ship that brought Papa from Boston to the islands when he was a boy. But as soon as Papa left the house—as soon as he straightened his vest and picked up his satchel, as soon as he harnessed Hoku to the buggy and rounded the `ōhi`a trees that gathered as if sharing a secret where our road starts down the valley—our house turned brown. I do not mean the brown of warm bread pulled from Mama's cook stove. I mean the barefoot brown the early missionaries were never able to get rid of, no matter how hard they tried.

On one of those long-ago mornings, when Papa had left and the house was brown as a calabash, I was in our garden weeding the beans. Mama and her sister Kalina had knotted their holokū dresses, waded into the water, and they were working in the taro patch. I overheard them talking.

"He needs to be moved." Aunty Kalina's voice was low.

I stayed quiet behind the stalks of ripening beans.

Mama stood up, shook water from her hands, and dried them on her dress. "So soon?" she asked.

I inched closer.

Aunty Kalina squinted toward the pali cliffs at the upper end of our valley. She pulled the back of a hand across her forehead.

"We can't let them find him," she said.

I stepped back.

That same evening was sweet as mint in hanging pots, and warm, so Papa and I had moved from the parlor to the lānai, our outdoor brick terrace, to do my lessons. Mama and my grandma Tūtū sat at a short wooden table mixing herbs for a dye. They left for Papa and me the place I loved to sit, the stuffed jute sofa. Finally Papa said the words I had waited all day to hear:

"It's time to hang the Chinese lanterns."

Standing on a crate, Papa lifted a lantern to the lower branches of the banyan tree in the center of our lānai. I wrapped around his leg the way wisteria clings to a fence, thinking I was holding him up.

When we finished, Papa lifted me up and we walked back and forth admiring our work: the Chinese lanterns hung in twinkling strands from the porch to the banyan tree. For each little circle of shining light, I made a wish. On one light I wished grandma Tūtū's eyesight would get better. On another I wished never to lose the peacock feather given to me by a man whose name I did not know, but I called him Manu, for the **`ō`ō** bird.

The brightest light of all was near the porch. On this light I simply giggled and said, "Keahi,"—the name of a boy who lived at the lower end of our valley. When our families had picnics at the beach together, he raced along the shore pretending to be the white stallion that ran wild on the Big Island. But he always ended up next to me in Tūtū's lap. My wish? That I would never be far from the sound of Keahi's laughter.

Many of my lessons with Papa were about other lands. I imagined elegant arches in England where the queen sat having tea, or magical China where a Moon Bear might sit under a mulberry tree scratching its tummy. At other times, Papa wrote stories about our island of O`ahu. Slowly, so I could read along with him, he ran his finger under the words, always in English. I sat beside him and leaned into the hospital smell of his white cotton shirt; he leaned into the light of the oil lamp.

From the moment I found a torn corner of a map blown into our pasture, I had been pestering Papa to make a drawing of our valley. Even at that age, all those years ago, Papa encouraged me to be strong and ask for what I wanted.

"I was born in this valley!" I exclaimed, wiping a spot of dirt from the scrap of paper. It is said that when the sun shines on Nu`uanu Valley, the whole island is sunny—I liked to think that was true of the whole world.

"That's right," said Papa. "Tūtū gathered up a bundle of herbs that were drying on the kitchen table and out you came. Splash, plop, right into my arms!"

Mama tells the story differently. I was born between seasons, she says, in the early morning when turtle clouds hung low in the sky, and a breathy fog whispered through the tulip trees. Tūtū named me "Mele," Hawaiian for "song."

Papa brought a large piece of butcher paper and smoothed it on a wooden plank laid across his lap.

"Here we go," he said, "a map for my girl of a hundred questions. And she will be worse when she turns six!"

I wiggled closer.

"Where should I start?" he asked.

"The ridges!"

I looked up past the Chinese lanterns to the place where I knew the ridge on our side of the valley came closest to our house, but all I saw were faint lines of sleepy gray. When I looked back, Papa had drawn two long wiggly lines, one on each side of the paper.

"Is that the pali, the cliffs?" I asked, pointing to the bottom of the butcher paper.

"No, that's where Honolulu would be. The pali is the other way. The top of the valley is at the top of the paper." Across the top he scribbled the jagged pali, where treacherous cliffs dropped straight down to the other side of the islands. To me, the lines looked like shark's teeth. Next came trees marching along the ridges.

"Why are there ridges in one place, but not another place?" I asked.

"A question you would ask," he said. "Maybe the land started out wanting to be a ridge, but then changed its mind and decided to be a valley. And in between, it was a little confused."

That satisfied me. *Papa would never be confused.*

Below the ridges he scribbled a row of tiny elbows. I was glad for a chance to show Papa what Mama had taught me.

"The ravines!" I explained proudly, "where the bird catchers hang their snares."

"Kāwili manu." Without looking up, Mama had reminded me of the Hawaiian name for the bird catchers. "Hawaiian girl ought to know her own language." She and Tūtū were making a gourd whistle for Keahi's sixth birthday. Mama cut the tip end of a tiny gourd to make a blowing hole. Then she carved three small holes along one side. Tūtū worked on the stain, mixing water and bruised herbs in a small calabash.

"I'm a bad artist, you know," said Papa. "You can't expect too much." He winked at me.

"But you're a good doctor!" I sat up tall, feeling proud of him. "You are going to cure *all* the Hawaiians of *all* the foreign diseases. I am sure of it."

Papa glanced at Mama. She looked away.

Papa's pencil moved again. He drew Nu`uanu Road going up the middle of the valley. Half-way up the paper, our two-story house appeared as if by magic. He did not draw Nu`uanu stream, where Keahi and I played, or the barn or pasture. But I knew they were there.

I touched the paper, wondering.

Something was missing.

I leaned forward in the light of the oil lamp and studied the map intently. I ran my finger along the butcher paper. Past the drawing of our house. Along Nu`uanu Road. It did not seem right—that is what Tūtū said. Who would bury their bones? Who would sing the songs? I touched the drawing where the valley began to narrow. Was that the place? Maybe farther up the valley.

"Now draw the people," I said.

He drew Mama, Tūtū, himself, and me, all standing in front of our clapboard house. My brother Pōki`i was not yet born. Above us was the small window of my bedroom.

I shook my head.

"No, Papa. The *other* people. The people *hiding*. Draw them, too."

The gourd whistle slipped from Mama's hand, making a tiny hollow sound on the bricks. Tūtū took a quick breath.

Papa's hand went still.

"What people hiding?" he asked.

I took the pencil from Papa and made stick drawings of people. One was part-way up a ridge. Another in a ravine. When I overheard Aunty Kalina talk about them, she never said where they were, or who they were. But I sensed that she knew these things.

On each stick figure I drew a sad face. Then lines to show tears running down. I drew hands, then hesitated. I turned the pencil around.

Then I erased the fingers.

Papa looked at me like he had just stumbled on a rock he had not seen.

"The *lepers*!" I said. "The ones hiding in the hills."

Back and forth he looked, from one stick figure to another. He turned to look at Mama, but she was leaning over to reach for Keahi's gourd whistle. Tūtū pulled the bottom of her dress into her lap, crushing its hem—her way of holding her breath.

I dug my bare toes into the hiding coolness of mossy bricks, not understanding why the air was still, why the smells of the evening were gone, why everyone was quiet. Mama dipped her broad thumb into the mixture of herbs and scooped a bit of stain into the tiny gourd. She slowly rubbed the mixture into the design she had cut on the outside of Keahi's gourd whistle: a fish hook with waves on both sides.

"Don't you worry, Mele," she said. Her voice was soft as cream.

Every native Hawaiian child knew about Moloka`i. After that night on the lānai, when I asked Mama to tell me more about the island, her answer was always the same: "The dry eyes of your papa, the wet eyes of your mama." When I asked

up and stomped down, will follow me through my whole life even if my face is never wet from tears again. Spreading out from the grave in every direction, and on the other side of the fence behind it, is a sea of faded white crosses. There are more stories than people left to tell them.

Gonggg...gonggg. I look down the valley to white church spires rising above a canopy of green. The ringing bells of Kawaiha`o Church will always remind me of the day earlier this year when I received a letter with the best possible news.

Papa and I were coming home from Honolulu. Locals just called it "town."

"Something arrived today." Papa's words had floated across the fragrant smell of hibiscus wrapping porches along Nu`uanu Avenue. Hoku shook his bridle and plodded along the dusty street, pulling our buggy toward the valley. Overhead, a plover slanted and leveled toward a small flock, finding a welcome in the trade winds that blew across the islands.

"For you," he said, grinning as he pulled an envelope from his vest.

I felt a smile begin. On the front, in the upper left corner, was a pencil drawing of a small gourd whistle. Below it were two words: "It's me."

Several months before, Keahi had gone to the neighboring island of Maui to help his uncle who, together with a Chinaman, owned a small noodle factory on the dusty main street of Lāhainā. The *Kilauea* was the little steamer that carried him to Maui and would bring him back to O`ahu. The vessel chugs back and forth between the islands, carrying chickens and mail and cargo. It stitches across the sea, sewing people to new lives as families sleep on wet decks through the foggy night, wrapping their keiki in their arms. I imagined the deck smelling as it had when Papa once took me on the

Kilauea—of chicken feed and sweat, of air tasting like salt hanging from old ropes.

I felt a flush rise in my cheeks as I tore open the letter.

Aloha, Mele!

Are you doing okay? We are all good here! We sell lots of noodles every day now. My uncle says I am magic for buying, that customers only want to come say hello to Keahi. But I think they want to buy noodles too. The Chinaman and I tell jokes every day now. At first, he only looked down and would not speak to me. Now we laugh good. Yesterday he laughed so hard his hat fell into the vat and came out with noodles all over it.

My aunty talked to my uncle and told him. I have missed too much school, she said. So, I will come back to O`ahu. She says I can go to Royal School. Where John and Hoaloha go! My uncle said ok, he will send me.

Is your Papa still teaching you at home? Maybe someday you will be able to go to school. Maybe Royal School with me?

Give my Aloha to Tūtū and your family.

Aloha, Keahi

I stroked the drawing of the small whistle. Sometimes a lie just falls out of a girl's mouth.

"Only Keahi."

"Of course," said Papa. He flicked the reins, and Hoku picked up his pace. "Just like Keahi is over on Maui, stirring noodles in a big vat, thinking of how your hair lifts in a breeze, and saying to himself, 'Only Mele.'"

My chest, throat, and face—I felt them all go pink. But I let Papa wrap an arm around me and give me a quick hug.

"You two!" he said. "Your mama and I have seen this coming for a long time."

When you want Papa to think an idea is his own, you need to plant tiny seeds in wandering circles, and not stomp them into the ground. The best time to approach him is during a storm, when he is distracted by the sound of branches skittering across the roof. So it was unfortunate that I decided on a sunny day, without a drop of rain falling from the sky, that I could wait no longer. I glanced across the parlor to where Papa sat reading files from the hospital.

"Papa?" I kept my voice calm.

He continued reading. "Yes?"

"We've been missing some of my lessons lately."

"Not too many. You catch up quickly." He kept reading.

"I know how busy you are!" I wanted to appear considerate.

"Not at all," he murmured.

I felt like a popped jellyfish! But Uncle Elia says I need to practice the art of being a soft branch the wind can go around.

"And now that you and Kalina are training doctors on Kaua`i—"

He glanced at me over the narrow rim of his reading glasses.

"You're far ahead of grade level, Mele. And your English can match that of any doctor on the staff. You can read every newspaper in the kingdom—or in Boston for that matter."

I left the parlor, wondering if Papa would teach me at home forever.

A few evenings later, I sat at supper listening to the gecko scamper up and down the back of the metal stovepipe. It did this almost every evening. From my chair next to Tūtū's, I could look across the table and through the screen door, past the lānai and down the valley. I could see the white steeple of

Kawaiha`o Church and the twinkling lights of town...the Fort Street docks...the masts of barkentines, and the sea beyond.

I listened to the gecko as I watched the moods of my family. I knew my mother's mood by the way she kneaded dough on the butcher block, my little brother Pōki`i's mood by the way he slapped his bare feet together under the kitchen table, and Tūtū's mood by the way she fiddled with the hem of her holokū dress. I knew Papa's mood by the way he laid his fork on the supper table, while my mood, more and more, felt tied to the moon.

I looked at my father, wondering if he ever wished he were back in Boston. He came to Honolulu as a boy of twelve, on a vacation with his parents. Mama found him sitting on a rock, crying his eyes out. Smallpox had swept over the islands, killing thousands of Hawaiians and foreigners, too. Among the foreigners were both of Papa's parents. Mama took him home to Tūtū. A few years later, off he went to Boston to become a doctor. I looked at Mama, thinking of why he came back.

At supper that evening, my father reached for his fork. Slowly. Deliberately. He lifted the handle and paused.

The seeds had sprouted.

"Mele is fifteen, and her English is as good as mine," he said to the fork. "It's time to enroll her in school."

A look of hope slipped out before I could catch it. Tūtū reached under the table and I felt the squeeze of her small cool hand—I always let Tūtū in on my secrets. Starting school at mid-year was not ideal, but I did not mind. There were over fifty schools in Honolulu, with students from all over the world.

"My work schedule won't allow me to teach her much longer," Papa announced. "Next week I'll enroll her at Punahou."

Punahou? I glanced at Mama and set a biscuit back down on my plate. For the first time in his life, Pōki`i did not move.

Mama sat up straight as a board.

"Punahou," Papa said, "is as good as any private school in America." Mama said nothing.

Haoles, foreigners, mentioned Punahou with pride. After all, it was a private school created for children of missionaries and wealthy foreigners. But when the haoles said "Hawaiian school," their voices dropped in contempt.

I watched Mama.

"When Mele finishes Punahou," Papa continued, "she can attend school in Boston, or New—"

"No." Mama's voice was like gravel. "Mele will go to *Hawaiian* school, stay in Hawai`i with *family*!"

Papa's voice grew louder. "Nahoa, I will not see Mele attend a second-rate Hawaiian school! She is meant for something more."

"You listen to me, Reed Bennett." Mama's eyes flared as she pushed her face toward Papa. "Mele can go to Kaumakapili, or Kawaiha`o. There are *many* good Hawaiian schools!"

"The Hawaiian schools are falling down, Nahoa! They are understaffed, and they rank dreadfully low on proficiency!"

"What do you expect? The government gave buckets of money this year to English schools, hardly any to Hawaiian schools! And Branch Hospital School? For children with the disease? Maybe U.S. nickel!"

Papa was almost crushing his fork. "Things are changing, Nahoa. All the Portuguese cane workers? Bringing their children with them? They are a growing voice. They want English, not Hawaiian. It's practically a dead language!"

Mama jumped up, waving her powerful arms.

"Dead language? You don't call me dead language! Mele will go to Hawaiian school because she is *Hawaiian!"*

Papa tore off his glasses and was on his feet. He slammed his fist to the table, and my plate bounced. "Mele is *half* -Hawaiian!"

I sank my face into my hands.

At that moment, Tūtū fluttered her small hands in the space between Mama and Papa. "Shhh," she said, "you talk like this, we all be lōlō crazy by morning!"

Everything went quiet.

"I have answer," Tūtū announced into the hush. She proudly patted the Bible on her lap. "Mele go *missionary* school, like when I was young girl. Learn better word of *Jesus*!"

Mama and Papa sank into their chairs—Tūtū had forgotten there were no more missionary schools.

I pulled myself up and aligned my shoulders to the back of my chair. This was not the time to be a soft branch. I lifted my chin as high as I dared and addressed my parents.

"I would like to go to Royal School."

Papa's eyebrows worked their way around this idea, though I could tell it was not a perfect fit.

"It's a highly rated English school," I urged, "and they use the same curriculum as students in Boston!"

My mother finally agreed because I reminded her that Royal School had been founded to teach the children of Hawaiian royalty. Tūtū was happy because when she was a girl, Royal School was taught by missionaries. When Papa stopped turning his fork over, when he stood up and took a deep breath and let it out, I knew I had won.

But as soon as Papa promised to enroll me at Royal School, I felt a chill along my arms. A few months ago, a new boy had come to town. From San Francisco. I had never met him, but from what I heard, I did not care to. My triumph in getting to attend Royal School was marred by this realization: in the same class with Keahi, Hoaloha, John Makahehi and me, would be this boy. His name was Daniel Livingstone.

Chapter 3

ONLY KEAHI

A week went by, the sky changed its mind a dozen times, and the day came when I knew the *Kilauea* would be arriving once again from its trip across the glistening waters between islands. I refused to allow myself to rush like a crazy girl down the valley to the end of Fort Street, to plant myself at the noisy pier and shade my eyes as I begged the *Kilauea* to bring Keahi back. That was for children, I told myself.

Instead, I agreed to meet my best friend, Hoaloha, at the swimming hole at Nu`uanu Stream. We always went for different reasons. I went to escape the constant questions from my little brother, Pōki`i. "When will Keahi come back? Will he take me torch fishing again?" Hoaloha had her own reasons. She went to watch the boys, and the less clothes they wore, the better.

We always met at the shade-giving `ōhi`a tree above the swimming hole. The tree stood on a rise not far above the waterfalls where Nu`uanu Stream rushed over flat rocks and dropped ten or more feet into a perfect swimming hole. Waiting in the shade of the tree and listening to the boys splashing, I felt a *tap, tap* on my shoulder, and smelled the sweet breath of someone who could always find a way to make me laugh. That was her gift. I gave Hoaloha a warm hug.

"You gone to land of dreams," she said. "Keahi comes back, I will *never* see you again."

"No land of dreams," I said, laughing, "only Keahi."

"Suuure," she said, smiling. She ran her hands down her hips, stroking rhythmic circles as she took playful hula steps. She spun slowly, singing in a low, wet voice. "On-ly Ke-a-hi. On-ly Ke-a-hi."

The earth shook beneath our bare feet as three kanaka, Hawaiian men, came galloping up the dirt road, forcing us to jump back. By the time the cloud of dust had settled, I was tasting grit and she had lost the music. I finished coughing and turned back to Hoaloha.

"You still angry?" she asked, pulling specks of dirt from her hair.

In the last few months, we seemed never far from an argument about my father. She loved Papa, and she knew he reserved a special place in his heart for Mimo, Hoaloha's tūtū. Let Mimo have the slightest temperature or the smallest cough, and Papa was off in the middle of the night, rushing down the valley to care for her. Each time he visited, he took rice cakes and pressed a small envelop into her hand as they hugged goodbye on her creaky verandah. He treated Mimo like she was the Queen, but still Hoaloha criticized him.

I shrugged and shook dust from my dress. "No."

"Why you get so upset yesterday?" she asked. "All John said is your Papa—"

"He doesn't hate them. It's for everybody's good."

"How you know that?"

"Because my father *says* so!"

Hoaloha threw her hands up. "Oh, here she go again. If the lepela so contagious, why is the fence at Branch Hospital so low, so they can just walk away! You ever think about that?"

"Hoaloha. Separating them is the law!"

"You try to convince everybody your Papa so right. Maybe you're not so convinced."

I turned and stomped up Nu`uanu Road. Hoaloha ran after me.

"Mele!" she called.

I kept going. A lost mule stood next to the road, with one ear forward and one ear back, staring at me with sleepy eyes.

"Can't you get all of yourself going the same direction?" I yelled at it.

"Mele!"

I stopped, turning like a squall. "My best friend. Don't you know how I feel when you criticize Papa?" I pulled the back of my hand across my dripping nose.

Hoaloha dragged her bare heel in circles through the dirt. "You want to throw me in the ocean?" she asked. A voice full of innocence.

"Yes!" I said, choking my dress with my fist.

She twisted a strand of hair and looked down the valley toward the docks. "Send me to China, never see me again?" When she looked back at me, she had a glimmer in her eye.

We bent over laughing, slapping at each other.

"Come on!" she said. She squeezed my hand all the way back to the `ōhi`a tree above the falls. While Hoaloha happily polished an apple with her skirt, I told her what I had noticed when I left home that morning. On our back porch, near the corner where Holoholo curled up for her catnaps, Mama always kept a crate of pears. To steal was a great shame in the old ways; it violated a strong tradition of generosity.

"The whole crate. Don't you think this is strange," I said as we walked, "that suddenly a whole crate of pears goes missing? A whole dollar worth. And all Mama does is shrug."

"Only pears," said Hoaloha, flapping a hand in the air, "nothing to worry about." Just what Hoaloha would say. "My father's paper fish go missing, too," she said, "all the time."

Hanging from bamboo poles in every part of town were brightly colored fish made by Hoaloha's Japanese father. Some were ten feet long. They filled the sky with festive movement, rolling, dipping, and spinning in the wind. Hoaloha's mother was Hawaiian. Hoaloha knew what it was like to be caught between two cultures. In the space between her parents, she found ways to laugh. In the space between my parents, I felt adrift.

We found our favorite spot in the shade. Below us, boys hung like a bracelet around the sunny pool, leaping off the rocks, yelling and splashing. Most were local boys. They wore the traditional malo with a cord around their waist from which a swatch of material draped down. "Cover their wishes!" Hoaloha said. She laughed like Mama, deep and rolling. Hoaloha had known the moon longer than I had. She knew boys in ways that would have taken Papa's breath away.

We unrolled our brown lauhala mats and flopped down. On our dresses we flattened a place and spread out rice cakes and pineapple. I was wearing a blue holokū, the dress introduced years ago by the missionaries. It gathered in a seam across my chest, had long sleeves, and fell to my ankles. Most of the time, Hoaloha wore cotton skirts with low cut blouses. But sometimes she got a certain look in her eye and swam without a top—sometimes she did not even need to be swimming. The local boys were accustomed to partial nudity. Most haoles pasted their eyes straight ahead as they rushed past any kind of nudity, and murmured things about the devil. No matter how much I tried to convince Papa that things were different in Hawai`i than in Boston, Papa insisted I always cover myself.

I picked up a slice of pineapple, wondering if the *Kilauea* had docked yet.

"That Keahi," Hoaloha said, "he's like a dream with hands and feet." She planted this delicious seed and then glanced at me, wrapping herself in a tasty innocence. Waiting.

"Well?" She nudged me with her elbow.

"Just Keahi," I said, trying to bury her in a long and wandering yawn. But on the exhale, we both exploded into giggles as Hoaloha poked at me with her finger. "You're not fooling me, Mele Bennett."

"Eh, Keahi, that good splash!" A shout from one of the boys at the falls.

Keahi?

My mind leapt over itself as I searched and found Keahi among the boys. He pulled himself up out of the pool, swung his legs onto the rocks, and jumped up. He was now taller than most of the boys, with lean hips and strong shoulders. He bent forward and shook water from his long hair, threw his head back, glanced up the rise, and saw me. And why not? I must have looked like a jumping bean turned loose on a hillside.

He cupped his hands and shouted up the hill. "That you, Mele?" Every boy turned to look.

Hoaloha grabbed my arm and thrust it in the air, flopping my wrist in a frantic wave. I jerked my hand back down. "Hoaloha!"

Keahi yelled up the rise again. "I just get back. I'll come see you!"

"Go again, one more time!" another boy called to Keahi. "This time do dive!" Sometimes the boys spoke Hawaiian, sometimes in broken English. Keahi and I usually spoke English.

Keahi looked down into the pool. The water level had dropped. The pool was not deep enough at this time of the season—not for diving. Sometimes the boys dove from a higher rock to get a better angle, but it was also farther from the deepest part of the pool, so less safe.

In one twist and a smooth leap, Keahi pulled himself onto the higher rock and stood up. Even from the hillside, I could see him take a deep breath. One of the boys quickly crossed himself. I pressed a strand of hair into my lips, holding my breath. Hoaloha covered her mouth.

Water dripped from the malo around Keahi's waist, turning to shiny the dull gray rocks. With one hand he wiped his face. His chest rose and fell again. I could sense him thinking. Trying to decide. Feeling with his eyes for the edges of the rocks hidden beneath the water. He stepped forward.

Hoaloha crushed my hand and closed her eyes.

"Keahi, *no*." I whispered.

One shake of his head, and water again flew from his long black hair. He bent his knees, drew back his arms, thrust them forward, and his body—sun glistening on his brown skin—sprang through the air.

I closed my eyes and heard a thin splash. Rushing at me was the memory of a day at the beach when we were children and he dove off a rock into the deep, deep blue. I was sure then, too, that Papa's white God had snatched him away. In the time it takes a leaf to be picked up by a breeze and set down in a new place, Keahi burst out of the water laughing. Hoaloha and I collapsed into each other.

"Boy like that," Tūtū would have said, "make a girl crazy with one smile."

Chapter 4

THESE BIRDS ARE SINGING

The next day, on my way home from town, I took one of the smaller paths that followed the stream and then veered through a small grove of papaya trees, where I had planned on gathering some papayas for Tūtū. Everyone in Hawai`i called their grandmas "Tūtū." Also, for our whole lives we called our parents "Mama" and "Papa." This was not considered a childish thing to do. Recently, wanting to feel more like an adult, I had called Mama "Mother." She frowned, looking at me as if I had just swallowed a pepper root.

Thump! I jumped back as a papaya fell to the grass in front of me. I looked up to see a pair of dusty feet and rolled up beige trousers wrapped around the trunk of a papaya tree, its bushy green top swaying against the light blue sky. A familiar face looked down. In his surprise to see me, he slipped, knocking several more papayas to the clearing. I watched his muscles pull at his white shirt as Keahi slid down and jumped barefoot to the ground.

"Eh, Mele, Aloha!" His hair, black and smooth and shiny, fell loosely across his shoulders. It was almost long as mine. "How are you doing?"

By the end of his sentence, I forgot what he said.

"Gathering tūtūs for my papaya," is what came out. *Mele!* "I mean— "

He looked at the ripening fruit he had already picked. "There is plenty here!" he said, starting to pick them up. I could not find my arms to help.

"Want me help you carry them home?" he asked, pulling up the front of his shirt to cradle the papayas. His stomach was smooth and brown. Rainbows wrapped around me.

We walked along the old trail, following the stream. At the lower end of the valley, where the ridges slumped down into lazy foothills, Keahi's green clapboard house sat in a grove of hau trees near an outcropping of rocks. His house was about a mile below mine. Living in the house were his aunt, another uncle, Keahi, and several cousins. "I came back to go to school," he said, "but everybody else, they stayed on Maui." Keahi's tūtūs and several other relatives had died during the smallpox epidemic. My tūtū had been like a grandmother to him.

"Eh, Mele," he said, shifting a papaya. His eyes lit up. "John and me, we caught a wild boar. Upper end of the valley! John lasso it from one side, me from the other. We sold it for a $1.75! One day, you watch. John and I will go to Big Island and lasso the white stallion."

Every child native to the islands knew the story of the great white stallion. For years, the stallion had eluded capture, lunging down steep ravines with scores of cowboys—paniolo—riding after. But always when the cloud of dust settled, the stallion was gone, the thicket still as a sleeping fern. "A phantom," some whispered.

"John, he knows how to make a lariat dance in the sky," Keahi said. "Waiting for okay to come down on whatever John says."

I laughed. A lariat, waiting for instructions? I imagined the two of them riding through brush for days in the upland hills above Hilo, until finally they caught a glimpse of the white stallion. I imagined the lariat, in Keahi's hands now, lifting into the blue sky. It eased over rocks and followed curves in the trail, peeking through trees until it found the stallion. Then the lasso hovered obediently, waiting for Keahi to tell it to drop.

"Why you smiling?" asked Keahi, poking at me with his elbow.

I playfully grabbed at the corner of his shirt and yanked, almost dumping the batch of papayas. He was all hands and juggling and trying to regain his balance. "You're nothing but one pail of trouble!" he said, laughing.

When we crossed the lānai, and Keahi ducked under the Chinese lanterns and straightened up with a smile on his face, Mama let out a happy shriek. She jumped up and ran to him as radishes flew from her apron and bounced across the bricks.

"You are back!" Mama laughed, taking a few hula steps. Mama's forearms are as big as Papa's and she can shove a mule right off a road. But when she dances, when the drumming starts and her hips begin to sway, she moves like a piece of magic! After Mama laughs, after the deep rolling music of her voice is anchored in your memory, the air seems different. Crisp, watchful. You just stand there, watching the soft brown square of her face, hoping she will laugh one more time.

Tūtū burst to life the moment she heard his voice. "That my Keahi?" She fluttered her hands in the air until he grasped them and hugged her warmly.

"Tūtū!" he said happily, "The birds, they keep singing about you." She slapped playfully at his chest and said how tall he had grown; he laughed and squeezed her hand. She took off her lei and put it around his neck. I stepped back and gulped. He had never looked so handsome.

Mama rushed inside to get food.

"Oh, I wish I can see your face," said Tūtū. She was almost blind by then. This is what she would have seen: eyelashes long and curving, eyes that danced, a mouth ready to say kind words. A safe place, high ground.

Keahi reached into his pocket. He gently took Tūtū's wrist, turned it upward, and opened her hand. He pressed something into her palm and folded her fingers around it.

"You remember this, Tūtū?" He dipped his face to hers.

She took a quick breath of recognition as shaking fingers went to her lips. She reached for Keahi, patting his face, wet running down her cheeks. He wrapped around her again.

"You honor us to remember us," she said. "Even as little keiki, you never far from your gourd whistle. So smooth now, like silk!" She turned the whistle over and over in her hand, as if in it the whole island was held fast and safe. Keahi never cared much for school; he stumbled over numbers like they were stones in a road. But he always knew two things. He always knew, even as a keiki, where the center of the universe was according to Hawaiian legend. "Aia la!" he would shout as a child, dragging Tūtū and me to a pile of rocks in Honolulu. And he always knew where his gourd whistle was. The cuffs of his brown trousers could be rolled up and full of sand, his white shirt tails could be hanging out or stuffed in, his hair could be tussled or glistening, but when he reached inside his pocket and pulled out his hand and opened it, there was his gourd whistle.

From the moment they greeted, Keahi and Tūtū were like two feathers floating down a happy stream. He had heard the story since we were little keiki, but he always let Tūtū tell him again.

"You know Kawaiha`o Church? I help build it! Mimo and me! Every native brought rocks and more rocks. Mimo and Tūtū get a basket, drag big piece of coral rock in it—all the way to place for the church." Keahi squeezed her hand, smiling. "We walk and walk, dragging the stone," she said. "We slap at each other in joy, thanking Jesus every step for good dirt for dragging this gift to God. We thank missionaries for this church to build. We tell workers, we want this to be *corner* stone! They say, okay. Imagine! Mimo and Tūtū, making cornerstone for the church!" Hoaloha and I had heard this story from her grandma Mimo as many times as from Tūtū.

Tūtū pulled a bin of sweet potatoes close, and we helped as she peeled them by feel. Strips of peelings, earth-colored and wrapped in stories of Mimo and the missionaries, piled up on the butcher paper at Tūtū's leathery feet. We cut sections of sweet potato and dropped them with a *clunk* into the calabash.

"You one cute little keiki," she told Keahi, "run around like sea crab, always busy. You get lasso and chase cousins up and down the beach pretending to chase white stallion; but lasso only fall once, around shoulders of my Mele. You two! One of you jumps onto rock, other one has to be on same rock."

He laughed to hear these stories.

"That Mele," said Tūtū. "Ever since she little keiki, she like a match on dry wood. Still that way. *But*—" Up went her index finger as if the whole island were listening. "Mele loves her Papa, big as the moon!"

Keahi's eyes twinkled as he looked at me in a new way. "She always walks proud, grand and swinging." His hands flew past his head. "Hibiscus flaming in her hair. I tell you, Tūtū, I'd rather face a shark than a girl so strong!"

I hit his arm. He pulled back giggling.

"And look at her now." His eyes followed my hair down to my shoulders and then down to my chest. I tucked to hide my smallness. "Too pretty. Enough to make an island boy tremble."

It was months away, but Keahi was already talking about flying a kite with Tūtū on her birthday.

"A dragon," she said, "with big head and ferocious eyes. Long licks of red tongue, like hot fire!" Never had I seen her wave her arms around so much...until she realized. "Where you get a kite?"

Keahi and I looked at each other.

"I will build it for you!" he said. "Dr. Netten got me a job at George Lucas's Planing Mill. I start next week helping Mr. Nott build cages for the haole doctor from Europe. Some kind of research—monkeys and rabbits, I think. There is plenty of wood left for a kite." He took the last cut of a sweet potato and added it to the pile at Tūtū's feet. "Maybe Mele will help me." He glanced at me sideways.

"I don't think so," I said, shaking my head at a sweet potato. Mama told me never say yes to a boy the first time.

"Eh, Mele, say yes." He looked at me and smiled. Strands of shining hair fell from his shoulder. I missed the calabash, and my sweet potato landed in the dirt. He leaned over to pick it up and his shoulder was the curve of the new moon.

"Yes."

Chapter 5

ROYAL SCHOOL

Nobody understood how nervous I was about facing my first day of public school, and not just because of Daniel Livingstone or because I knew that Keahi could not enroll for another week. As I pulled on my best white holokū dress and looked at my bare feet, I realized how much I would miss the security of the lānai as the only classroom I had ever known.

"This daughter of mine!" said Mama, shaking her head. "One day she is strong sea rising, telling her father what she wants. Next day she is wai puhia." She meant the water streaming down the face of the pali cliffs, where Nu`uanu Road stops and the treacherous road winding down the other side of the cliffs begins. When the wind is fierce, it sweeps up the face of the cliffs with such force that the falling water is thrust back on itself, shooting straight up the cliff and into the sky, creating an upside-down waterfall.

My mother's worry that day was not my churning stomach, or my fear that I would not prove as smart as Papa thought, but the lice outbreak at school. She burst into the parlor, scooped up the hairbrush and plopped me down on the chair like a sack of rice.

"Four times already this year!"

"Can't Papa do something?" I asked, wincing as she tugged at my hair.

She gave me an impatient look but slowed her strokes of the brush. "Always thinking your Papa and a wish can fix all things. Board has more important things to worry about."

My eyes followed their usual path along Mama's arms. Even though Papa checked us every week, I found myself watching Mama and Tūtū for discolored spots on their skin. "You mean the ma`i Pākē," I said, the Chinese disease. Many Hawaiians believed the disease came from China, but nobody knew for certain.

She nodded. "Getting bad, Mele. We dying out."

Who was *we*? One minute I wanted to be included when Mama said "we," and the next minute I did not. Did I think I could just pick and choose? Be Hawaiian when it came to dancing the hula, and white when it came to escaping the disease?

"Family of twenty chiefs, whole royal family," she said, pulling the brush through my hair, "and only one baby." Everyone knows you cannot run a kingdom on one baby. "Our men are not so good at baby-making anymore...all the foreign diseases."

She thrust a load of schoolbooks into my arms and opened the screen door. Holoholo meowed, flew off the porch, and scrambled up the banyan tree.

Papa was waiting for me in the buggy. During the trip down Nu`uanu Road, I did nothing but try to escape my fear. I tried to hide it behind white picket fences lining the streets of expensive homes, tried to bury it among bougainvillea cascading over porches. Soon our buggy was rolling past the beautiful home of Mr. Afong, a man wealthy enough to send his dozen daughters to school in America. But I agreed with Keahi—who would want to go to America? I knew Keahi's cousin had stowed away twice on the *Amy Turner*, trying to get to Boston to attend an American school; and the Americans bought our sugar by the ton. But all I could imagine of America was smokestacks and robbers.

A new buggy pulled out from a driveway of a lovely tall home wrapped in white fences and hibiscus. Mr. Carter, always cheerful, waved to Papa. "Morning, Dr. Bennett," he called. I was glad for something to occupy my mind.

"You look like a breeze carrying good news," said Papa.

"That is true! My favorite bark is on her way to Honolulu, the *Amy Turner*. With fair winds, she'll round Cape Horn and arrive in decent time, my good friend Capt. Newell with her!"

The *Amy Turner*? I perked up. Keahi's cousin, Kalua, would be on the ship, being brought back to Hawaii after he was caught stowing away. Though I did not like more ships coming to our islands, I loved hearing the names: the *Amy Turner*, the *Hazard*, the *Mariposa*.

"Papa," I asked, thinking of how Mama wondered what disease might arrive on the next ship, "Why is it Hawaiians who mostly get the lepela?" I craned my neck to peek into the corner of a garden where a peacock stood, all purple and midnight eyes, jeweled in the morning sun. The peacock moved in the same way my stomach felt: nervous and unsure of which direction it was going.

"Hawaiians haven't had time to build up immunity yet." He knew to tell me again. "I think you are safe, Mele. I think your white blood will protect you."

"No Hawaiians are immune?"

"A few have natural immunity, but not many. A few others can have the bacilli in their system, but for some reason, it stays inactive. The bacilli just sit there, dormant—sometimes for years, sometimes for a whole lifetime—hiding like a rogue wave. It's a tricky disease."

"What about Mama and Tūtū?"

His voice dropped. How many times had I asked this question? "Your mother and Tūtū aren't around the disease."

"But Kalina works at Branch Hospital. She treats patients all the time."

"She's careful, as are the Catholic sisters. Besides, mostly males get the disease."

I felt relief and right behind that, guilt. It did not seem fair that my white blood gave me protection that Mama and Tūtū and Keahi did not have. I felt as if I had cheated, stolen something that should not have been mine.

Snap! I turned to see the rear door of a paddy wagon fly open and slam into a bougainvillea, snapping a branch in half. Men piled out. Inmates wearing black and white striped uniforms often worked on the streets of Honolulu. Clinking ice wagons, foreign ships arriving, inmates from O`ahu Jail, peacocks dragging their jeweled tails through the dusty streets—these were all parts of daily life in Honolulu town.

The other rear door flung open. Inside, a powerfully built Hawaiian prisoner rose from his seat, grunted, lifted a heavy bale of wire, and hurled it from the paddy wagon. The bale landed hard on the street, scattering dust. Keahi was strong for his slim build, but nothing like this man! The prisoner turned to watch our buggy approach. My eyes met his briefly, giving me chicken skin. As Papa and I drove past, the prisoner turned away to join others slumped in the shade of a hedge. For several moments I saw the frightening face of the prisoner everywhere: in the pocked leather on Hoku's harness, in the pitted dirt of the road. I had no idea who the man was—not that day. None of us knew that the story of this man, and the frightening thing he traded to escape a hanging, would be told among doctors all over Europe. On that day, I knew him only as a man who made me shiver.

"We're here." Papa's voice.

I pushed away images of the prisoner's face, glad for the sight of grass and fence and a long building of white adobe that seemed to grow out of the earth between monkey pod trees. I had seen Royal School a hundred times, but never with my stomach flopping like a landed fish. I saw a pigeon flap away from the long white verandah, and wished I had wings.

Papa halted the buggy and Hoku shifted patiently under his harness. I climbed down, watching a long line of gray pigeons bow and strut along the roof. In the blossomed shade of the veranda were gathered students from all over the world: Hawaiians, plus students from Portugal, China, England, Scotland, Japan, Germany. And of course, America. I knew they could hear, not far above their heads, the sounds of pigeons cooing. I wanted to hear words from my father that would soothe my fear. I wanted him to tell me that his daughter was smart enough, good enough. That I was wonderful and brilliant and the best daughter he could ever wish for and—

"Don't be late," he said.

I must have given him a pathetic look, straightening my dress, trying to pretend I was the same strong girl so sure of herself a few evenings ago at the kitchen table. I hoped to sit next to my friend, Hoaloha, but the thought of Daniel Livingstone filled me with dread.

When I walked into the classroom, Hoaloha was seated near the front, trying to contain her joy at seeing me.

"You're here!" she whispered. "And Keahi will be here next week."

A week seemed forever away. But it reminded me of why I wanted to attend Royal School: to be near Keahi and my friends. To my fifteen-year-old mind, nothing else mattered.

I looked around the small room with high plaster walls, then through the window in time to see Papa turn the buggy toward Queen's Hospital.

The door opened, a hush filled the air, and Miss Spencer swished like an ocean of petticoats across the room to where I stood, trying not to blink. Like most teachers at Royal School, she was American. She tucked her chin, and her white bonnet popped out behind her ears, as if sprouting wings. Even in my nicest white dress and a new pink ribbon in my hair, she looked at me as if I were lacking. Rather, as if my brown half were lacking. Mama said I look more Hawaiian than haole because that is what happens, the darker features step forward.

"Mele Bennett?" she said, as if chopping onions. Her petticoat banged against my knees.

I nodded. My chest was not exactly flat, but there was not much to crush my books against. Miss Spencer lowered her glasses, frowning.

"A bit short, aren't you? Well, at least you're not a plump one."

I could feel Hoaloha cringe in offense. *Miss Spencer and I were not going to get along.*

"And your Christian name is—?" She waited with raised eyebrows.

I knew this would happen.

"I don't use a Christian name," I said calmly. Taking Christian names was another idea brought by the missionaries, another way the haoles wanted us to be more like them and less like ourselves. "My father says I don't have to." I tried to sound respectful.

She drew back indignantly. "You *do* know the law? That *every* Hawaiian is *required* to take a Christian name?"

Laws made by foreigners, I wanted to say. I did not mean to, I was not aware until it was too late, but I let my shoulder lift in a tiny shrug. From that shrug forward, the space between Miss Spencer and me was filled with bitter yams. I could almost feel Hoaloha sink into her chair. My first year in public school, ruined, and class had not even started.

"Take a seat in the third row," she said curtly, lifting her nose an American inch. "Next to Daniel."

I glanced up to see a boy I had never met. Then why, I wondered, did he look familiar? He had dirty blond hair that fell in short angry waves and a thin mouth ready to curl in contempt. There is a saying on the islands: "When a boy is cruel, look to the father." Then I remembered. I had never met Daniel's father, but who else would ride up on a dusty horse to collect this curly haired boy from the sheriff's office? I had seen this one day on my way home from town. Even from a distance, even with his back to me, I knew what sort of man the father was from the moment he slapped this boy across the face and kicked him as he fell. I had turned and gone down another street, my hands shaking. Papa knew of Daniel and his father through the deputy, and of course through trips to the hospital by boys who had already encountered Daniel's fists.

"Would you mind if—?" I looked around, desperate.

"Be *seated*, Mele."

"Yes, Ma'am." As I set my books on the desk and started to sit, Daniel hooked his boot under the leg of my chair and pretended to sneeze. My chair jolted sideways. I almost fell, and my books scattered across the aisle. John Makahehi, usually slow to anger, turned red-faced at this rudeness and picked up my books. John was Keahi's best friend.

"Oh, gosh. S'cuse *me*," said Daniel, smirking.

"Daniel!" Miss Spencer gave him pinch eye and he gathered himself back into his space.

Miss Spencer looked at me with half respect—for the white half.

"Mele," she said, "we do verbal assignments every Monday morning. I understand that, thanks to *excellent* instruction from your father, you speak *proper* English."

I folded my half-proper hands. "My mother is teaching me Hawaiian."

Miss Spencer cleared her throat and drew a dainty finger across a perfect eyebrow.

"How sweet of her. I am told remnants of the language linger still. But your *English* will take you a long way, I'm sure."

"Oh, yeah, girl like you go looong way." I already knew who murmured these words under his breath.

Everyone knew the rule in English schools—English was the only language allowed. For me it was easy, and Hoaloha and Keahi spoke good English when they wanted to. But most students were caught between languages. They were not allowed to speak their native language at school, nor were they yet proficient at English. I pushed away a twinge of guilt; feeling again as if I had gained something through no effort I could call my own.

Miss Spencer rapped her knuckles briskly on her desk and glared. A small Portuguese boy named Theodore bolted upright and pulled his face to attention. "Yes, Ma'am!" he almost shouted. I liked Theodore.

"For today's oral practice, I will ask each of you to describe a building. Speak in full sentences, using only *proper* English. Use good descriptive verbs, appropriate adjectives, correct grammatical syntax."

Theodore, twisting the top button of his frayed shirt and smelling of chicken coops, would not know those words.

Nor would many other students. He was new to the islands, his family was poorer than most, and his mother sold eggs for the dollar and a half needed to keep Theodore in school each month. The income hardly paid for the chicken feed, but even a few pennies a day made a difference to a family like Theodore's.

A boy seated nearby pressed a bare brown toe into his other foot. A simple gesture, but it turned my thoughts to Keahi. I recalled a time at the beach when Keahi and I were little keiki. We had curled into Tūtū's lap like two butterflies sharing the same hibiscus. Keahi had reached out his foot, pressed it slowly into my thigh, and smiled.

At thoughts of Tūtū, I turned to look out the row of small windows running the length of the classroom. Between the canopies of monkey pod trees, the top of a tall white spire rose to a blue sky. It was the bell tower of Kawaiha`o Church where Tūtū attended.

"You may wish to describe the legislative buildings," said Miss Spencer cheerfully, "or one of the mission houses. Perhaps a bank. Honolulu has *two* banks now, and I hope you will think about saving your extra money!" She smiled, looking expectantly around the room.

Students looked at each other and grimaced. What extra money? Many families on the islands made only one or two hundred dollars a year, while the king made over $20,000 and the foreign-run government set their own salaries, according to how hungry their pockets were. Between King Kalākaua and Claus Spreckels, the sugar baron who saw dollar signs on every inch of our soil, it was no surprise the kingdom was deep in debt.

Whispered words floated toward me. "How about describing a whorehouse?"

"Daniel, be quiet!" I snapped. I looked right into his eyes—the blue of shallow water.

"Theodore," continued Miss Spencer, "please go first. Try to describe a building that could be influential in your life, significant to the future of the island."

Influential? I thought. Significant? The only future Theodore worried about was that even a single hen might be stolen, and there would be no money for his schooling. Theodore pulled himself from his seat. His eyes nervously searched the wall of the classroom, fixing on a section of crumbled plaster where narrow slats of wood showed through. It reminded me of the cages I once saw in Theodore's back yard when Papa and I took a calabash of soup to Theodore's mother.

"My chicken coop!" he blurted out.

Miss Spencer forced a smile, probably wishing she were back in San Francisco with doilies, pink chalk, and students with shiny foreheads.

"Next to house! Like this—!" Theodore slanted his hands to the side and leaned his body. "Old wood, falling down, tired." He sat down and immediately jumped back up, inspired. "Nails! Some get rusty. One day last year, I step—"

Miss Spencer stopped him with a flat palm and a wearied look. He dropped into his chair in a cheerful heap. That was Theodore, always in the last canoe. Would I like to go next, Miss Spencer proposed, to set a good example? The worst thing she could say....

My first thought was to describe Royal School. Built in the heart of town, Royal School was the pride of the Board of Education. The school had one story, built long before the $10,000 went missing that had been set aside to buy more land for public schools. "Fell into foreign pockets," Mama said. The school sat a few wrought iron fences away from `Iolani Palace, the residence of our king.

"I would like to describe `Iolani," I began, "the old palace, before the new palace was built last year." I hesitated but went on, knowing I was already doomed. "Before King Kalākaua traveled around the world and came back wanting the islands to be something we're not." John Makahehi and other Hawaiian students nodded. I continued, trying to hide my distaste for the new royal building. "The old palace was a structure of wood poles, looking like other homes in Honolulu, only larger. It was lashed together with coconut fiber and vines and banana leaves." Hoaloha sent me a look, pleading for me to stop.

"And mana," I said, "with power."

The room went silent.

"You don't like the new palace?" Miss Spencer's lip twitched. Every foreigner loved the sight of `Iolani Palace glistening in the sun: gold-gilded mirrors, splendid jewels, cascading satin, massive Grecian-looking columns. Even by European standards the palace was extravagant. But with the sandalwood forests stripped years ago, the days of affording such luxuries were long gone. The kingdom had gone into terrible debt to build the palace, most of the money owed to Claus Spreckels.

"It's elegant. But every day our king loses some of his power." Bare feet filled the aisle as Hawaiian students in the front turned to look back at me, nodding in agreement. "King Kalākaua is a pretend king." I tried to sound like a textbook. "The real power is in the hands of—"

Hoaloha put her head down. Miss Spencer looked at me as if I had just burned down the school.

Chapter 6

QUESTIONS

By the time the last bell rang, my teacher despised me, I was miserable that Keahi would not enroll for another week, and my promise to Papa (that I would not forget my manners) was in shreds.

"I don't want to be the model," I said to Papa as I climbed into the buggy and told him what had happened.

"We can still enroll you in Punahoa," he said, a little too patiently. "Though you would still have an American teacher."

"Wouldn't it be awful," I said, working up a smile for Papa, "if Miss Spencer had a twin sister? Who came to the islands with her?"

Papa caught my smile and returned it. "And she taught at…."

"Punahoa!" we both blurted out.

Papa laughed. "Royal School. I see. This is all about Keahi, isn't it?"

"No, Papa. I'd be willing to go to Punahoa."

He gave me the kind of smile a papa gives a daughter when they both know she is knee deep in a delicious lie.

"Mele, you will succeed anywhere. Just remember your goal."

Hoku clopped along for a few moments of silence.

It came unexpectedly. "What is Keahi's goal for his life?"

I felt silly to realize—I had never asked Keahi. Surely a goal is larger, I thought, than something you can do in an afternoon, like lassoing a white stallion running loose on the Parker Ranch. Maybe that was a difference between Keahi and me. I knew my vision for my life was to become a nurse. But who was I to say what Keahi's vision for his life should be?

"I don't know, Papa. Is it important to you?"

"I think it is, yes." Hoku shook his bridle into another silence. "Is it important to you?"

I wanted to tell Papa what I knew he would like to hear. But I also wanted to tell the truth. *Is it important to me?*

"Not today," I finally said.

With Hoku's harness clicking in the sun, we set off for Branch Hospital. On the front seat of the buggy, between Papa and me, was a pile of medical records. We clopped along, passing keiki running barefoot through the streets, local women balancing fruit-filled baskets on their heads, an ice wagon, pigeons pecking at the dirt, and another paddy wagon carrying prisoners to a different work site. Honolulu was a town of 18,000 people who lived from sun to shade in the middle of an ocean stretching to places I had never seen.

At the first drop of rain, I reached for the corner of my skirt and draped it over the medical records. Why I felt the urge to protect them, I do not know. In a few weeks, the files would be largely forgotten, left among others in a damp corner of the clinic where my father worked. But, for now, they were anything but forgotten. Neatly stacked and double-bound with string, the medical reports might as well have been gunpowder. The whole island fought and prayed and wrung hands over the contents.

Inside were photographs of arms…backs…faces. Tear-stained letters from families of those afflicted with the disease. Sheriff's reports. I glanced at Papa, his back straight against the buggy seat. He had been up late again last night, signing authorization papers while raindrops divided our parlor window. His signature was like he was, tall and sure and holding much inside.

Papa was the last to sign before the patients were sent away.

"Are more going this week than last?" I asked. For a long time, those with the lepela were sent away once a month. Now the little steamer *Mokoli`i* chugged across the channel to Kalawao every week—carrying tears, Mama said, more than anything else. A drop of wet sky landed on my arm.

"More than ever." His voice had no tears it.

I watched two keiki chase each other along the shaded verandah of a white clapboard house. Many homes in Honolulu looked much like this one, as if at any moment the slanting verandah and all its blossoms would sink sideways and be swallowed by a jungle of ferns. The keiki leapt from the railing, found paths through the banana trees, and hid among the curling ferns. I hesitated, listening to the sound of giggles coming from the yard.

"Are any of them children?"

Papa would answer, I knew, without flinching. Not flinching is part of a doctor's job.

"Two boys, handsome, actually." He held the reins steady—Papa held *everything* steady.

I stroked the railing of the buggy, peeling back a long splinter. *Such things will never affect my life.* Then I pressed the splinter back into place. *Papa would never let that happen.*

I turned to look at clouds ladling their way across the soon-evening sky. Below them were the hushed buildings where my father worked. Branch Hospital was the holding station for those with the lepela. No one knew who brought the disease to the islands, but everyone was full of pointing fingers.

The whole compound perched nervously on Fisherman's Point: the single-story hospital, stark cottages, a cook house, and laundry. In a falling-down school, Mr. Unea taught eighteen infected children for $50 a year. He asked and asked, but still had not been paid in six months. Male teachers in public schools made $1,000. Even female teachers made $500. Almost all of those examined at the clinic were sent to Moloka`i. A few who were wrongly diagnosed were released to their families.

Surrounding the entire facility was a fence of varying heights. When a kona wind blew across the island, the shoreline backed up, seeped under the fence, and turned the whole compound into a wretched mess—even Mother Marianne said the facility needed more than a prayer. I studied a low section of the fence, wondering.

A week later, Papa and I worked together in the pasture. A chain of blurry clouds linked across the sky as Papa and I straightened the last of the kiawe fence posts we had set along the leeward side of the pasture to replace the rotten ones. We had soaked the new posts in salted water for three months. They now stood dried and strong and ready to withstand the beetles. Back to the barn we went, the fence like new.

"Papa," I said, hefting as best I could the remaining wire into the corner of the barn. My muscles looked like pieces of string compared with the huge arms of the inmate we had seen in the paddy wagon. I looked at my father cautiously and stepped into uncertain waters. "Why is the fence at Branch Hospital so short?"

Papa reached for the pail. "Seems to me like that fence is plenty tall."

"But not in one spot." I straightened a large square-headed nail and hung the wire cutters on it. "A patient could practically step over the fence and escape."

"I don't know." Papa threw out the salt water. "Maybe it needs repair."

"But if the lepela is so contagious—"

Papa gave me a stern look that made me swallow my questions. I twisted a scrap of wire and watched the saltwater soak into the ground as Papa walked around the corner of the barn and toward the house.

Why was I listening to Hoaloha? For the next week, I stomped out questions like they were fire as Hoaloha and I continued to argue about my father's beliefs—no, *my* beliefs. The more I took Papa's side, the more Hoaloha grew quiet on the topic of the disease when I was in her presence. So did Kalina and Mama. I felt surrounded by shrugs, unaware of what was coming.

Chapter 7

MUSTARD SKIES OVER WAI`ANAE

If you stood on our lānai and threw a stone down the valley toward town, walked to pick it up and tossed it again, the stone would land in the red dirt of Kalina and Uncle Elia's yard. To know Kalina was to know where walking ends off and floating might one day begin. Her eyes were soft and large, holding oceans of laughter. But she had bays of sadness, too, like dark shelves dropping to the ocean floor where no fish would go. Kalina was Mama's younger sister. As a nurse at Branch Hospital, working with those with leprosy, she also worked with Papa.

Kalina's English was much better than Mama's, and she knew all the good swear words, too, like "damn" and "hell" and "bastard." She usually saved them for when she talked about the legislators, who had more than a few of their own as they stomped across the legislative floor waving their arms and shouting that America needed to protect Hawai`i from Hawaiians.

"Hell no!" she would say. "We don't need the haoles to save us from ourselves!"

Between our houses sat a large vegetable garden. The garden was a magical mixture of talk and stories; a place where dragonflies flitted across lava walls holding our taro patch; where bees wove among apple trees, and bean stalks pushed up through the red earth. A third person lived farther down the hill and sometimes shared the garden. Her name was Liona.

One day, I was making trips back and forth from Kalina's shed to our garden, carrying tools to Kalina and Liona. Mama was in town. I walked to the garden feeling like a morning star, or like a leaf swept down a mountain and out to the sea. Threading along the ridge was a wisp of white, so different from the way Mama described the turtle clouds on the morning I was born. And why not? Keahi was back from Maui, and everything was light and bright.

I had ridden my horse Miki home from town, relieved when the final school bell stopped ringing and I could escape the bouncing petticoats and insults of Miss Spencer. Coming from the other side of the bamboo was the deep, rich, singing voice of Liona.

Tousled are the feathers
of birds in the morning rain...

If a grotto were a person, I think it would be Liona. Everything about her was large and round—her body, her laugh, and her spirit. She had more cousins than a tree has apples. Some cousins came to visit every week; some came once in ten years.

After a while, Kalina sent me down the hill to get a garden rake from her ever-leaning shed. The beans were tall, and the bamboo was ever shooting to the sky, so Kalina did not see me return. I stepped behind the bamboo and leaned to reach for a hoe.

"I think Mānoa, at least for now. There are good places there." Kalina's voice found its way through the leafy jade-colored stalks of bamboo. Liona stopped singing.

I paused, trying to remember why this sort of talk felt familiar. Something from what seemed a long time ago....

"They'll be burning the cane fields soon, you know," Kalina continued.

I inched a section of bamboo aside and watched. Kalina stood up and turned to look toward the distant sky over Wai`anae. At the end of every season, the sugar cane fields were burned flat to the ground to make ready for the next crop.

Liona kept working, bent over, hacking at weeds between the rows of cabbage. "There is still time," she said without looking up.

I stayed quiet. My stomach churned as I recalled a similar conversation in the garden when I was a child.

"But the lunas!" urged Kalina, wiping her hands. She meant the field bosses. "These are lean times for the lunas, too. You know how they can be when they are drinking; ten dollars is a lot, even to a luna. If they find him in the fields—"

To see better, I widened the space between bamboo stalks. Liona stopped working and stood up. She, too, looked across the valley to where the rising smoke of burning fields would soon darken the land, turning yellow and smoky the skies over Wai`anae. The burning had already started on the far side of the fields.

"Next week, then," Liona said in a worried voice, "we'll move him to the cave above Owl Hill. He will be safe there."

Every native child on the island knew of Mānoa, the valley next to Nu`uanu. At the base of the Ko'olau range, Mānoa Valley sat like a giant tipped bowl of green facing the sea. It was one of the first visible features of O`ahu as ships approached the island. Mānoa meant, "The Place Where One Can Be Free." And everything did seem free in Mānoa: rocks cascaded down to a quiet halt at the foot of the valley; water rushed over the rocks, scribbling wetness all down their front. But all of this was hidden from the eye. In Mānoa Valley, it was said, there were places so good for hiding that nobody could ever find you.

I stepped bravely through the bamboo.

"Move *who*?" I asked.

Kalina turned quickly. She and Liona glanced at each other. Was I imagining or did Kalina slightly shake her head at Liona?

Everything stopped at the sound of the buggy as Hoku curved the rise and headed toward the barn. I had a strange feeling as they watched Papa bring Hoku to a stop at the barn.

"Move who?" I asked again.

Kalina reached for the cane knife, turned it over and over in her hand, and slipped it back into its sheath.

"The wind," she murmured, watching Papa.

I felt a shiver too small to find the surface of my skin. I looked toward the upper part of Nu`uanu Valley where the hills held hiding places, too, as images carried me back to that evening in my childhood. The Chinese lanterns...the map...the stick figures I had drawn...the look on Papa's face that made me dig my toes into the moss-covered bricks of our lānai.

Over the years, I had forgotten about that night. Why had I not realized? *No,* I said to myself, *not the wind.*

During all those years, Mama had not once scolded me about that evening, not once said a word. She must have realized I had no idea what I had done. And yet I felt, standing there in the garden, as if I had betrayed Mama not once, but twice; for my feelings on that day did not support her belief that the lepers should be allowed to stay with their families, but rather my father's belief that they should be sent away.

I stood looking down the valley and across the foothills to smoke beginning to rise above the cane fields, remembering an old Hawaiian saying. He imu puhi, the smoke will rise. It related to an old proverb about secrets, that no matter how much one covers a steaming imu, or earth stove, the smoke will rise. The secret will be revealed.

My father was doing everything in his power to send the lepers away, while behind his back, my mother— I reached for a stalk of bamboo, trying to steady myself. *Pears go missing from the porch...a box of bandages disappears...a pot of poi larger than needed for our family.* I clung to the bamboo, feeling like you do when you are standing on sand one moment, and in the next you realize that the sea has been coming for a long time and washing the sand away, and you have been sinking the whole time.

So this was the silence. For years it had painted the walls of my house and been stroked by Tūtū into the hem of a dress.

How could I not support Papa? He only wanted to protect the remaining Hawaiians. Wasn't that a right thing to do? But how could I not support Mama? She only wanted to keep families together. Wasn't that a right thing to do, too?

Just when I thought I was old enough to make my own choices, I realized that the power of choice could be an awful thing. Whatever I did, I would be betraying one of my parents. Maybe, I thought for just an instant, I could do nothing. *No. To do nothing was making a choice, too. Silence, too, was taking a side.*

I had no truth of my own, nor did I know where I would find it or at what cost. What if the cost was losing Papa? What if the cost was losing Mama? What if I lost them both?

Chapter 8

THE PAPAYA TREE

The sky was full of purple clouds a few weeks later as Keahi and I started home from school. He had finally enrolled. Papa was allowing me to ride Miki to and from school, and Keahi rode Ali`i, a black stallion. Only a few students, mostly those attending Punahoa, rode horses to school. We rode through town, past Kawaiha`o Church and toward the valley. Nothing in town seemed to have changed much since he left. We passed every imaginable home: older grass huts and more recent clapboard houses like mine, homes of coral rock and lava, mansions and falling down structures. Each home had a deep verandah that swam in the shade of its own jungle. Banana, papaya, coconut and breadfruit trees grew fast as you could blink. Visitors found it hard to believe that tucked inside these pockets of shade, and including the outlying areas, lived thousands of people.

The paddy wagon from O`ahu jail was not an uncommon sight, so I was not surprised to see it parked again with one wheel on a rock and the crew standing in handfuls along Beretania Street. They were preparing streets for when the current gaslights would be replaced with electricity. That was not going to happen soon; only a few businesses had the luxury of electricity.

A large and muscular inmate leaned on the handle of a shovel and watched us pass by.

"Mele." Keahi reached toward me. "That's Keanu!"

Without thinking, I turned and looked back to see the man I had seen before.

"The man in the newspaper," Keahi said. "He ambush his girlfriend's husband."

The thought sent chicken skin up my arms. I had read about the case. Murder was rare on the islands, so the case was followed with fascination by haoles and Hawaiians alike. The man in the photo wore this man's face—the eyes of a man I imagined could kill someone. I watched him lift a mighty piece of timber and drop the load at his feet. Those were arms that could be brutal. Was it true? He had ambushed the man on a road, and beat him to death? Other inmates turned to watch us as Keahi and I rode past. Did Keanu ever feel remorse for what he had done? The only person I knew who never seemed to question himself, was Papa.

To take a short way home, Keahi and I left the streets and veered off toward a path through the papaya grove. He wanted papayas for his aunty, so we stopped and tethered Miki and Ali`i. They munched on mountain apples while I stood at the bottom of the tree, watching Keahi.

It was not like Miki to shy suddenly and lash out a foot. I spun around and stepped back so fast I almost fell.

He smelled of alcohol, wearing the same smile as the day he pulled a slingshot from his pocket and shot a dove off the verandah of Royal School—for no reason. In an instant, Keahi was down the tree and had stepped between Daniel and me. He cautiously offered a papaya to Daniel, keeping his eyes on him.

"Aloha. How is it going, Daniel?"

With a grunt, Daniel ignored Keahi's hospitality. An islander would not do that. He glanced up the narrow trunk of the papaya tree, its small top clustered with fruit and swaying lightly in a breeze.

"Looks easy enough," Daniel mumbled as if to the tree. His droopy eyes appraised the bumpy skin of the trunk. He tugged at the hand axe hanging from his belt and dumped it onto the flattened grass at the base of the tree.

Keahi stepped back and stroked his chin.

"You don't think I can," slurred Daniel.

Keahi shrugged.

"Well, island boy," said Daniel lurching sideways, "if you can climb it, so can I."

Daniel looked at Keahi's bare feet, tough as leather. He pulled off his badly worn boots and threw them in a heap alongside the axe. Hopping around the grass on one foot and trying not to fall, Daniel tugged at the other sock. Dirty and half-full of holes, it landed next to his boots. He hoisted up his trousers and shook hair from his eyes.

I did not know a haole boy who could climb a papaya tree—not all the way to the top.

Daniel clenched his hands around the narrow trunk. He cupped his feet around the base and gradually pulled himself up a few feet. But when he eased his grip to move his hands higher, he slid to the ground...bark tearing at his feet. He tried again and again, each time cursing the tree. I cringed. Soon the dirty sock on his foot was turning red, and his hands were raw. He glared up at the top of the tree, swearing and kicking at the trunk as if the fault were in the tree.

Keahi winced to see Daniel's hands. "Eh, Daniel, not that impor—"

"Shut up!"

Keahi clenched his fists.

"Come on," I whispered, hauling Keahi across the grass toward Ali`i and Miki. As we left, we looked back to see Daniel swatting at the tree, swearing loudly, and trying again to climb it. I do not think he even saw us leave.

The sky grew dark and moody as we rode toward Keahi's house. As we reached the rise and his house was in sight, I reined in Miki with a sudden realization.

"Keahi! I left a sack of schoolbooks back at the papaya tree. Lying in the grass where Miki was tethered."

"Daniel's gone by now, come on," said Keahi.

We turned around on the trail and started back to the clearing. Within minutes a drizzle turned to hard rain, then to sheets of slanting silver that stung my arms. Branches drooped. Waterfalls poured down from the leaves of wild ginger. Miki's hooves made sucking sounds as they popped out of the soupy trail, and squishing sounds at the next step. The level of rainwater in the streets of Honolulu often rose fast like this, until mud oozed under the front door of a feed store or a bank and spread across the floor. As we reached the clearing, the rain stopped as quickly as it had started—we were drenched and the sky was blue.

Keahi saw it first and pulled Ali`i up fast. When I realized, I dug my fingers into the soaking reins. We sat staring, with water still running down our faces and arms. I could not tell the difference between rain and the wetness of sudden tears.

The papaya tree, beloved by Tūtū and us all for its wonderful fruit, with its green bushy top so majestic against the sky a few moments ago, lay in a long sad puddle of mud. The stump was covered with axe marks. Next to it was one of

Daniel Livingstone's dirty socks. Rain mingled with my tears of frustration, sadness, and anger. Keahi tightened his jaw as if chewing tough meat, as if more than a tree had been chopped down.

"How can a boy be so cruel?" I asked Keahi. All over the islands, haoles were showing disrespect—for our culture and for our land.

We stood staring at the fallen tree. A breeze lifted a small mangled branch, then let it sink back into the reddish-brown mud. An almost-ripe papaya, turning golden yellow and still attached to the tree, bobbed up and down in the murky water, rising as if longing to go home with us, then sinking. Was this so different, I wondered, from what was happening to our islands?

"You watch," Keahi said. "Going to come back to Daniel someday."

Over a period of weeks, the stump dried and turned gray as if to signal the cane fields to burn, sending their plumes of smoke jumping to the sky. For weeks I had watched for the smoke over Wai`anae, wondering about the man hiding in the cane fields.

I was beginning to feel pulled along, not by my own choices, but by events outside myself. Then came the tragedy on the little steamer *Mokoli`i* during its latest trip across the channel.

Chapter 9

A SPLASH IN THE NIGHT

A young woman had been put on the steamer on the previous Sunday night, Kalina said. Shipping Day. Like others forced up the gangplank and herded onto the decks of the *Mokoli`i*, she had to be peeled away from her family. In the air was the sound of despair as families and patients wailed over their common pain: loved ones leaving forever.

"That night," said Kalina, "the weather was worse than usual. The trip across the channel can be rough as it is."

Passengers, all of them lepers being exiled to Kalawao, were crammed on the midnight decks along with horses and cows and crates of chickens. Wood, sacks of rice and cargo were also making the trip. I knew that long into the night there would be sounds of crying, with people holding onto each other for whatever comfort they could find as they huddled together across the channel to an unknown life. If one could call it that.

"Part way across the channel, the others heard it," Kalina said. The sound cut through the wailing, encircling it afterward with a sudden silence.

Splash!

At the sound, the passengers ran to the side and looked over the rail, cupping their eyes to try to see. Perhaps a cage of chickens, they thought at first. Or a piece of luggage knocked from a tall hold and sent over the railing by a nervous cow. They saw nothing but moving darkness. They knew what can happen during the unbearable loneliness as the little steamer crosses the deep channel, how sadness can drive a person to do something they might never have considered until that moment.

The next morning, Father Damien, the priest who cared for the patients at the settlement, checked the passengers who had arrived against the list of those sent. A young woman had set out on the steamer but never arrived at the rocky landing. Rather than Kalawao, she chose the sea.

"It happens sometimes." Kalina said this as she rubbed her wrist. "At other times, when they arrive at Kalawao and are told to wade ashore..." She hesitated. "Some turn toward the open sea and swim."

Kalina had examined the woman before her departure and assured her that Father Damien would care for her. But even I knew that a hundred Father Damiens could not replace the woman's husband and children.

The news found its way to the streets of Honolulu.

"One less leper mouth to feed," whispered some as they hurried down the muddy streets under pink parasols.

"Good as dead anyway," nodded others.

"Nothing but a nuisance."

"The Will of God."

My face felt hot to hear of these words. To so many haoles, those with the disease were no more important than a piece of bark, than brown leaves falling to the earth. Mama and Tūtū and Kalina cried and held each other. Keahi dug his hands deep into pockets and said nothing. Even Papa pulled a hand across his mouth and shook his head.

A few evenings later, the sun set orange and alone and barely visible beyond the pali cliffs dropping to the windward side of the island. Not far from the shrimp cages in Kāne`ohe, just as a fisherman turned his boat toward shore to go home to his family, he felt a tugging at his line.

It is said there are some things a fisherman hopes never to pull over the side of his boat. He pulled up the remaining clothing of the woman's husband. A note in a pocket was partly eaten by fish. "We are ho`opili," the note said, "bound together."

There was grief under many roofs, on both sides of the pali. The couple's children were hānai'd, taken in and cared for by the woman's mother. The woman's father had disappeared. It seemed strange to me that nobody knew where he was...but nobody seemed to ask, either. That was sometimes true on the islands: things happened, people went missing, the mouths of families clamped shut.

The missing man—the father of the drowned woman—was Liona's cousin.

For days we heard wailing come from Liona's house, ebbing at night, rising with the morning sun. This was the first time I had a connection with anyone—if only through someone with whom we shared the garden—who had been sent to Moloka`i. For some reason this surprised me.

"What," Mama said, "you think the lepela only touches somebody else? Never someone we know?"

That evening, the air was balmy and the valley quiet. It was one of those nights when you think you can hear the kāwelu grass growing outside your window. Sometimes in the evenings, I heard gunshot bouncing off the ridges and zigzagging down the valley; someone hunting a wild boar, perhaps. But on this night, even the hills were without sound. Papa and I worked together in the barn.

"Papa," I started to say as I held new shelving and he nailed it in place. Then I felt silently numb. I wondered how old the woman's children were. What it would have been like to lose Mama when I was a child, then to lose Papa. I felt the shelving slip.

Papa glanced sideways at me and repositioned the shelf. "That mind of yours looks pretty busy," he said. He stood back and eyed the shelf, then lifted one side and renailed it.

I never expected to say what came out.

"Why can't the lepers be cared for at home?"

Papa stopped hammering.

"I hope you're not saying you think they should be."

"I...I don't know." What *was* I saying?

Papa took a big breath and set the hammer down.

"Mele, I don't understand why suddenly you feel the need to question your father on this. I've had more years of dealing with this disease than you've been on the earth."

I did not doubt Papa at all. I knew he was right—or did I?

"Do we really have to send them away?"

Papa gently sat me down, right there in the hay, with Miki munching behind me and the slightest breeze coming through the window. He sat facing me, reached out, took my hands, and held them in his. His hands felt large and warm and safe. He rubbed a thumb along the inside of my palms as he watched me.

"Mele," he said, "maybe I've never fully explained to you why I feel the way I do. Or why I do the work I do."

I shook my head. He had not. I knew how he felt about separating the lepers, but not totally why. He continued rubbing his thumb into the palm of my hand, as if he might find there a way to make everything simple.

"We are dealing with an unknown in this disease," he explained, "so, if we err, we need to err on the side of practicalities and caution—not on the side of emotions. If research bears out that the lepela is not as contagious as believed, which Dr. Arning says might be the case, then all these years of separation were not necessary after all. Families will have been put through unnecessary emotional pain."

He continued. "But if the disease *is* highly contagious, and we let the lepers stay with their families because they are miserable when separated, then we have erred unforgivably, and we have put the survival of the population at stake. It's an awful trade, I admit. But the disease is epidemic in the islands, it's deadly, it's incurable, and..." he said, shaking his head, "... it's not going away."

He tried to give me a little smile. It faded.

"Mele." He was squeezing my hands now. "I love you so much. I could not have asked for a more special daughter. But we can't risk losing a whole race, and an entire culture, simply because Hawaiians are sad about the measures necessary to preserve them. Is this making sense?"

I nodded.

When Papa explained this, his reasoning did make sense. It made sense as we walked to the house. It made sense all the way through supper, all evening long as we talked and ate pineapple on the lānai with Kalina and Uncle Elia and his sister's family. The haole way made sense right up to the moment when I lay down that night and closed my eyes.

And then my father's words were gone. I tasted the salty night air...heard the splash...felt the tug on the fisherman's line. I thought of how much I loved my father, how the haole way of solving a problem is to put it on a boat and send it out into the night. I fell asleep among tears I did not want to admit were my own.

Chapter 10

A PIECE OF SILK – DR. AKITA

One morning in early April, it rained so hard the dirt jumped. By the time I fed and brushed Miki and Hoku, the earth was crusted dry and I heard a buggy coming up the hill. Our visitor was Dr. Akita, a friend of Papa's from Queen's Hospital. At the end of his visit I would hold in my hand a piece of white silk from a faraway place called Nepal, and in my mind a picture of meeting Father Damien, the priest on Moloka`i who realized someone had disappeared from the *Mokoli`i* during the night crossing to Kalawao.

Pōki`i and I watched Dr. Akita's arm shoot straight up in a friendly wave. He was a man of corners and edges, smiles and laughter, and always moving.

"Mele!" whispered Pōki`i, "isn't that the doctor who went to China?"

"Yes, and don't ask about snakes!" I warned. We had none on the islands, and Pōki`i was fascinated with foreign places that had these huge colored worms.

"I have gifts for you both," said Dr. Akita as he jumped to the ground and reached to the seat of the buggy. I had forgotten what shiny, clean hair he had.

"I brought them from Nepal."

Pōki`i smiled widely, holding out both hands. Into them was dropped a nest of brightly colored silk string, perfect for a boy who spent hours sitting under the banyan tree on the lānai, making intricate string figures. In my hands, Dr. Akita placed a lovely wooden box. Painted on the lid was a cherry tree. Its pink flowers were so bright that I stroked them to see if they were real.

"Did you go to visit your family in Japan?" I asked.

"Not this time, no. This box was made in Nepal." His voice and face became animated. "It's a place so high in the mountains you feel like you are in the sky. In these mountains live hooded monks. They take small amounts of brown rice with bits of vegetable and eat in silence. Sometimes they walk the hills of the steep valley or work in the monastery gardens while long poisonous snakes lie in the grass nearby. They share the earth quietly, everyone moving slowly...*veeery* sloooowly." Dr. Akita snatched a quick grab at Pōki`i—"Hrarhh!"—who jumped back laughing.

From the box I lifted two pieces of pure white silk and held them to the sunlight. So soft!

"How do I thank the silkworm who made these?" I said, opening my arms. Dr. Akita knew how to hug! Not like some haoles who lean forward and are relieved when the hug is finished, and they can get their shoulders back.

"Good to see you again, Gavin," called Papa, walking toward us. He gave me the look, mostly of raised eyebrows, meant as an invitation to leave them to talk. Pōki`i ran off to show the colored strings to Tūtū and Mama. I pretended not to know what the look meant, and invited Dr. Akita to have some fresh pineapple on the lānai. It was the first time my father allowed me to stay when he spoke with an associate—a sign he saw me as an adult?

Dr. Akita politely let me quiz him about his visit to Nepal, then he turned to Papa. "Have things changed much between the Board and the Hawaiians? A hotbed of tempers when I left."

"All the worse now," answered Papa, reaching for a piece of pineapple. Was he referring to the woman who had drowned? The frustrated letters her family wrote to the Board of Health?

"Long battle," said Dr. Akita. "Surely the disease will be under control soon."

Papa swirled ice in his glass, frowning. "That's what we've all hoped for. But, no, it's here to stay."

I swallowed. Everybody sensed this about the disease, but I had only recently heard Papa say so.

"What's this about the German researcher, Dr. Arning, is it?" asked Dr. Akita.

I moved closer, trying to remember why the name was familiar.

Papa nodded. "He arrived in November, while you were gone. The Board of Health paid his way over, though I hear he took his sweet time, visiting Niagara Falls on the way. Arning thinks he can trigger the disease by inoculating animals, and maybe learn more about how it is passed. He has monkeys, rabbits—cages all over the place. We gave him that shed next to Branch Hospital, but I doubt—"

"Papa! That's the doctor Keahi is building cages for. He and Mr. Nott at the Planing Mill!"

Papa gave me his eyebrow look. I sank back into my manners.

"Why not just improve conditions on Moloka`i?" continued Dr. Akita. "For God's sake, the inmates at the jail eat better.

And what has it taken, almost 20 years to get the settlement a *doctor?*" He pulled a penny from his pocket and studied it.

"It's not only that, Gavin, though it seems that would be obvious to the legislature." Papa hesitated, frowning as the energy left his voice. "Hawaiians want their lepers at home—now more than ever."

I felt my skin prickle. Was it so hard to understand why the drowned woman's family would want to care for her at home?

"Hawaiians don't even seem afraid of the disease," observed Dr. Akita, scratching the penny. "In fact, they seem downright reckless in having contact with them."

"You're right. Their lack of fear is unique the world over."

I felt myself holding inside the words I wanted to say. The woman and her husband did not care about being protected by haole laws; they just wanted to be together. I thought of what Hoaloha said: if the lepela was so contagious, then why, after eleven years at the settlement, did Father Damien not have the disease?

"You'd think there was something else going on," said Dr. Akita, spinning the penny on the table, "the way the Board resists every dime spent on the settlement. They always have."

"Look at Damien," said Papa, nodding in agreement, "a Catholic Priest devoting his life to the lepers—known and loved for his work. And look at the Protestants, so far barely a shred of help at the settlement."

"Who holds the money strings?"

"That's my point, Gavin. Most of the Board is Protestant. You think they are anxious to give money to Damien? He already makes them look bad; last thing they want is to advertise their own shortcomings."

"Phew!" Dr. Akita stopped spinning the penny. "So, it's really *Damien* the Board is saying no to?"

I straightened up. What did he mean?

"You'd never get me to say it publicly," said Papa, "but that's my hunch. You know how these things can slide along on the underside of what is seen. Nahoa and I have our differences about this, but we do talk. She says Hawaiians are growing disillusioned with the Protestant churches—more and more Hawaiians are moving their membership to the Catholic Church. Mimo tells me the same thing. The Catholics seem to care about the lepers, and that goes a mighty long way with Hawaiians right now."

"At least the Catholic Church isn't after their land," said Dr. Akita. "At least the Catholics aren't pushing annexation for personal gain. It's a far different story for many Protestants I know, though they would deny it the whole day long."

"All of which," said Papa, "might explain the shift in church membership. Nahoa tells me Hawaiians are leaving the Protestant churches."

It was true. Hoaloha said if Mimo joined the Catholic church, she would too.

"Well, Damien's no angel!" said Dr. Akita, suddenly laughing. "He does as he damn well pleases—drives the Board nuts. I hear even the Catholics are getting fed up with his constant harping to help the settlement."

Papa chuckled and reached for a slice of pear. "He's the only person I know who can exhaust Mother Marianne. I have only met the man a few times, meetings at Branch Hospital. Maybe he thinks his work has earned him the right. After all, Gavin, the man's given his life to the lepers when nobody else would."

I barely remember the rest of the conversation, but by the time Dr. Akita climbed into his buggy and waved good-bye from the bottom of the hill, I was a girl with a plan. I turned the pieces of silk over and over in my hand, held them to the light and through them saw the blurred circle of a shining sun. Surely there was a way to meet Father Damien, and I would find it.

Not many days later, Kalina and I were in the kitchen making kukui nut candles for Pōki`i. He loved the candles, made from stringing together the roasted, shelled kukui nuts. I reached for a handful of nuts, laid them in a row, and began threading them along a sliver of bamboo.

"How often does Father Damien come to Honolulu?" I avoided Kalina's eyes and reached quickly for another nut.

Kalina took one long look at me and shook her head.

"No!" Fooling Kalina was impossible. "Mele, do not even *think* about this idea hatching in your head."

I dropped the nuts and practically leapt at her. "Please, Kalina! There must be a way. I know you can!"

"And what would your Papa say if I took his daughter—already finding ways to challenge him—to meet the hero of the lepers? Sticks already smoldering, and you want to add more kindling?"

Papa says (with a warm scowl) that Mama and I show no mercy in wearing down an innocent person. Soon the candles were made, the table was cleared, and Kalina's resistance was gone. "Father Damien is coming soon, to talk to the Board," she said. "Maybe we could see him come off the *Mokoli`i*." She sent me a warning look. "But only from a distance. You must promise you won't try to meet him!"

I thought of Pōki`i, the way he scooted up to the edge of a lie and slowly leaned into it; the way he blinked part way through as if trying to remember the last half. I stroked a kukui nut, my thinking fingers running along the smooth side, feeling for the right words. The screen door banged open and Pōki`i flew inside, saving me.

When Kalina first asked why I wanted to meet Father Damien, I had no answer. When a pond of water is disturbed, it takes a while for the dirt to settle and the pond to become clear. Maybe I needed Father Damien to do this for me—to make everything clear again. To make me remember why Papa was right.

Chapter 11

FATHER DAMIEN

Each day took me farther away from the sadness I felt about the drownings and closer to the day when Kalina said I might get to see Father Damien arrive on the *Mokoli`i*. Finally, the day arrived. We would shop first, she said, then go to the docks.

On market day, Honolulu swarmed with excitement—the colors, the noise, different languages, the taste of dust as riders on horses galloped past. Rows of vendors leaned over their crates to hand vegetables and fruits to customers and opened their palms to coins from all over the world: dimes, pence, reals, sovereigns and gold pieces. Customers smiled at handfuls of change just as mysterious—silver coins of Napoleon III, a Peruvian dollar, Mexican coins not distinguishable in value—and made their way to the next vendor. It occurred to me that nobody seemed to care about the value of the coins so long as they had something shiny in their hands when they walked away.

Everyone dressed as if for a feast or coronation. The men wore red scarves tied in a knot around the neck, and their best shirts. Dressed in brightly colored holokū dresses, native women walked like gifts down the street. Some looked elegant! Children grasped the hands of their mamas or tūtūs. Everywhere were leis of ginger, jasmine, plumeria, and the traditional maile that hung in long dark green strands from the necks of men. People jumped back and spat bits of dust as horses galloped past carrying kanaka, native Hawaiians, from outlying valleys. Up and down the streets they dashed, shouting and laughing, reckless with joy at seeing their friends. It was impossible to avoid the smell of delicious food.

Everywhere was talk of our recent election or gossip about how so-and-so was arrested for doing the hula without a license, though that law was rarely enforced now. "Why do we need a license to do our own dances?" people asked.

I grabbed Kalina's arm when I saw a massive man leaning against a brick building. "That man," I whispered leaning toward her, "he looks like the murderer, Keanu."

"It can't be," she whispered back. "Keanu is in jail until his trial in August." Then he will be hanged, I expected her to say.

Kalina and I finally moved along to get the items we needed, and then Kalina stepped into a shop. Just as I turned from looking at a scarf, I saw the shopkeeper quietly reach out to hand a bottle of Chaulmoogra oil to Kalina, and with a gesture of his hand, refuse payment.

"Why are you getting Chaulmoogra? And why didn't he charge you?" Even as I asked, I realized. Chaulmoogra was an expensive oil from India used with some success to treat leprosy.

"In case someone needs it," she answered, wrapping kerchiefs around the bottle. I said nothing but tucked the knowledge away, certain the oil was for the man she and Liona talked about moving to a cave in Mānoa Valley.

Market was not far from the harbor, especially with me hurrying us along in the hope of seeing Father Damien. Kalina now carried sugar, cloth, and fish wrapped in ti leaves. I slung over my shoulder a sack filled with syrup-soaked ginger, peaches from Kona, and ramie. In a flat blue box tied with pink string, I carried moon cakes and sugar pineapple. Around my neck hung the shiny green lei I had bought for Father Damien.

Craaaagh! Craaagh! "Look, Kalina!" I said. An arrogant peacock had rushed into the street and planted itself in front of a wooden cargo wagon, refusing with flaps and squawks to be shooed away. Pīkake, peacocks, often wandered in from the rice fields on the other side of Kewalo Basin. They dragged their jeweled tails through the dusty streets of town, strutting as if the islands rose out of the sea just to adore them. A barefoot little boy turned to watch, still pulled along by his mama's hand.

Lying in the dirt, shimmering and blue in a patch of shade, was one of the peacock's feathers.

I never repaid his kindness. A single memory made me stop, staring at the feather. Suddenly, just for a moment, I remembered myself as a little girl, and the day I met one of Liona's cousins.

I had been playing near Kalina's shed when I heard a tiny sound, like something soft landing with a thump against something hard. I walked around the corner of the shed and saw, below the window, a tiny \`ō\`ō bird lying in the grass. At the sight of the injured bird, I began to cry. Around the corner of the shed came Liona's cousin. I never knew his name, but I called him Manu, bird, for what he did that day. We sat together, cross-legged in the grass, watching the last breaths of the tiny honey eater. Its black wings covered the few yellow feathers beneath.

"We have to help it," I had cried, watching its twisted neck and fluttering heart.

"Cannot," said Manu.

Two blinks of its tiny eyelids, and its chest went still. Using an old copper soup ladle we had found in Kalina's shed, Manu dug a shallow dip in the red earth. In it we laid the `ō`ō bird, patting handfuls of tear-stained dirt on top. Manu wiped away my tears, but more tears took their place. He stroked the tarnished handle of the soup ladle as he told me the bird felt no pain. But nothing soothed my loss.

He patted my hand. "Wait here, a gift for Mele." He returned with a peacock feather of dazzling turquoise. The instant I ran a finger across the delicate colors—so silky—my tears were gone.

Standing in the street and looking down at the feather, I wondered what happened to Manu. Maybe he moved to Maui, I thought, or the Big Island. Lots of people moved around on the islands, changing places of work.

By the time I caught up with Kalina, my thoughts of Manu were mixed with crackling noises, smells of oil, and the general confusion that fills the senses as you get closer to the docks. Being at the docks is what it must be like at the center of a beehive on a sunny day. The scene varied from day to day, but at any hour the docks were a noisy place. Sailors, together with an occasional parrot perched on a shoulder, shouted words that shocked ladies passing by. On Steamer Day, sounds of the Royal Hawaiian Band welcomed arriving passengers. The little inter-island steamers such as the *Kilauea* wove their way between the longboats. Rigging slapped in the breeze, tall-mast ships rubbed against oily pilings, and rats scratched about at night.

"The docks are trouble," said some. Drunken sailors staggered back to ships visiting from foreign ports, tired from what Kalina called "loose-trouser trips" to certain parts of town. They laughed and tilted bottles and wiped their mouths, then with a massive heave sent the bottle spinning far out into the harbor where it bobbed up and down among the seaweed. Wine barrels creaked and rolled down the gangplanks, sending bare-chested men jumping back. The wine barrels slammed against a pile of Oregon lumber and rested on their sides until loaded into carts and hauled away. Wine was everywhere, and the newspapers said too much of it went to our king. Always there were smells and sights and sounds that offended one sense while pleasing another, all of it sending you on a wild journey of the imagination.

At last a steamer inched its way around a tall vessel, and the faded name *Mokoli`i* appeared on the bow. The little steamer bumped against the pilings, ropes were thrown down and tied off, and the plank dropped with a loud bang against the dock.

From his beginning steps down the gangplank, Father Damien seemed a lonely man. He swayed back and forth while moving forward, as if trying to find his place on the salty gray planks. It seemed odd, since he so well knew his place in the world. He was a burr of a man, a moving dark figure wearing glasses and a hat, and smoking a pipe. When he walked, leaning hard on the railing, I winced.

"His feet hurt," I said. "Look how he is walking."

"Father!" someone called from the deck. In a few strides, a crewman hurried down, tucked an old wooden box under Father Damien's arm, and ran back up the gangplank. Father Damien took a deep breath of harbor air. He was only forty years old, Kalina said. But with a beard already turning gray and with deep lines in his face, he looked like an aging man.

"We met only once," she said, "when he came to talk to Mr. Gibson and the Board of Health."

"Would he remember you?... About what?"

"No," she said, "he wouldn't remember me. He requested an orphanage for girls at Kalaupapa." An area of the settlement.

"What did the Board say?" I remembered what Papa told Dr. Akita about the board being mostly Protestants, irritated that a Catholic priest had done so much for the settlement. But it was not Father Damien's fault, I thought, that others had done so little.

She looked at me flatly. The jasmine lei hung in double strands around her neck and sweetened the air; she stroked it.

"They said no."

As Father Damien reached the bottom of the ramp, a woman in a long shawl, possibly Portuguese, stepped forward. Only a few words were exchanged, but I sensed they were important. He placed his hand on the lid of the wooden box, bowed his head briefly, crossed himself, and handed her the box. At first, she looked as if she did not know quite what to do. She stroked her hand across the lid and around the corners. Then she clutched it to her chest, leaning over it, rocking. Father Damien touched her arm and crossed himself again as she suddenly wailed, "Auwē! Auwē!" Of everything happening around us, her cries were the only sounds I seemed to hear. Father Damien's head bent over hers. His old tattered hat, with strings going from one side to the other and across the top, almost covered her, too.

I stood there holding the lei I had purchased, planning to put it around his neck. But now I knew I had no place in what was happening. I wondered if other mothers had received such a box bearing the last of a loved one's belongings. Maybe a hole-filled shoe, a cap, a ramie bracelet. Maybe a daughter's lock of hair. Had other mothers stood here on the dock and like this woman flung their grief onto Father Damien? How many on Moloka`i had leaned against that chest and been held in the safety of those arms, and then died? I knew Father Damien dug all the graves himself, two or three a week, and he had been doing this since I was a child.

At that moment I thought of these deaths not as graves, not as crosses or even as people dying. I thought of them as an endless stream of small wooden boxes handed to mothers waiting on docks. I knew there were many lepers whose names had been scratched out of family bibles the day they went to Kalawao—and never spoken of again.

What went on in Father Damien's mind, I wondered, in the span of even one day on Moloka`i? What did he tell someone who had let the land seep into his bones…and then was exiled from the very land that gave him life? What did he say to those unable to endure a continual sense of separation? What would I say to someone dying in *my* arms? What could I, so eager to be an adult, offer someone who had been taught to believe they were condemned for getting a disease brought by foreigners? Cursed for a sin they did not understand and could not remove? Until the missionaries came, Mama told me, the Hawaiians had no word for sin, no concept of it.

"I met you once."

I had become lost in my thoughts. Standing before us, Father Damien was addressing Kalina. He tipped his hat, if you could call it that when a thick hand bumps the rim of a hat and knocks it even more sideways.

"At Branch Hospital," he added.

I did not expect him to be built solid as a tree trunk. There were small areas of discoloration on his face and neck. Bumps on one ear. I clutched the lei in my hands.

Kalina nodded. "Yes, I admire your generous work at Kalawao. Very much."

His face was ruddy and tough as an old piece of beat up leather, and almost matched his battered hat. He had such a look of sameness that I can say this: if I were to find scattered around the streets a trampled-looking hat here, a pair of old wire-rimmed glasses there, a wrinkled and worn cloak even farther away and asked to whom they belonged—I would say to this man.

The most opposite person on the islands would be Dr. Arning. He was stiff, Keahi said, with a long narrow head, a thin nose, and glasses he seemed to hide behind.

Father Damien did not look like a man who hid from anything.

"I understand," he continued, "that you are helping in your own way here, so we are working together, yes?"

They smiled and nodded. I wanted him to notice me, too.

He started to turn away. "Father Damien?" I almost jumped forward.

When he turned to look at me, his eyes were intent. They had seen everything, and here I stood before him, a silly girl with a lei in her hands, feeling suddenly selfish that all I could think about was meeting this important man, when all he could think about was bringing respect and dignity to the lepers. This was the man who stood up when the Catholic Superiors asked, "And who will go to Moloka`i, to help the lepers?"

This was a man with a vision for his life, while sometimes I did not even want to help Mama with supper. I stepped back, feeling suddenly distraught at the smallness of my world.

"Would you be Mele?" His hat tilted with his head.

"Yes…sir."

He had to lean close to hear my voice. He smelled like layers of sawdust and pipe tobacco and earth. A smell of something sad lingered around him; it was the smell of sickness gone deep into the fiber of his clothes. Then he straightened up again and looked through his dusty glasses. From his nose to his toes, he was almost straight down.

"As I recall, your father is Dr. Bennett. At meetings for the Board of Health, he mentioned a daughter your age. A good guess on my part, yes?"

None of the words I wanted to say would line up into sentences, so I just smiled. I could see why those who loved him, would love him deeply; and why those who did not, would find it easy to say no to him. He seemed not exactly lovable in the usual hugging way, but lovable in a way that stretched this way and that in directions I had never thought of but found myself willing to go. After parasols and doilies, Miss Spencer and painted eyebrows, I found him refreshing.

His eyes blinked a bit of a smile. By the time he had walked to a waiting buggy and was helped into the seat and gathered his cloak around him, I realized the lei I had brought for him was still dangling from my fingers. As I turned to watch his buggy start down Queen Street toward the legislative buildings, I saw across the street someone else watching him, too. The woman clutched the box with one hand as she fluttered the other at Father Damien.

By the time Father Damien touched his hat as the wagon rolled past, I knew why the lepers called him their hero. Nothing owned Father Damien but his own conscience. He was a man who saw only one star and dug only one well—a deep one. Some said Father Damien was lōlō, crazy to go care for the lepers. But not my grandma—Tūtū was certain as nutmeg that he was an angel.

My hand holding the lei dropped to my side. I had never been committed to anything. Did I even know what it meant? Father Damien left me longing for a moment that would define me. I wanted the same kind of moment that must have defined him the day he stood up before the Catholic Superiors. A telling moment.

Standing there, watching his buggy disappear around the corner, I knew Father Damien had become a stone dropped into the pond of my mind, causing everything to ripple out in a new direction. But not in the direction I had expected.

Chapter 12

MULE TRAIN

The house always had a shuttered look when Tūtū was not feeling well. Upstairs, her head lay heavily upon her pillow. The grayness that covered her eyes almost matched the color of her hair. Her chest rose and fell quickly, stilled, then quickened again. I tucked another soft pillow under her head and tried to cheer her.

"Tūtū," I whispered, "Keahi is excited for your birthday. I know he will make you a wonderful kite!"

She closed her eyes and sunk deeper into the pillow.

"I'll come say goodnight later," I said. She did not answer, and I closed the door.

After an early supper, Papa and I sat together in the parlor. I was reading the newspaper daily by now, sometimes for school assignments but mostly I enjoyed talking with my father about the latest news. Another military ship had come to our harbor, and we both agreed—there were already too many.

"Why here? Why Honolulu?" I asked. Russia, France, America...everyone seemed to want to fly their flag above our palace.

"A good question. What do you think?" he asked.

"But if it's true that we are just small islands in the middle of the ocean, why would they care?"

"Ah," he said, putting down the newspaper. I imagined him sorting through a box of words, looking for the right ones. "Remember the day Daniel Livingstone came upon you and Keahi at the papaya tree?"

"Yes, but—"

"What did Keahi do?"

"Offered Daniel a papaya."

"He did something else. Before that," said Papa.

I thought for a moment. "He slid down the papaya tree."

"Yes...and then what did he do?"

"He stepped between me and Daniel...facing Daniel."

"Why?"

I tried not to blush. "To protect me."

Papa picked up the newspaper and started reading. "Always good," he said, smiling to the newspaper, "when we can answer our own questions."

I finally gave up trying to grasp the mind of foreigners, and reached for another section of the newspaper.

A brief article reported little progress in the work of Dr. Arning. He was still trying to reproduce the leprosy bacillus. Now he had added a monkey to his growing collection of animals. *Good,* I thought, *more cages for Keahi to build.*

"Is Dr. Arning any closer to a cure?" (I asked this only after making sure I could not answer it myself.)

"Probably not. They just recently isolated the bacteria—Dr. Hansen in Norway."

"But can't they do more...to accelerate their research?"

He lowered the paper. "Accelerate?" There was a tiny edge to his voice. "Mele, this disease has been with us for thousands of years."

A long ride often soothed me, so I went to the barn, haltered Miki, and reined her toward the pali. We galloped at first, spurred on by my frustration with Papa. Queen Emma's gardens, her barns, and the open pasture flew past us. Papa said he wanted me to have a good mind, to think for myself. But on the topic of the disease—? I dug my heels deeper into Miki's sides.

The wind whipped through my hair, as if lashing me for my thoughts. One moment I was worried by even a thread of separation between Papa and me; the next moment I was sharpening knives to slash those threads. I felt afraid. Not the hot fear of danger, not the vague fear the darkness holds. What frightened me, especially after meeting Father Damien, was my own path. I was afraid that one day I would turn and reach back for Papa's hand, and he would not be there.

I paused and looked across the sky. Pig clouds—it would rain by morning. For a while, Miki and I had the road to ourselves. She trotted up the middle to avoid the deep and hardened ruts made by wagon wheels. A few miles up the road from our house, the valley began to narrow. It was an area where wild boars, often with broken tusks from rooting among the rocks, roamed the hills. From lack of use, some of the old trails had already grown over.

Ahead of us was a mist that sometimes reminded me of a person. A stringy mist reminded me of Pōki`i. A lifting fog was like Tūtū. But this was a tireless fog, spreading its arms across the valley as if trying to hold together everything that would otherwise have fallen apart—a Father Damien fog. Out of the fog's belly came not the hero of the lepers, but a line of moving forms linked to each other with slack rope. One by one, the mules stepped out of the mist to take on softened visages of black, brown, and white. They were part of a pack train coming over the pali from Kāne`ohe.

Their backs swayed from a life of heavy loads. White sacks of rice hung down, rubbing against worn and hairless skin. By the time they reached Honolulu, some sacks would be leaving a trail of rice. Others would be streaked with fresh blood.

I leaned forward to stroke Miki's neck, grateful for the life she could have. The smell of fresh manure made her nose twitch as the mules came closer. The lead mule dropped some cakes and swished its tail. The second mule seemed too tired to step over the piles of shiny brown. Flies gathered, buzzing with joy at their new treasure. The mule train would have left Kāne`ohe early, or maybe Waimānalo, to get up and over the pali before a fast darkness could spill across the islands.

On our side of the pali, the road was not bad. But at the top, everything changed. From pleated cliffs that only birds could reach, the mountains fell away and the pali dropped suddenly to the valley floor below. The road down the other side was treacherous. In some places it was barely a wide path, worn smooth by the bare feet of generations of kanaka, Hawaiians, carrying supplies from one side to the other. The trip from Kāne`ohe over the pali to Honolulu was ten miles or more—a day's work. I had not made the trip in years.

Often the winds sweeping up our side of the valley were strong enough to blow a man off the cliffs if he stood too close. Even horses had been lost in this way. I dug my legs against Miki's side, my way of giving her a hug, and felt glad we were away from the windy cliffs.

One by one, the mules approached like plodding ghosts. Their heads hung low, eyelashes sticky and thick with flies. Halters jangled with each effort to shake the pests away.

Empty metal jugs bounced against each other with a clinking sound—no wonder the poor beasts appeared thirsty.

"Hey, girl."

I had stopped, glancing at the hills on my side of the valley as I wondered where the old trail was. The voice made me turn to see the driver.

"What you lookin' at?" He stopped the mules—who were barely moving anyway—and shifted on his horse, watching me. I did not like being talked to that way. Mama said I flared fast when treated badly. I pulled my face back.

"Is it your business?"

"Could be." He chewed gum around the words.

A straight back encourages men to respect a woman. (Finally something useful from Miss Spencer.)

He glanced in the direction I had been looking.

"You'd best stay away from those trails," he said. "Nothin' there but bones and wild boar."

"I'm old enough to take care of myself." I looked back at him just as sharply, refusing even to blink.

"Old enough's different than smart enough."

I kicked Miki and galloped past him, the insult stinging my pride. *Not smart enough? You fool! Papa says I could go to Harv—.* A feeling of disgust came over me. I had done it again. Why did I take pride in being half-Hawaiian one minute, and in the next minute think the only respect was in being half-white?

I felt angry that a stranger could poke at my fear that I would never be Hawaiian enough for my mother or white enough for my father. I turned Miki and urged her into the hills, wondering why the driver would try to frighten me away from an old trail likely grown over and not even usable.

Soon, something rustled the underbrush. When the air grew quiet again, there was a new sound. It was a woman's voice. Not a beautiful voice, but a voice filled with mana, spirit. I slid down from Miki, pulled her a few steps into the underbrush, and petted her neck to quiet her while I listened, wondering why the voice was familiar. She was singing one of the parts to "A Song of Kane," celebrating the god Kane and his life-giving waters.

...Over the near-shore sea, over the far sea,
In the wind-blown rain at sea, in the rainbow,
In the reddish-brown billowing cloud, in the low red rainbow,
In the low hanging clouds,
There is the water of Kane.

I pulled back a branch and saw a woman with her back to me. She wore a purple holokū dress that folded as she bent over something on the ground. She pulled the object closed—a sack maybe—and bound the top. A straw hat hid her face, but there was something familiar about the way her lei curved into the hollow above her chest. When she lifted the sack onto her shoulder, I could see beyond her a tethered horse. She turned toward the brush between us and stood up.

Liona!

She glanced around as if to confirm she was not seen. Then she quickly turned up the trail. The sack she carried was half-full, poking out in places. I started to call out but stopped, watching as Liona disappeared around the first bend.

Branches of kiawe and hau pulled across my dress as Miki made her way through the brush back toward the road. I did not need to wonder what Liona was doing, from whose kitchen any poi in the sack might have come, or from whose porch any pears in the bag might have disappeared. Who was up the trail? And the man with the mule train...was he trying to protect someone?

By the time we reached the barn and I slid off Miki, there were only a few places for moonlight to drop through the rolling clouds. Rain was sneaking along the ridge. The house seemed worried as I walked to the back porch and tried to ignore the sound of a mud hen. The old belief was that the sound of the `alae mud hen near a house at night was a sign trouble could be expected there. The worlds of the haoles and the Hawaiians did not easily meet. Tūtū's world lived by these old beliefs, while Papa's world called them signs of ignorance.

The mud hen went quiet.

The downstairs was dim but for an oil lamp in the kitchen. I turned to look down the hill toward Kalina's house. Darkness. I promised myself to say nothing to Kalina about seeing Liona on the trail—not yet—but I felt my chest pulling with guilt and fear that Papa would look into my eyes and see the truth: without a word, Father Damien had spoken to me in a way I could not easily ignore.

I pulled open the screen door and saw Mama leaning hard into Papa's arms. Papa stood like a crumbling statue. His voice was hoarse and exhausted. I learned later that he had been out searching for me.

"It's Tūtū," he said.

Chapter 13

TŪTŪ

Maybe I thought everything in my life was like a photograph, that it would never change. When I was young, I thought I would always stay young; and when Tūtū was old, I thought she would always stay old. But I never really believed I would lose her.

The island had always seemed touched with the feel of soft air and the smell of fragrant flowers. But as Keahi and I sat with Mama and Pōki`i in the long silent corridor of Queen's Hospital in the middle of the night, feeling one with the dull gray walls, that fragrance was gone. In its place was the smell of a jar of disinfectant next to the wooden bench on which I sat. I listened for Papa's footsteps...hid in Keahi's strong hand. I watched the dark space in the empty room across from me, thinking of everything that was missing.

I thought of the last time Tūtū and I walked through Chinatown in the pink of early evening, and a gas streetlight flickered. Old Chinamen with pigtails sat in the alleys and burned joss sticks. Chinese lanterns hung like rigging, while tiny women draped in embroidered dragons rushed in and out of tiny doors. Their voices were like the chirping of birds, like Tūtū's voice when she was excited. I longed to hear her voice again. I thought of the time Tūtū took Keahi and me to the place in Honolulu that legend says is the navel—the center of the universe. I had stood looking down at a rock placed exactly at the spot and grown over with morning glory, wondering: *If someone picks up the rock and throws it, will the center of the universe move too?* Would I have felt the same jolt that I felt now?

A door swung open and slants of light fell into the hallway and across my bare feet. Dr. Netten gently squeezed Mama's arm and stroked Pōki`i's sullen hair. I do not know why he addressed me.

"We can't expect too much in cases like this," Dr. Netten said quietly. He gave Keahi's shoulder a light squeeze. I hated knowing what he meant.

The nights dragged on; the days lasted too long. The pneumonia stayed and stayed. Next to her bed, I watched Tūtū the way I had watched the wounded bird with Liona's cousin, Manu. The `ō`ō lay in the grass, its tiny mouth opening and closing—like Tūtū's now—as if asking for something. When Keahi came to visit the hospital, he pulled a chair close by Tūtū's bedside. He played his gourd whistle for her, and sometimes his `ukulele. He leaned close and stroked her tiny hands, telling her how the wind would lift her birthday kite. How the red dragon would dance in the sky.

She said nothing.

Mimo and Hoaloha came every day.

"I lift my face," Mimo said, "and ask, why these new afflictions? Why these new ways of dying should fall upon the people?" Tears rolled down her face. "I pray to gods, old and new both. But no comfort comes—only silence."

I shivered to hear these words. So many of Tūtū's generation seemed caught between gods—feeling abandoned by the old gods, and not understanding the ways of the new God. Mimo rocked herself in the chair next to Tūtū's bed.

"It is not the right time to tell her," Mimo said.

I looked up fast. "Tell her what?"

"I am leaving our Congregational Church. I will join the Catholic Church."

I watched Tūtū in her sleep, wondering how she would feel when she learned this. For years, Mimo and Tūtū had cherished the early Protestant missionaries. But then—

"Father Damien, Mother Marianne..." she said, "...they care for our lepers."

I gave Mimo a long hug.

On one of the nights at the hospital, as Keahi and I again sat in the hallway, I told him about encountering the mule train driver and discovering the old trail. He already knew how torn I felt after meeting Father Damien. I took a deep breath and shared what I learned about Liona. Keahi snapped a twig into smaller and smaller pieces, watching each piece drop to the floor.

"You going get everybody in trouble," he whispered.

"I won't," I insisted. "I'm just wondering how I *feel* about things. I'm not going to *do* anything!"

We turned to see Dr. Netten walking toward us.

After a brief chat, Dr. Netten turned to Keahi. "How's your aunty? Your uncle stopped by the other day to say hello. I always like it when he does that."

"She is doing good!"

Dr. Netten hesitated. "Keahi...your uncle told me you didn't seem well last week." He looked concerned. "I checked your records. Your last physical examination was before you went to Maui last year. I can't go around worrying about a boy I watched come into this world, you know."

Keahi's eyes darted to me, then away. "Something in my stomach. It's all gone now."

"That's odd," said Dr. Netten. "Your uncle said you had a cough."

Barely had I a chance to look from Dr. Netten to Keahi when Mama and Pōki`i walked around the corner. Dr. Netten watched Keahi for a moment, then he told us all goodnight.

I can't say how many times my hands picked up Tūtū's Bible and carefully set it back down, wondering if she would ever touch it again, before Dr. Netten told us to prepare the house, for on the very next day, Tūtū was coming home.

"Almost get to meet Jesus!" Tūtū chirped. She smiled like she had won a prize. How good to hear that voice! She giggled and swatted playfully at me as I patted her all over and grabbed at her and pumped her hands up and down. Mama brought a new blue holokū dress for Tūtū to wear on the way home. We made an appointment in two weeks with Dr. Netten to confirm the medications were working.

"Dr. Netten is gold," said Papa. He had reason to be proud; it was Papa's suggestion that Dr. Netten join him at the hospital. They had gone to medical school together in Boston, though Dr. Netten was younger.

The thing I liked about Dr. Netten, other than his bushel of sandy hair and a smile that welcomed everyone, was his respect for the culture of the islands. He was Keahi's family doctor as well as ours and had been present at Keahi's birth; in honor of Hawaiian tradition, he had stood apart unless needed. He was a haole and fair-skinned like Papa, but Dr. Netten did not think like most foreigners. He told Mama many times how he wished Keahi were his own son. This made me like Dr. Netten even more.

Tūtū coughed and I took her arm, looking at Dr. Netten for reassurance. Papa opened the buggy door.

"Bed rest for a week, Tūtū," Dr. Netten said. Even he seemed to know her tricks. "And I do mean down. *Flat*!"

"Flat like…sit up flat?" She found a mischievous smile.

"Nooo," said Dr. Netten, stirring up a firm look, "flat like *pancake* flat." He shook a friendly finger at her, though I think she saw little more than a blur. "Come back in two weeks," he said, "for a check-up."

I would not have chosen to miss my footing as I stepped onto a slippery rock in Nu`uanu Stream on the morning of Tūtū's next appointment with Dr. Netten.

"Is this the leg of my daughter too old to be flying across rivers? Too smart to be falling on whiskey bottles thrown into a stream?" Mama shook her head at the jagged cut below my knee.

After Dr. Netten exclaimed how well Tūtū was doing, he reached inside the pocket of his white uniform, removed his glasses, and set them on his nose while Mama took Tūtū to the waiting room and I propped up my leg. He tilted a small bottle of iodine and drew the bright purple swab along the cut. It would need stitches.

I held my breath and winced as Dr. Netten sewed the stitches, then watched him prepare a bandage. As he began twisting the cap onto the iodine bottle, I asked, as if trying to make the words come from somewhere else.

"Do you do research to cure the lepers?"

Dr. Netten's fingers hesitated, then turned the cap more slowly. He glanced at me, as if considering the wider direction such a question can take. He closed the iodine bottle and turned it over in the palm of his hand.

"No," he said at last, "but if it were my choice, yes, I would be doing research to help them. Like Dr. Arning."

I considered my words, then realized there was only one way to ask. "Do you think they should be sent away to Moloka`i?"

He cleared his throat. "Mele. I'm a physician."

"There is talk of centers being set up," I said hopefully. "Kalina told me. On each island so patients can be near their families."

He hesitated. "That could be a good thing."

"Would you help them?" I asked, glancing again through the door. Mama and Tūtū were talking to a friend. I had a little more time alone with Dr. Netten.

"Help who?" He turned aside to wad up used cotton balls and drop them into a basket in the corner.

I swallowed, watching his back. He could get more bandages, more medications. But what if he told the health authorities?

"Those who are hiding." My words were partly drowned out by Mama's laughter in the hallway.

He turned, looking puzzled. "What did you say?"

Was I crazy? *Mele, he is the health authority!*

What I did next was a pathetic effort at a skill Hoaloha had developed to an art when she wanted to get away from a boy. She said it worked perfectly. Every time.

"MOON!" I blurted out. The moon visiting a girl's body, she said, is a topic NO boy ever wants to pursue with ANY girl.

Dr. Netten's eyebrows jumped as he looked at me over the rim of his glasses. "Ex...excuse me?"

I flew off the table and bolted from the room.

On the way home, Mama let me drive the buggy. Still, every bump in the road hurt my stinging leg and jostled me to the bottom of my doubts. While the adults in my life seemed so sure of what they believed, I was not sure where "right" ended and where "wrong" began, where the law must be turned aside, and where compassion should come to take its place. As if he had long ago agreed to settle this for me, a boy named Jacob Maila came into my life.

Chapter 14

JACOB MAILA

When a kona wind sweeps across the island, you board up the windows and hold your breath. A gale changes little for dancing pili grass or a cloud already moving across the sky. But a tree half-uprooted and already hanging over a cliff? It will never be the same. How can the wind know how desperately the tree clings to the only soil its roots have ever known? The wind merely yanks the tree away and lets it fall, with no plan for what will happen next.

An island boy named Jacob Maila was my kona wind. I had never met him. He came into my life for a few moments, tore me from the security of my childhood beliefs, and was gone.

Keahi knew Jacob from Steamer Days. When the steamers arrived from America, the moment was grand for visitors and islanders alike. The Hawaiian Royal Band greeted the ship with beautiful songs and alohas of welcome. The local boys swarmed into the water like bees around a honey hull. Visitors, shaded by hats and parasols, were ecstatic to be off the water after months of open ocean, seagulls and swells. They rushed to the rails, waving at the cheering crowds and tossing coins into the water to watch the local boys go feet up. The boys were equally delighted at the attention. They scrambled up the chains and swung from the stanchions. They leapt, all arms and legs and naked joy, back into the water, shouting the whole time. Afterwards, Keahi and John Makahehi emptied their trouser pockets to show me their fortune of pennies and dimes, and maybe a quarter.

"Look, Mele!" Keahi sometimes said, "only Jacob Maila got more than me!" Jacob was younger than many of the other boys who dove; he was only ten years old. To me, he was just another island boy. But some people you like without ever meeting them.

Tūtū was recovering nicely from her stay at Queen's Hospital, so Mama and Papa and I took her to visit Mimo for a few days. Mimo still lived with eight other people in one of the older pili grass huts in town. Every year, as the number of clapboard houses grew, there were fewer and fewer grass huts. I knew that Tūtū and Mimo would spend hours sitting in the shade wiggling their dusty toes, reminiscing, then take turns reading the Bible aloud. For Tūtū, "reading" meant tapping her finger along the place where print was likely to be found, turning a handful of pages now and then, and cooking up as best she could a stew of phrases from what she remembered hearing years ago from the missionaries. Her favorite was, "I am the Way, the Truth, and the Oil Lamp. Only visit God when I go, too!"

As we said good-bye to Tūtū and Mimo, my father pressed an envelope into Mimo's small hand. She tried to say no, but Papa hugged her. "Mimo," he said, "this is nothing compared with the debt I owe you. Please."

With Mama and Papa in the front seat and me behind them, Papa reined Hoku onto a quiet dirt road that skirted around Honolulu. We talked about the coming lū`au at Kūhiō Beach; everyone would be there. Even better, it would be Keahi's birthday.

Our quiet did not last for long.

I heard a woman's shriek. The sound, on Mama's and my side, came from a clapboard house and sent a rattle through me. Hoku came to an abrupt stop. He pawed at the dirt, jerking his head at the sound of a screen door slamming. The buggy shook.

Two white men climbed down from horses tied up in front of us. A woman ran from her house, pleading with them. The men shook their heads and thrust a piece of paper at her as they pushed away her arms.

"You know the law," one of them said gruffly.

They brushed past her, up the porch and into the house. She ran in after them, crying, "No, please!"

Mama's chest moved up and down fast. She grabbed the handrail, turned and glared at Papa. One of the men wore a badge on his brown shirt. Mama seemed to know who they were and why they were there—so did Papa.

"Who are those men?" I asked, but nobody answered me. I pulled nervously at Mama's shoulder. "Mama?"

The men came out of the house, one of them tugging a boy by the hand. On his cheek was a patch of discolored skin. Mama stood up fast. The buggy rocked hard to one side.

"Nahoa, sit down!" Papa's voice was huge. Hoku jerked his head.

The boy drew back and began to whimper. His mother reached around his face and covered the mark with her hand. She begged the men. "Please!" She pulled the boy close. "I will keep him in the house! I promise!" But the man yanked at the boy's hand, trying to pull him away.

Mama threw open the side door of the buggy. Papa reached to grab her arm. "Nahoa, no!" But he was too late, she was out of the buggy. Mama ran toward the house, pulling up the hem of her dress and shouting, "No! Let him be!"

Hoku stepped sideways then backed up, trying to get away from the scene. The buggy jerked. I grabbed at the railing. Papa threw down the reins, jumped down and started around the front of the buggy.

The boy cried out, "*Maamaaaaa*!"

Hoku lurched forward in fright, almost knocking Papa over. Papa grabbed Hoku's bridle, yanking it downward.

The boy clung desperately to the doorframe. His grip broke loose. In panic, he grabbed at a torn piece of metal screen and I felt the sting in my hands. Crates fell over as he kicked his bare feet at the men. The boy's mother grabbed at his outstretched hand, pulling him back toward the door.

Then the boy screamed.

Hoku lashed out a rear leg. He whinnied and tried violently to shake loose from Papa's firm grip. Then Hoku's shoulders went straight up. The buggy jolted backwards. The front wheels lifted in the air. Papa jerked down on the reins, hard, but he did not dare turn loose of Hoku—even to go after Mama. The front wheels slammed to the dirt and I was thrown to the floor.

I could hear the boy's mother shouting at the men, "It could be something else! A rash! So many times the doctors are wrong!" Two small children watched from the doorway of the house, crying for their mama.

I pulled myself up, knees throbbing from my fall, and watched.

"Let him be!" Mama grabbed the shirt of the man with the badge, trying to drag him away from the boy. He shook Mama loose. Her lei broke, scattering white petals across the dirt

"Nahoa!" yelled Papa. "This is none of your affair!"

She spun toward Papa. "Look at you! You who can *do* something! You will watch this child go Moloka`i. And do *nothing*!"

Moloka`i.

"He's got to be separated, Nahoa, for the sake of the rest!" Papa tightened the reins, still struggling to keep Hoku under control. I watched through my tears as the men pried the boy loose from his mama's shaking hands and took him away.

The boy's mother fell to the ground, holding her sides, rocking. "Auwē! Auwē!" Mama rushed to her and held her tight, stroking the woman's face and hair, then grabbing her again and pulling her close.

"I should have hidden him!" wailed his mother. But there had been no time for that—it all happened too fast. I can still see Mama wrapping her arms around the small woman, rocking her and asking God to shed His grace upon the boy.

I felt sick as the meaning of what I saw cut its way into my heart. Is *this* what the policy means? Is *this* what it was like when the woman was taken from her husband and children? It shook me to a depth I did not know I even had. All the way home, Mama sat in the back seat of the buggy and held me. I covered my ears to shut out the angry words between her and my father.

"Signed into law by your own King, I might add!" The words flew like hot stones over Papa's shoulder.

"And who writes the law? American attorneys! So worried! What happens to property value, what happens to money in pockets if visitors see a leper on the streets?"

I did not know how to contain the loss I felt. I did not know what was worse, watching a boy be taken away, or the realization that I had argued on so many occasions that exile was the right thing to do because my white father said so.

But that was before I saw, right in front of me, what the policy meant.

"We will control this disease!" Papa said angrily. "That will happen when *all* the lepers, on *all* the islands..." He punched the words into the seat with his finger. "...When every last one of them has been found and removed!"

I thought my lungs would burst with grief as I pictured this scene on porches all over the islands. Such a short time ago, I had looked up at a blue sky and so casually asked my father, "Were any of them children?"

"You say 'removed' like we are talking about corpses after a fire!" Mama's body was hard as iron.

My father's voice crawled out of his throat. "This is not called 'the living death' for nothing!"

I could only feel the burn in my lungs from holding in gulps of horrible truth. The sound of the woman's wailing clung to my mind as our buggy approached the elegant McKibbon residence. I gazed through swollen eyes at the splendid gardens, the vast green lawns, the white pillared verandas wrapping the house. White guests were playing a game of lawn tennis—toasting drinks, flashing smiles as ladies in long white dresses and white hats opened their parasols and sent ripples of laughter into the air. I felt my jaw tighten. What did I expect? That life should come to a halt because a boy with leprosy is taken from his mama? Oddly enough—just for a moment—I did. The laughter forced its way across the lawn, crashed against the sounds of wailing in my head. These two worlds had nothing to say to one another. It was this way all over the islands, cultures standing apart. I closed my eyes and covered my ears.

We came around a grove of trees and I saw on the knoll a blurry white house with dark green trim—home. I had no words to describe my feelings. 'Sad' was not a big enough word. I had only the image of a storm, the kind that bursts over the ridge in the night, and when you wake up the next morning the heart of the valley is changed. Everything old has been uprooted and thrown aside. New roots have set down, underground runners search to find their place in the earth. Something in me, too, took root that day. From the moment I saw the boy's face as he turned to look back at his mother, I knew I was now on the side of the families who were losing their loved ones.

The house felt white that night, full of Papa's whiteness. Was this the Papa I loved? The man who rushed out in the middle of the night when Mimo had only a slight temperature? The man who took a stitch in the torn leg of a gecko because Pōki`i could not bear to see it in pain?

What would Papa do if Mama or Pōki`i or Tūtū got the lepela? What would he do if *I* got it, or Keahi? Back and forth I went, relieved one moment that my white blood protected me, and afraid the next moment that the Hawaiian blood of those I loved could make their lives so short.

I walked to the barn and leaned heavily against Miki as she offered comforting nudges with her nose. Shadows hung in the corners of the barn, keeping the light out and holding the pain in. I lifted a turquoise feather from where it hung near the window of Miki's stall, felt a pang of longing for the sunny noontime of my childhood when the simple gift of a peacock feather could dry my tears.

I learned only afterwards that the boy's name was Jacob Maila.

When I thought of Jacob after that day, I saw in my memory Keahi and me as little keiki at the beach. When the sun began to go pink in the evening sky, we would run to the edge of the sea, drop to the sand, and cross our legs. We stayed there, facing the sun and believing that so long as we held our breath, the sun would not set—Na'u, a child's game then. We believed and believed, even as the setting sun fell across our shoulders, even as the ball of orange sank below the horizon and was gone.

This is what I did with Jacob Maila, too. I admit that at the age of fifteen, though longing for the treasures of adulthood, I clung to this silly notion of power with child-like faith—told myself that so long as I held Jacob in my thoughts...he would live. Someday he would return from Moloka`i. At night, listening to the tick-tock of new rain on the roof, I drew pictures for Jacob—of his mama and his little sisters, of people tossing pennies from the decks of steamers, of men shouting victoriously into the darkness while torch fishing at night—imagining my pictures consoled him. I whispered to him.

"Don't be afraid. Shut your ears to the sounds that might frighten you. May the Night Rainbow, Ka Pō Mōkole, hold you as you sleep."

But in the same way that I finally learned the sun would always set, I knew that Jacob Maila would never walk up the steps of his mama's porch again.

Exile. The word now chewed holes in my heart. After meeting Father Damien, I had longed for a telling moment. A shiny moment! Like when a firebrand is hurled over the cliff and lights up the night sky. Instead, my telling moment was the memory of the look on a boy's face as he turned to look back at his mama for the last time. Exile. The word felt like a knife ripping through a piece of silk.

Chapter 15

THE LŪ`AU

Keahi and John Makahehi rounded up the boys who dove with Jacob on Steamer Days. They loosened the reins of their horses and leaned toward exotic foliage around town and gathered fistfuls of elegant blossoms. From trash bins they dug colorful containers and filled them with water. When they had gathered armfuls of flowers to express their grief, they took their gifts of aloha to Jacob's mother. They tethered their horses to the porch and slid down and did the chores that Jacob had always done. Each time they did this, Jacob's mother held onto each of the boys for a long time, and everybody went home with wet hair where her eyes had touched their heads.

It was all they had left of Jacob, a patch of wetness behind an ear.

For weeks, none of them felt like diving at the docks. Visitors with white parasols and jeweled arms arrived on the tall ships and wondered why the boys they heard about did not come to meet them, climb the stanchions, and leap into the water shouting with joy.

The memories of Jacob Maila were still fresh in our minds as Keahi and I joined our families for a lū`au at Kūhiō Beach. Everyone would be together. We always looked forward to these picnics. But this time, best of all, it was Keahi's birthday. When the day came, he went with my family to the beach. Keahi and I put Tūtū between us in the back seat of the buggy, but that did not keep the boy in him or the girl in me away from each other. Keahi reached behind Tūtū, his fingers finding spaces in my blowing hair. He lifted strands, drawing them into the breeze, watching them wrap around the back of his hand. When he let the strands of hair fall, they slid down the front of my white blouse. It was useless to try to keep from blushing.

"You two like a puddle of giggles!" Tūtū said, slapping playfully at us.

Ahead of us, along the beach of Waikīkī, there was only the stillness of fishponds and coconut groves. On the other side of the road, large square ponds of water had been turned from old taro patches to new rice fields now operated by Chinese. Above us, Mānoa Valley jumped up green and alive. Even more than tales of other lands, I loved the stories Tūtū told of Mānoa Valley, and how the spirits of the chiefs still lived there. Mama looked for a long time at the upper slopes, then reached back and took Tūtū's hand. I looked up, too, wondering if Mama knew about the cave Liona and Kalina had spoken of.

"Look!" Pōki`i called from the front seat. "On the footbridge!" Even Hoku pulled at his harness to watch.

Between the rice fields, a Chinaman and a peacock were doing a strange dance on the old footbridge. The Chinaman flailed his arms, shouting in Chinese, pigtails flying, trying to shoo the peacock off the bridge, then jumping back. The peacock flapped and shrieked, trying to back the Chinaman out of its way.

"Who win?" asked Tūtū, excitedly.

The Chinaman bounced off the railing as the peacock burst past.

"The pīkake!" shouted Pōki`i.

At the picnic, we followed our noses to the delicious smells of roast pig. The very words were enough to make my mouth crazy with joy. With so many families at the lū`au, the lauhala mats spread down the beach like a woven floor. Everywhere was food and music and waves of laughter. People sat in overlapping circles, wanting to be part of all the conversations at once. Some men wore western-style clothing; others wore traditional malos around their waist with the swatch of cloth hanging down, and the elegant all-green maile leis around their necks or heads. For beach picnics, Keahi wore a malo. I wore short skirts and a light blouse.

Full of delicious juices, the pig had been cooking all day. The steaming meat was lifted out of the smoldering ti leaves and hot rocks lining the imu that had been dug in which to cook the pig. All around were greetings of aloha, hugs and laughter. With so many fragrant birthday leis around his neck, Keahi looked like a rainbow.

Talk at picnics was always lively, with people laughing one minute and sad the next, then happy again when a new thought lifted their spirits. Conversation happened so fast it was sometimes hard to follow. I was not sure that I cared. I just wanted to be with family and friends. The talk was all the same anyway, whether at picnics, market, or the horse races. Keahi and I dropped to the sand in the middle of a loud discussion about our royalty.

"Queen Emma is last of the royal Kamehameha line." A fist shot into the air. "We owe her our allegiance!"

"But Kalākaua is King! Royal blood or not." Someone threw down a crab shell.

Keahi crossed his legs in the sand and leaned toward me. "You look `ono," he whispered. He meant delicious. I pressed a foot against his. Keahi and I waved to Hoaloha and Mimo to come sit near us. Papa got up to greet Mimo and help her get settled. Then John Makahehi appeared, lumbering happily along in his usual relaxed way. Hoaloha dropped onto a mat.

Hoaloha's father busied himself attaching a flying paper carp to a bamboo pole stuck in the sand. He let go fast and the fish found the wind, spinning in the sky. Two men behind us talked about the recent fistfight on the legislative floor. I tried to listen, but my eyes were busy watching Keahi's thumb stroke circles on a piece of bamboo. He inched his toes into mine and we buried them among the flattened grasses, still touching.

Keahi reached in front of me for papaya. Spread around us on mats were lomi salmon, mango gathered from our tree, raw fish, poi, roast pig, the best and fattest mālolo—flying fish. I smelled fragrance as the leis around Keahi's neck fell across my chest and into folds of light cotton. I glanced at Papa. He would stop breathing if he knew my thoughts. Not Tūtū—she would smile.

"How many of us laughed at the idea," said Liona, "that the land and the sky above it could be lost? We thought nobody could own the land. So we played along with the crazy foreigners. We signed our name or put an X on a piece of paper in exchange for a bolt of fabric, a few dollars, or a jug of wine, not knowing. And when we looked up, the land was gone."

"Who needs telephone and piece of wire?" said Tūtū. She flitted away the idea with her hands. "Mimo and I use coconut telephone! Talk long as we want, eh, Mimo?" They burst into laughter.

Mimo told a story to heaps of laughter, of a Chinese cook in Honolulu who made his first telephone call to another Chinaman, also in Honolulu. They struggled through the entire conversation, speaking only in broken English, and hung up exhausted. When the owner of the telephone asked the cook why he did not speak to his friend in their own language, the Chinaman was shocked. They thought the telephone spoke only English!

I watched two peacocks do a poking-head walk down the beach. Several peacocks wandered around `Āinahau, where Princess Ka`iulani lived. She was nine years old, the only child among the whole royal family. Keahi and I recently had seen her riding her pony Fairie across a footbridge near Waikīkī. It was hard to imagine being the only child in all the royal line—everybody watching you, nervous, afraid you will die. And even then, not even certain there would be a kingdom to rule.

I looked at Keahi, watched him gather sand and pick out shreds of coconut bark. He flicked them away. What would happen to us when America annexed the islands? Everyone knew this was coming. Would we have any rights? What would happen to my goal of being a nurse?

But my worries were lost when the smell of roast pig floated by. The sound of a ukelele came near, and one more birthday lei was placed around Keahi's neck.

"Eh, Keahi, where's your cousin, Kalua?" John Makahehi asked. Of Keahi's cousins, Kalua was my favorite. He was my age and always ready with a song. He was short but stood properly, not slouching like many of the boys.

Keahi tossed a coconut into the air with one hand and caught it with the other. "Gone to America!"

Hoaloha crunched up her face. "*Again*?"

"Yeah, stowed away...again," said Keahi, laughing.

"You are making this up!" exclaimed Hoaloha.

"No, I'm telling you!" said Keahi, "He sent me a letter! For three days he ate only onions, then came out. Captain Newell caught him good!"

I wrinkled my nose, imagining the smell of onions in my hair.

Each time Captain Newell had discovered Kalua, and each time the *Amy Turner* was too far out to sea to turn around and bring him back. So when they reached New York, Kalua was turned over to the U.S. Consulate, scolded, and sent back to Honolulu on its return trip, again with Captain Newell. He was too young, the Consulate said, to be away from his family.

I could not imagine spending three years trying to go to school in Boston.

"Back and forth, back and forth. He will be here in June." said Keahi. "This time, I'm going to make him stay!"

"Should never have left," murmured Hoaloha as she reached for more pulled pork.

"Why not?" asked John. "Nothing to come back to—not anymore."

Keahi and I could not understand anyone wanting to leave the islands. Only barely did I listen to talk until I heard, "Moloka`i."

My fingers drew guilty lines in the sand, circling in and out among the grasses. I had made a silent promise to Jacob Maila the day he was taken away that I would stand on my new conviction. But what did that mean?

"How many of us at the settlement now?" someone asked.

"Maybe eight hundred...still alive anyway," said Uncle Elia. "About two thousand gone so far." I wondered how long Jacob would live once he reached Moloka`i. Most patients lived only a few years.

"Used to be mostly the poor who got the lepela," said Uncle Elia. "Not anymore. Now teachers, ministers, choir boys. Queen Emma's cousin has had it for a long time."

I looked to where Papa had been sitting, but there was only an empty mat lifting in the breeze. John Makahehi glanced at the empty spot as well. "How many are hiding from the Board?" he asked quietly.

"Not enough," said Liona, peeling a mango. I watched her closely, waiting for her to look up. All I saw was a hiding silence.

"Eh, Liona. You hear anything about Peter Kohala?" One of her cousins looked over toward Mānoa Valley.

My fingers stopped moving.

Liona glanced at Papa's empty place in the circle, then in my direction. "How would I know?" she said.

I took in a quick breath and leaned toward Keahi. "She *does* know," I whispered. "He's the man I told you was hiding in the cane fields. I am sure of it! Kalina and Liona took him to Mānoa Valley."

"Do you know him...Peter Kohala?" Keahi whispered back.

"No, but—"

"Sshhhh," he said, "your papa is coming."

Papa stepped over a mat and into a circle of conspiring silence. Everyone, now including me, had drawn an invisible fortress around Mānoa Valley. The most important things, I learned that day, are often unspoken—slipped into the silence between words.

Finally, Keahi's uncle spoke. "King's boathouse sure noisy last night. Playing cards late again, I bet."

"We don't even know how the lepela is spread," said Keahi's aunty into the strange quiet. "What you think, Kalina? Through vaccinations?"

"A crazy idea," Kalina said. "Leprosy was around long before vaccinations."

Papa nodded. At least he and Kalina agreed on that.

"Losing more of us all the time," one of the men protested. His hands shook as he tied a section of coconut husk to the fishing line on a bamboo pole held between his bare feet. I knew where these words were directed.

"We hope it will be under control soon," said Papa.

"Board of Health been saying that since the first ones were taken. Eighteen years ago!" said another man. He picked up a fistful of sand and threw it back down. "Gets harder on us all the time. You don't know, Reed, what it's like to lose loved ones."

Papa's face creased, as if he were hurting somewhere.

Mama gave the man pinch eye.

"I do know," Papa said, "I lost both my parents to a haole disease."

A slow nodding silence worked its way around the circle as people remembered this. Then someone spoke up.

"I hear at market it's from mosquitoes," she said, and the list grew. Poi, sex, kissing...a curse from God. Papa usually kept quiet during this kind of talk.

I knew what Hoaloha would say later, that behind the jokes and stories everyone was casting for wish fish, hoping things would go back to how they were before. I looked at the pattern of sand clinging to the side of Keahi's foot. Not me—I wanted things to go forward.

"Eh, Mele." Keahi leaned and whispered in my ear, his leg pressed against my thigh. "The sea is waiting for us. You want to go swimming?"

I jumped up as he pulled off leis and ran with arms held high. A waist-high wave came toward us. I dove over it, with Keahi close behind. The breeze blew through my imagination, woke the warmth of the lifting sea and Keahi as they both wrapped around me. Keahi went under, stroking a finger down the length of my soaking blouse as he disappeared. I turned to search for him, saw the shadow of the malo around his waist. He burst out of the water, laughing. He went under and came up again. I was suddenly on his shoulders and plunged backwards. We swam out further, my skirt floating up to my waist. Each time we dove deeper, under the rolling waves. Then we were beyond the reef. Alone.

The sea was calm. We floated and bobbed among the gentle rolling swells that lifted us and sometimes concealed us from the shore. We shared delicious moments when we had the starless evening sky to ourselves—a sky deep as the look in Keahi's eyes, cool as the blouse that clung to my chest. Beads of brilliant wetness flew in every direction as he threw his head back and his hair circled his shoulders. He dropped further into the water in front of me, and the shadow of his malo disappeared.

If ever there was an evening sky to make me hold my breath, that sky was unfolding before us. The canopy stretched from sea to distant hills, as if rubbed with mango juice almost sweet enough to taste. And if ever there was a thought to take my breath away, that thought was unfolding in my mind. I could no longer deny my feelings for Keahi. They were not the feelings I had for him as a child.

Chapter 16

CONVINCING KALINA

If the rotting beam in Kalina's shed had not collapsed in the middle of the night, I might never have met Peter Kohala. The morning after the shed caved in on itself, Kalina and I struggled with the wretched sight.

"Helping someone?" She pulled stringy cobwebs from her hair. "I don't know what you are talking about."

"You do," I said. I exerted as much strength as possible to lift the beam, but not a splinter budged. I turned to face her. "I know what you're doing. I know about the missing pears and the bandages, and what you did with the Chaulmoogra oil you got at market the day we saw Father Damien. When I rode Miki up the valley the evening Tūtū went to the hospital, I saw Liona carrying a rice sack up one of the old trails."

She turned back to her chore, tugging more furiously at the beam.

"Kalina, you are helping the lepers to hide. So is Liona."

She stared at me.

"And a man named Peter Kohala," I pressed, "whoever he is." I looked around in exasperation. "You hid him in Mānoa Valley."

Kalina looked from the wooden beam to the crates crushed and scattered about. She said nothing. What could she say? She could not deny it.

Enough for the moment, there was work to do. I tugged at a small piece of crushed metal, trying to pry it from beneath the heavy beam. Kalina saw my struggle and lifted an end of the beam. I was tugging so hard that I almost fell backward when the piece was released. In my hand was a scrap of twisted copper.

"Kalina! This is it!" The handle was split, the rest was crushed flat.

"Just an old soup ladle. Give me the hammer."

Kalina stopped suddenly, taking my shoulders. They were shaking. "What's wrong? Mele?"

"This is the copper ladle Manu and I used to bury the little \`ō\`ō. I never saw him after that. I never got to return his kindness."

Kalina put a hand to her mouth.

"Nobody mentions Manu," I said. "Why not?"

She gave a resigned sigh. "Someday you will know anyway."

I felt a flash of irritation.

"At the lū\`au," she said, "we talked about...Peter Kohala."

I nodded. "One of Liona's cousins. But I only met Manu. I don't know Peter Kohala." I stood clutching the crushed soup ladle.

Kalina's arms dropped to her side. "Yes, you do." Her eyes slid across my face. "You met him when you were a child, but you didn't know him as Peter Kohala. You gave him a nickname."

I stared at the crushed ladle in my hand, felt myself step back.

Manu.

"He has the lepela, Mele. Bad."

I sat on the collapsed beam, settling my gaze on a crumpled cobweb at my feet. Kalina lowered herself next to me.

"I'm sorry, Mele. We didn't want to have to tell you."

"Does Mama know what you are doing?" Useless words when I already knew the answer.

"Your mother has a way of saying she does not want to know certain things. She gives me food, I take it, she asks no questions. Sometimes she adds extra treats, like pieces of ginger cake she got by trading eggs or mangos."

Eggs? I thought of mornings when I had gathered eggs with Mama; she put them in a basket, went off to market, and came home with items I never saw in our cupboards.

"I want to go with you," I said, "to see Manu."

"No, Mele." She shook her head and stood. "I can't let you be part of this."

There was never a chance to do anything for Jacob Maila—everything happened too fast. This was a chance to do something, not only for Manu, but also for Jacob.

"I could make biscuits for him!"

"Letting you help a leper hiding from the Board? From your *father!* No, Mele, you cannot ask me to do this."

"How would he find out?"

"Best you not even *know*."

"I already know! You help them, so does Liona. Even Ma—"

She put her hands up to stop me.

"Listen to you...as if the law is nothing! It is now a crime to have the disease! Do you know the fine for helping a leper to hide? A hundred dollars!"

I had never seen a hundred dollars, not all at once. It was almost as much as Hoaloha's father made in a year selling his paper flying fish I saw around town.

"And what would be said about your papa's daughter helping the lepers?"

"What would be said about Papa's sister-in-law helping the lepers?" I asked. Her silence fed my bravery. "Aren't *you* putting Papa at risk, too? Aren't *you* risking *your* job?" I felt sudden irritation.

"I don't like this," said Kalina, shaking her head again.

"You mean you don't like that I am no longer a child." These words came out harsher than I intended.

Kalina stood folding and unfolding a piece of oilcloth, not looking at me.

"No longer a little girl," she said. But it did not change anything. "No," she said quietly.

There was a moment when the only sound in the shed was of Kalina breathing deeply.

"Kalina," I finally said, "if it would bring him joy to see me, please don't take that from him."

She lifted the soup ladle from my palm, hesitated, and handed it back.

"You know...that if you go again and his hiding place is found...what that will mean. Do you understand?"

I knew. If found, he would be sent to Moloka`i—and I could not be the cause of that.

We planned the trip to Mānoa Valley in a week or two, enough time to finish the gift already taking shape in my mind.

"Where is Peter hiding?" I asked.

"A cave in the upper valley, above Owl Hill."

"How long has he had the ma`i Pākē?"

"A few years. But it took hold fast, the way it does sometimes."

"Can he ever—" I stopped, unsure.

"Go back to his family? I don't think so. Not safely."

"But he will be safe in Mānoa?"

"Yes."

I did not know—not that day—why I felt the need to ask. "Are you sure?"

Kalina looked at her hands. I had always believed those hands could accomplish anything.

"No."

It should have been difficult for me to walk into the kitchen that evening and kiss Papa hello; it should have been impossible to meet his eyes at the supper table when he scooped yams into my calabash. But it was not. If I turned and walked away from doing this for Peter Kohala, I would never find that wide line that would connect me, not with parts of my parents, but with all of myself.

I'm sorry, Papa, I thought to myself as I looked across the table at him, *but I need to do this. For Manu, to repay his kindness. Jacob never had a chance to run away; he never had a chance for anything! I also need to do this...*

"...for Jacob Maila."

Papa looked up as he reached for a bowl of bamboo shoots. "What's for Jacob Maila?"

A face turning color has a tiny sting to it. Frantically, I searched for what to say. I looked at Mama for the answer but realized I must hide this from her too, so she was not caught between Papa and me. The beans in my calabash looked up at me, waiting.

I stared at him blankly. Out came an answer rather witless for a girl preparing to be a criminal. "A song," I said.

"You going to end up in jail, you and Keanu," said Keahi the next day. We sat on the school's verandah. "A hundred dollar fine!"

I hushed him. "I won't end up in jail!" I whispered loudly. "Besides, I won't get caught."

He rolled his eyes. "Oh yeah, she won't get caught. Her father is all sweet potato with the Board, and she is sneaking around behind his back."

"Keahi, this is important to me! You know how I now feel about sending them to Moloka`i."

"Why not?" He looked away and his voice went empty. "They going to die anyway."

"Stop! Keahi, you have never talked this way before!"

He pushed himself away from the wall and stood. "Mr. Nott is waiting for me. I see you tomorrow."

I stood unbelieving and watched him ride away. "Die anyway?" This was not the boy I knew.

Chapter 17

FENCES

Miss Spencer should have known better. It was a Monday morning and she had instructed the class to present a personal opinion on any topic we chose. We needed to sharpen our analytical processing skills, she said—words that would make students like Theodore want to run and hide. While I would not upset a teacher on purpose, Hoaloha was right: I did not mind that my opinions might cause Miss Spencer to stop breathing for a moment.

"You better be careful," Hoaloha warned me before class.

"Hoaloha, I have a right to state my opinion," I whispered.

"Sure," she said. "And Miss Spencer, she going to squish you into pickle relish!"

I sat looking at Miss Spencer, wondering why she came to the islands, especially when so many haoles complained about mosquitoes and the heat. The mosquitoes had not always been here; Tūtū and Mimo both remembered when the annoying pests first came to the islands not many years after the missionary schools opened. Tūtū said a Mexican ship had been moored at Honolulu, not far offshore. One day a massive swarm of mosquitoes rose from the ship's hold, hovered in the air, and turned toward the island. People at the docks, and in town too, saw the dark mass moving inland. The mosquitoes had been here ever since.

My habit, as soon as I sat down, was to turn and gaze out the window toward the hills. The morning was bright, and a few clouds flitted over the school in quick shadows. It was hard not to blush as Keahi, back to his usual mood, walked past my desk and leaned down. "Eh, Mele, you are more `ono every day. I will have to fight off the boys!"

I slapped at his knee. "Go away." What I meant was, *come closer*! Keahi, always an undertow pulling smiles out of me. Hoaloha gave me her look that said, "Oh yeah, we're just friends."

Keahi walked down rows of feet; mostly brown, mostly barefoot, some with shoes. It was like this on all the islands—feet from all over the world. Theodore's father came to work in the cane fields and brought his family. The new Portuguese workers almost always brought their wives and children. The Chinese rarely brought their families; most intended to return home after two or three years of hard labor on the plantations. Several of us were half-white, or hapa-haole.

Students began their presentations. Of all the students, I was most curious about what Daniel Livingstone would say. Of course it would be something ridiculous. He went first.

"What's the big deal about the petroglyphs?" he argued.

This is not a boy with leadership qualities, said my look to Hoaloha. The knife-etched initials of "D.L." and others had damaged the ancient sacred stone drawings at the bridge.

"Doesn't everybody have the right," he said, "to carve his name on a rock? I mean, a rock's just a rock—nothin' sacred about it."

From the look of John Makahehi's fists as he listened, I thought Daniel would be smart to bolt at the closing bell for the protection of the pa he bragged about. John was easy as pudding, but he'd had his fill of Daniel's disrespect for the islands.

Several students gave good speeches. Keahi wondered why we were required to learn American history, but not allowed to learn Hawaiian history. Hoaloha suggested Hawaiian teachers be paid the same salary as white teachers.

Miss Spencer ran out of foreheads to rub, and began looking haggard. I was certain we would never have this assignment again.

Next, Theodore gave the shortest speech in history, but it made me smile: "Which eggs better, white or brown? I say brown." And down he sat.

When my turn came, Miss Spencer started gathering a frown before I even stood up. Difficult as it might be, I had made myself a promise: I would endeavor to become the docile student she wished me to be. I tugged at the nutmeg-colored skirt Mama had made for me the week before, reminding me it was full of respect...as should I be.

"My Aunty Kalina helped me with my report," I began carefully.

Be docile.

"She is a nurse at Branch Hospital in Honolulu." Every Hawaiian student knew that was the clinic for diagnosing and treating those with the lepela. I turned to Miss Spencer and added with a look of polite assurance, "She studied nursing in San Francisco." Her chest dropped in relief.

"My topic is Fences." Miss Spencer's face changed from the frown when I first stood up, to a look of sudden hope.

Daniel Livingstone spread out into the aisle and leaned back. *What could you say that I would possibly want to hear?*

"On the north side of Moloka`i," I said, "a long time ago, a massive lava flow poured over the steep cliffs, downward and out into the sea. It pushed rocks and land ahead of it, forming a peninsula."

Theodore sneezed and pulled his sleeve across his face. "S'cuse me," he said, sinking into himself with a shy look. I smiled at him.

"The peninsula is almost inaccessible. On three sides there is nothing but crashing surf. Behind the peninsula are cliffs so high they seem to start in the sky and drop to the sea. So high that the peninsula below is without sun for most of the year."

Hoaloha smiled to encourage me, but I knew Miss Spencer might not like what was coming. Mama told me what the problem was with Miss Spencer and me. "You are letting too much brown show through," she said.

"It is here," I continued, "to this isolated peninsula..."

Miss Spencer hid a yawn.

"...that the lepers are sent."

Miss Spencer's yawn caught in her throat and out came a sound like a frog choking on a fly. A few students fidgeted. John Makahehi nodded.

Docile...docile!

"They do not return."

Miss Spencer's neck grew longer as her chin lifted. "I'm sure," she enunciated, "they are quite happy there, and well cared for."

"Moloka`i no good," murmured Keahi. Almost all of us knew of the settlement at Kalawao; even Papa said the conditions were bad.

All of us knew except Miss Spencer. She crossed her arms tight against her chest. Against the truth.

"While those exiled to Moloka`i are imprisoned by crashing surf and giant cliffs," I said, "the patients at Branch Hospital have the same disease. But they are separated from the rest of the population, at least in one spot," —everyone was quiet as I hesitated— "by a fence low enough to step over."

I did not need to look at Miss Spencer to imagine her face.

"Though the rest of the fence is high," I continued, "this part is low. Perhaps our foreign-run government does not really believe the lepela is as contagious as it claims. If so contagious, why are patients allowed to mix with visitors over a fence so low? A patient could step over the fence and walk away."

Miss Spencer's hand went to her throat. A Hawaiian girl in the front row began to sniff. "My aunty step over fence and go home," she said. "Next Shipment Day, she gone." A Portuguese boy whispered something to John Makahehi, then snapped his fingers. "Like that!" the boy said. Miss Spencer blinked fast and commanded the class to silence.

"Please hurry along now, Mele," she said. "Remember: brevity is the hallmark of a lexically advanced speaker."

Docile? I continued, adding new material to my speech.

"And when the government imposes its policy of separation, why is it strict one year but looking away the next year? Up and down like a wave."

"You poor, you worth nothing," said John Makahehi. "You poor and have the ma`i Pākē? Worth *double* nothing!"

"If the lepela is so contagious," I continued, "why do so many Hawaiians live next to the disease for years without becoming infected? Like Father Damien. He has lived at the settlement for eleven years!"

Several students nodded vigorously.

"Mele, I think you've said enough!" I ignored these words from Miss Spencer.

My resolve to be docile was crumbling beneath an anger that had been smoldering since the day I saw Jacob Maila taken from his home.

"The Board has the letters!" My voice was rising, faster. "Doctors all over the world now say the disease is not very contagious. The Royal College of Medicine! Even the researcher Dr. Arning, right here in Honolulu. If anything, he says, the lepela is hard to get. He has tried and tried to infect monkeys and rabbits—and he can't!" *Still* our Board of Health refuses to end their policy of separation. Why? This is 1884!"

"I'm sure it's best for *everyone*," interrupted Miss Spencer, "and we are fortunate to have such a nice place to send...*those people.*"

I spun toward her, my notes scattering across the floor. All I could hear were the cries of Jacob Maila. All I could think of was Manu sitting alone in a cave in Manoa Valley, longing for his family. "Best for haoles! *Such a nice place?* Would you want *your* bones—"

Miss Spencer bolted forward, slashing her hand through the air. "*Enough!* Mele Bennett, take your seat! I will not tolerate such disrespect in my classroom!"

My mouth felt like a vice trying to close on my final words. "They should be at home, where they can die with dignity." I sat, my chest heaving at her ignorance of what was important to us.

Yes, *us!*

Almost out of control herself, Miss Spencer sentenced me to detention for rudeness. "And you shall go immediately to Mr. Mackintosh's office," she almost shrieked. "Where you will write, two hundred times, 'Respect for authority is the foundation of democracy.'"

Hawaiian students looked at each other. It was useless to tell her this was a kingdom and a monarchy—at least until America annexed us, claiming this, too, was for our own good. But before I gathered up my books and marched out, she reminded me in front of the entire class that half of me, the half I hated at that moment, was white.

Keahi waited for me after detention. I wanted to feel exhilarated, as proud of myself as Keahi said he felt to hear me speak the truth. At the same time, I realized I had spoken to a teacher in a way that would be shocking to adults. As Keahi and I started home, I only felt miserable. Miki and Ali`i plodded along with heads down, seeming to sense our mood.

"Even right words not going to change anything," said Keahi. "Maybe a handful get justice, and the rest of us?" He shrugged. "Saltwater."

Maybe he was right. We turned toward Emma Square where the Royal Hawaiian Band held their outdoor concerts, then stopped to get rice cakes to lift our feelings. On our way home, Keahi pointed to Mānoa Valley.

"The new moon is coming," he said, glancing at me sideways and wiping crumbs from his mouth. A little smile crossed his face. "The cereus will be in bloom!"

I tingled. When the moon is new and young, the night-blooming cereus unfolds along the upper slopes of Mānoa Valley. There was a tradition for young lovers to go see this occur. B*ut Keahi and I are not exactly young lovers!* He gave me a smile that would send a butterfly spinning.

"You want to go?" he asked.

Chapter 18

MOON FLOWER

Going to see the Moon Flower bloom! I imagined how to ask my father, then how to hide my thoughts. Tūtū and I hatched a plan: at suppertime, she would happen to mention to Papa what a fine boy Keahi was. "Don't forget to say how *respectful* he is of me!" I reminded her. Then I would ask about going to see the Moon Flower bloom.

Suppertime came, but before Tūtū could even begin, and just as I scooped bamboo shoots onto my plate and leaned over to blow away the steam, the words tumbled out.

"Keahi and I want to go see the Moon Flower bloom."

I glanced sideways at Papa, feeling the wet steam rise past my face. Would part of me be relieved if he said no? Papa looked at me, then across at Mama. I gave Pōki`i a look that said I would destroy him if he breathed a single word. Tūtū smiled slyly into the silence. She secretly loved times like this, when everything turned upside down and she could be young all over again. Not me, I wanted to be older. Papa took a deep breath and pulled his collar away from his neck. He slid his hand down the side of his face and across his lips, studied me with eyebrows together, as if he were counting. *Thirteen, fourteen... fifteen.*

Never had I seen Papa lay his fork down with so much jostling of his eyebrows. He rubbed his finger along the stem. He straightened the top of the fork, then the bottom. He pushed the fork away from himself, then pulled it back. When he spoke, his voice was like an anchor finding deep water.

"Nnooo."

Pōki`i began slapping his feet together. Tūtū started humming.

"She should be able to go," said Mama. She reminded Papa of when they themselves were young, the first time he and Mama went to see the Moon Flower. Papa looked like he remembered; maybe that was why he was holding his breath.

Papa looked at me again. All at the same time I tried to look taller and older, but innocent and obedient; to pull back my shoulders but hide my growing chest. I felt like a mess of lies.

"No."

At that moment, Tūtū remembered her speech and chirped into the air, "Never do I see a boy *so* disrespectful of a girl!" She smiled proudly.

Pōki`i slapped his hand over his mouth, but the giggle had already escaped.

Mama reached for the calabash in the center of the table. "She is no longer a girl, Reed. If we do not give permission, do you want her run off, do it anyway?"

Pōki`i was shooed outside.

Watching Mama was like watching a blacksmith set a horseshoe. They discussed what "someday" meant; how things were different in Hawai`i than in Boston—that was one nail. She reminded him of their own youth when she was even younger than I. Another nail as Papa struggled for an answer. She pointed this out, too: even Papa hoped all along that Keahi and I would be together. By the time she set the final nail and promised Papa she would speak with me, a lump was filling my throat.

"Mama," I asked as we sat close on the edge of my bed, "how does Papa feel? About Keahi and me?" I stroked a pleat in my skirt.

She stilled my nervous hand. "I reminded him," she said, "that he has a beautiful girl who loves her father. Don't you worry, your Papa will stand on the side of his daughter's happiness."

"Up go the sails!" Tūtū said the next evening, grinning. Keahi gave her playful nose kisses. We said goodbye to Mama taking hula steps and to Papa looking like he had rocks in his mouth. He patted Keahi on the shoulder, but it seemed to me like he wanted to grab him and put him in jail! I laughed, kissed Papa good-bye, and contained my temptation to tease him by saying he would never see me again.

With leis around our necks, we rode Miki and Ali`i around the slumping foothills toward Mānoa, the next valley over. Everything was alive and lovely. In the upper part of the valley, on the slopes above Tantalus, we would find one of the places where the Moon Flower grew.

"Listen!" said Keahi as we turned onto a side path. I leaned to look around a bamboo fence. On the verandah of a green clapboard house, afloat in a sea of jasmine, sat an old man, happy as honeyeater. His cracked bare feet were perched up on the railing. In his lap was an `ukulele. He chatted with an old woman as she wove pieces of lauhala laid across her lap. Beside the house, a natural corral was carved from a thicket of hau trees. Huddled in the corner nearest the house where he could hear the `ukulele, was an old black donkey. A patch of white hair trickled down his left front ankle. As we approached, the man waved the `ukulele in the air and called out.

"Aloha! Where you going?"

If ever I wanted to be invisible, that was the moment.

Keahi's voice boomed like the cannons at Punchbowl celebrating a great event. "See Moon Flower bloom!"

Everyone looked right at me, even Ali`i! The old man and woman smiled at each other with knowing looks. The man hobbled to meet us, snatching a handful of yellow hibiscus along the way. He tucked the flowers into Ali`i and Miki's halters, adding color to the leis already around their necks.

"*Go*! *Go*!" The couple hooted and waved us on with strips of lauhala.

My insides felt like rice rattling in a tin.

Seen from a ship, they say the island is a splash of purple hills and leaping streams. Seen from the island, the white sails come and go, no larger than butterfly wings on the horizon. For me there was only the feel of warm air, bits of pink sky that hung down among the trees, and the sound of Keahi's voice. The trail, coiling like a dropped rope, followed the talus of a hill and started up the valley. Keahi sat loosely, with one leg crossed and the other dangling down Ali`i's side. Usually we galloped at high speed along these trails. But not this time. He played his gourd whistle and sang, swaying in rhythm with Ali`i's steps. The trees, as if waiting for this night the whole time they grew out of the mountain, opened to the music.

The valley unfolded before us. The trail was easy, then rocky, then easy again. Ali`i shifted, kicking out a rock. With a snort, he regained his foothold and took the next careful step as the trail became steep. Soon the forest hummed with eyes of early night. Miki's ears perked at the *hoo-hoo* of the pueo, the owl connected to traditional stories of the valley. Two large circles looked down at us from behind white feathers. Blinking, blinking. Even as a child I had loved this part of Mānoa Valley. For me, this was the most alive part of the whole island. Of course I would be here with Keahi.

At a small clearing, we stopped. Ahead was the denseness of the bamboo forest, always a place of mystery and the unknown. In China, a gale would send people running toward such a place, where they would be safe among roots set deep in the earth. Not me. I would run to Keahi.

Feeling the press from Keahi's heels, Ali`i had bounded up and over a short rise of root-bound lava. But Miki held back. She shied at first, making a deep throaty sound, then took a step sideways. Keahi stopped to look back. I had never seen Ali`i do this, but Keahi coaxed him backward along the narrow trail until they were closer, where Miki could see them. She pulled her head around as if to make sure I was still there. I soothed her neck, or maybe I was soothing myself, and encouraged her to go on. She paused, rocked back, and heaved herself up and over the rise.

Within steps, as if lifted by something beyond, we entered a tunnel of green stillness. Gone was the breeze that had followed us up the valley. The air was heavy. Pressing in from both sides were vertical lines of green and yellow stalks. Within moments, the trail seemed to question itself. One could blink and become almost dizzy from the lines crossing one another. The trail took us deeper, roots everywhere, bamboo encircling us far as we could see. Miki startled at shadows.

I felt the sudden panic one can experience deep in a bamboo forest—everything looking the same. Closing in. All around us was the sound of dripping water, as though streams hung in the air. I looked at Keahi, his back relaxed and his head bobbing. Did he ever feel frightened? He did not seem to. He leaned forward and I felt relief to see beyond him a circle of widening moonlight. We left the bamboo forest as quickly as we entered it, and now, suddenly, I felt a twitch in my stomach.

Miki hung back as Ali`i picked his way along the rocky trail and chose his footing. Keahi bent sideways as fingers of the forest brushed across his white shirt, lifting the leis I had placed around his neck. I wanted the touch to be mine!

When the trail became too rocky for the horses, we slid down and tossed the reins over their shoulders. The soft leather curled among ferns that seemed as everywhere as my thoughts of Keahi. I looked up. The moon was a sleepy eye, trying to open.

As Keahi and I approached the first bend in the mossy trail, I turned to look back. In the small clearing among the shadows, Ali`i and Miki stood as if horses by day and phantoms by night. They huddled close together, wrapped in their own cocoon—nuzzling, silent, as if they too were captured by strands of moonlight. Ali`i shook his head and the rings of his bridle jingled through the mist. He shifted. Miki moved with him. I felt Keahi's hand flit across my palm and close around it.

Human touch. I wondered if this, more than anything, was what Peter Kohala longed for. I squeezed Keahi's hand, wanting the moment to last even as I wondered if there were Moon Flowers near Peter's cave.

Keahi led us up the lower section of the trail. Bits of moonlight seemed hungry to find spaces between leaves so it could show us the way. We came to a boulder, large and wrapped in *hau* branches. In the mossy moonlight, it seemed almost to grow out of the cliffs.

We made our way through the hushing forest, ducking under branches and lifting the cool ferns aside. My panic in the bamboo forest turned to awe as moonlight reached down and found us. Mossy rocks filled the trail; we slid over them.

The trail widened, the forest thinned, and we climbed over the last mossy boulder. It filled the trail as if reminding us: *You must come back. The way will be the same. But you will be different.*

As if waiting its whole lifetime just for us, there it was. Near the top of Tantalus, the Moon Flower lay in the light of the new moon, just as Mama said it would. It was tightly rolled, hiding its face. The Moon Flower was finished with waiting for us. Now it was our turn to wait.

"Watch," Tūtū had said, "until new moon begins to rise, until mist begins to rise, until sun meets the sea. Then watch for first sign of Moon Flower wake up. Moon Flower like Love. Make you wait and wait, but worth it."

We lay listening to the sounds of the whispering night, watched the dove-gray clouds turning in their sleep. We waited among the moving grasses, the touching ferns. My heart opened to everything—the twinkle of a star, a leaf dropping from an `ōhi`a tree nearby, the curve of new moonlight on Keahi's face. Keahi watched for the first sign of the Moon Flower's opening as I lay in hihi`o, the wandering mind while dozing but still awake. In that mind, I saw Keahi diving, washed in glistening sun. I saw him carrying little Pōki`i on his shoulders, playing Horse. "Fast, Keahi. Go fast!"

I saw him with a small child in his arms.

"Your dream belong to you, or someone else?" whispered Keahi. A slow smile came to his face. The Hawaiian view of the dream life said that often we had dreams which, when we woke up, we knew were not ours, but someone else's.

"My dream." I could feel my eyes telling my feelings for Keahi.

"Eh, Mele, what this dream which is smiling your face?" He tickled a piece of grass across my forehead and down my arms, and in small circles in the palm of my hand. "Maybe Keahi have the same dream."

He glanced back at the Moon Flower. "Look!"

Gradually, the petals of the Moon Flower began to stir and reach for the moonlight. Their inner surface began to unfurl. Finally, the Moon Flower revealed its innermost parts of pure white, and its movement ceased.

Something since childhood, something slumbering until recently, scooped up our deep-felt dreams and poured them into whispered words. Keahi's breath moved across my hair. His lips, warm and safe, moved down my neck and across my bare shoulder. I felt the softness of his tongue.

I flew through those moments, leaping across the stream of one untamed thought to the next, embracing a quilt of feelings I could not name or speak. I felt myself being pulled along, into footsteps new and strange and yet as much a part of me as my very name, knowing in my heart there was nowhere else to step. I always knew they led to Keahi.

Chapter 19

INSIDE THE APPLE OF GOD'S EYE

A week later, every drop of water on every leaf sparkled. Or was it just me as I clutched my gift for Peter Kohala under my arm, passed the rain boundary of Pueo Hill, Owl Hill, and continued toward the rain-washed slopes of Mānoa Valley? We followed the overgrown trail—Liona, then Kalina, then me—with each step of rocks and roots leading us higher into the valley. Liona and Kalina had quietly brought him here on horseback during the full moon. Turning from the trail, Liona quickly leaned down and spread her arms in front of her, reaching into the brush. Branches of thicket rustled as she lifted them over her head, passing the branches back to Kalina, and Kalina on to me. As if passing along a promise.

When I emerged from the passageway of branches and stood up, I was in a small opening in the thicket; one could walk right past the spot without a thought. How did they ever find such a place? It is like that with so many places on the islands, where one world leans up against another. We crossed this space, and yet another passageway opened to us. We wove through tangled hau trees and turned to see another clearing. It was large for being so well concealed; a perfect hiding place, I thought. The clearing had a gentle dip, sloping down toward the valley.

I immediately saw the small cave at the other end of the clearing. On the right side—where the clearing sloped down toward the sea—a rocky shelf reached out. Within an arm's length, the shelf dropped into the treetops below. At night it would be treacherous. On the left side of the cave, a large kukui tree had fallen years ago. I wondered why. By now it had become a long mossy sofa. In the middle of this green cushion, with a tin cup in the dirt beside him, a man sat with his hands resting on his knees. Manu—Peter Kohala. When he saw us, it took effort for him to stand.

Part of his face was ravished. As if the hand molding it had intended one thing but done another. As if the hand had used a hot iron forged of lava, pushing away skin in places and leaving gulches that wept without stopping. The weeping skin, along with places where there were bumps on his face and ears, must have cried out in despair and pain.

And yet, Peter Kohala smiled.

"Long as I can see my family sometimes, I'm okay." His voice was breathy as wet moss hanging from trees, but full of certainty. He stood draped with dark smells and muted colors. He had chosen to be alone in the heart of Mānoa Valley rather than in the company of agony on Moloka`i.

The cave seemed to me as if Nature had been expecting Manu all along. As if it knew ages ago to take a deep scoop from a massive boulder in a place such as this. We stood in the clearing: Liona bearing a calabash of fresh poi, Kalina bringing sacks of fruit and vegetables, and me clinging like life itself to the gift I had sewn for him with Kalina's help.

Then I realized, he would not remember me.

"Peter," said Liona, "do you remember many years ago during a visit to my house? A small neighbor girl found a dying bird. It hit the window of Kalina's shed."

"Yes, her name was Mila. A little angel, I thought. How is she now?"

Angel? That is not what Miss Spencer would call me.

"Mele," I said, smiling. "You gave me a peacock feather."

He laughed. "Mele! Is that you?" He looked at me, up and down and all around, shocked. "You grew up!"

I nodded, offering the wrapped package. My hands were shaking. "Is it too late to thank you?"

"It is never too late," he said.

Peter opened the wrapping and eagerly unfolded his gift. He proudly held it up to his chest.

"Mele, this is a nice gift you brought for Peter Kohala. Very nice! Imagine how many heads would turn at market to see this shirt walk by! And my wife, the kisses she will plant all over it!"

He turned the shirt this way and that to admire it, tugged at the buttons. "Yes, good strong buttons. And my hands can still do buttons! Mele, this is very good of you."

Everything slowed inside me as he saw the collar and his face opened in awe. He drew in his breath and then, as if touching the wings of a butterfly, stroked the soft white silk Dr. Akita had given to me. I had sewn the silk inside the collar. He opened the note attached. "To Manu," he read out loud. "Thank you for the peacock feather. I have never forgotten you."

A tiny moan came from his throat. His mouth opened and closed, but no words came out. Finally, he spoke. "Silk." He looked at me. "Peter Kohala never had anything of silk before. Are you sure—?"

"Yes!" I blurted out, then I let myself smile and laugh.

He laughed then, too. The gulch along the side of his face lifted into a new shape. I'm not sure why—even now—but I felt myself being reshaped, too.

"Shall I wear it now, or save it for —"

My stomach jumped. *For what? For market? For church? The horse races? Luaus?* So many, robbed of their rights of inclusion, while I could go anywhere without a thought of what others had lost.

"Now." Peter nodded with certainty and pulled off his old shirt. It was tattered and thick with dirt, with leaves clinging to the back. He thanked me over and over as he sat in the middle of a quiet green forest where we hoped nobody would ever find him and pulled on his new white shirt. He turned around and round so we could see.

"Look, Mele!" He led us toward the cave and stepped into the entrance, smiling as if he had made it himself. As if the cave might help him to scoop something out of this valley—peace of mind, a chance to see his family. Peter Kohala's cave wrapped him every night in loneliness, but it saved him from despair. Here he could die with dignity, and his family could bury and honor his bones. At least he had that. Not like on Moloka`i, where Father Damien struggled to keep up with the number of shallow graves to be dug; where animals foraged at night, pawing and rooting in the soil.

"This is a good cave. I can almost stand up!" said Peter. As he turned back to us, he stumbled on a rock and teetered. I reached out and grabbed his arm to steady him, glancing down as I did at the new sores on his left foot. No wonder he had almost fallen.

"Peter, I need to look at that," said Kalina. "I brought clean bandages for you."

His face brightened. I tried to grasp what this moment held for Manu, but I could not. Only a week ago, my own feet had carried me over the coolness of mossy rocks as I thought only of Keahi and my dreams. Yet there were patients hiding on all the islands...grateful to receive something as simple and life-giving as a clean bandage.

Kalina and Liona watched as I guided Peter back toward the fallen kukui tree. Kalina washed his foot, little more than a stump now, with rainwater he had stored nearby. I fought dizziness.

"Ah, Kalina, the feeling in them is going, you know? The way it does with this disease. But my legs, up here." He patted at his thighs proudly. "They are still good, and my arms too!"

I looked at his strong body and remembered. The lepela will take anyone, not just the weak.

Kalina scraped away dead areas of Peter's foot while he chatted with Liona about news of his family. The whole time, he stroked his new shirt. With every slice of the knife, my own feet dug into the cringing rocky soil. But Peter never blinked.

"I wish I could do more, Peter," she said, "but I brought more chaulmoogra oil, and noni leaves, too. Can you mix a poultice if I leave them?" He nodded. She bandaged his foot. An oozing wetness soaked through, even before she finished.

"Worth it to me," said Peter.

"May I go see your cave again?" I asked.

"Of course," he said. "It is the best cave in Mānoa Valley!"

I pulled my gaze from the quickly discoloring bandage and crossed the clearing.

The small opening held a mixture of light and shadow, of hope and despair. In a crack next to the entrance, Peter had stuck a large twig. On it, he hung various leis, most of them dried by now. For a place to sit, Peter and Liona had dragged a flat rock inside the cave. For a bed, they had gathered fallen leaves, twigs, and grasses, and covered them with tapa cloth.

He had a blanket, but in the dampness of the cave, I knew he would never get warm.

I could climb out of bed, open a drawer to lift out a second blanket, climb back into my soft bed, and fall back asleep.

Turning my head to look around, I felt awash in the presence of what I could not name. I knew that hidden lepers on all the islands were tormented at the thought of apprehension. Yet, this man seemed to have no fear. He seemed to be a soul built inside out. He had something special, as if he had been living for hundreds of years, patiently waiting for the rest of us to be born. Peter Kohala seemed more at peace in his small cave than I sometimes felt on Miki's back as we thundered up the open valley.

I turned when I heard careful steps behind me. He pointed to a lei draped over an outcropping of rock. It looked as if the lei had been drying for some time.

"From my daughter," he said. "You ever meet her?"

I barely shook my head. "Does she come to see you?"

Kalina and Liona exchanged quiet looks. Peter stroked the tin cup in his hand, then spoke.

"She gone now."

"I'm sorry," I said, wondering why Kalina had reached out to touch my arm.

He looked blank as a wall. "Drowned."

My knees felt it first.

"She sent to Moloka`i," he said, "but she never—" He turned and straightened his bedding, his face away from us. I knew the unspoken words. *She never arrived.* It was Peter Kohala's daughter who never arrived at Kalawao, his son-in-law who could not bear the separation. Peter's wife, still living in Wai`anae, had taken in the children.

Was this happening all over the world?

I looked from Peter to Liona. Tears had left wet spots streaking down the front of her dress. She reached out for Peter. Through blurry eyes I looked at a Bible placed with care on a rock shelf next to Peter's bed. Its pages seemed somehow too white for a place like this, where I knew his tears must flow each night into the lonely air. And yet, Peter Kohala worshipped God with all his heart, and gave thanks every day for the love he received from his family and friends. It seemed to me that Peter Kohala showed more respect for God than God showed in return.

Everyone hugged as we started to leave.

"You will come again, Mele?" he asked.

I gave Kalina a hopeful look.

"Peter," she said, "it was important to Mele that she come today. She was such a pest until I said yes! Now it is important that she protects you. But she can write letters, or make treats for you, and Liona and I will bring them. Would you like that?"

His eyes were full of yes.

It is hard to say good-bye when you know you will never see someone again. I never had to do that before.

"Tūtū," I said that evening as we sat alone in the kitchen, "why does God let the lepers be sent away when they should be with their families?"

She began rocking. Each time the leg of the rocker hit a different plank in the floor, there was a different sound. She pulled the hem of her calico dress into her lap and followed a thread back to where it was attached.

"Ah," she said, "why you blaming God for what people do to each other?"

"Do you think God has abandoned the lepers?" I asked.

She rolled the thread round and round between her fingers and her thumb. "You think God push the lepers out of God's heart?"

"Isn't it so? The lepers are told they are loved by a loving God; then they are told they are cursed by the same loving God."

She squinted at me through the thin smoky curtain covering her eyes. "Here is what your tūtū think. Mele is apple of God's eye! Loves her very much! Tūtū think lepers..." She stopped and smiled. "...*inside* apple of God's eye!" She pressed the hem against her leg and patted it once, as if in her mind the matter was settled—the lepers were held in the most precious place of all.

She reached out, feeling for my hand. "What you think, Mele?"

"But the missionaries say leprosy is a curse for sins."

Tūtū stroked my hair. "Maybe lepers more sinned against than sinning."

A breeze came through the window, curving the curtain into a new shape.

"If God give leprosy to punish sinners," she said, "and if we all sinners, then we all get leprosy, yes?"

I waited.

"If God curse the lepers, then God must also curse Father Damien."

My eyes snapped wide open. "Father Damien? Why?"

She felt for the cross dangling from her Bible. "Dr. Netten told Kalina. They think Father Damien has it, too."

Chapter 20

PROPER ENGLISH

What I did not know about Papa was that he had his own cliffs, his own kona winds. Nor did I know that one of those gales was on its way toward what had always been a protected cliff. The gale came while Papa was on the Big Island for two weeks training a new doctor. Other doctors were filling in for Papa's work in Honolulu.

On the Monday morning that Papa was scheduled to return on the *Kilauea*, I saw Theodore reach both hands under his school desk and cross his fingers. I smiled. He did that every Monday morning, asking Jesus to please keep Miss Spencer home today. I looked out the classroom window, daydreaming. How was Peter Kohala? Was he able to make the noni poultice? What were Father Damien's thoughts when he realized he might have the disease? How old was the monkey pod tree near the palace? As old as Tūtū? She was older than all her childhood friends, except Mimo. I turned to smile at Hoaloha, but she had her head down on her desk. I had arrived late and had not been able to talk with her before school. Maybe she was awake until late the night before and was tired. But something did not feel right.

The classroom door opened, Keahi walked in, and my thoughts scattered like tiny sand crabs. I smelled the soft grass beneath us the night we climbed the winding trail up Tantalus to see the cereus bloom, felt the sea stroking and lifting us the day we swam out beyond the reef.

"Eh, Mele." He leaned down and whispered as he passed my desk. "I built two rabbit cages last night. Dr. Arning gave me tip—a whole dollar!"

Before I could answer, Miss Spencer swished into the room. She reached for a stack of slates and set them on her desk. Before handing them out, she neatly unfolded a clean white handkerchief. We all knew what that meant! John Makahehi leaned back. "Oh, here it come," he whispered to me. The white handkerchief was to remind us of her motto.

"Purity of Thought, Precision of Word." She tilted her head forward and looked over her glasses to tell us what no haole had to tell any Hawaiian.

"Students. If you want respect, if you want a good job and a secure future, you must abide in Standard English. American English. I have tried to impress this upon you and cannot emphasize it enough. Speak like Americans. We are a tuh-*rea-sure* of good English and are all around you! Listen to us, emulate us!" She spread her arms like Moses when he parted the sea so all the animals could run across to dry land. I knew how they must have felt.

"Each of you will deliver a one-minute exposition," she began.

Theodore's hand started to inch up.

"A *talk*," she said impatiently. "Last week we talked about our dreams and goals. I was hoping you might have more lofty goals, but perhaps...in time." I waited for her to sigh, and she did. "Today, in contrast to goals, our topic will be things we would not want to have happen in our lives." She smiled weakly. "Then we can talk about how we might use knowledge and skills, and of course proper English, to avoid those things." She looked around as if waiting for applause. "Use precise thought, Standard English, and Standard English only."

Everyone started fidgeting. John Makahehi slid down in his seat. Theodore blinked fast, then kept his eyes closed tightly. I wondered what he was asking of Jesus.

Daniel Livingstone stood up, volunteering to go first. "The worst thing that could happen to me, but it never would, is to lose my pa. He taught me everything I know, like how to shoot and how to hunt wild boar." He smirked, and I could tell he was hunting something else, too. At night, maybe, like stealing chickens. He sat down and spread out like he owned the air.

Theodore was called on. He turned and looked at me as if begging for help. I wished there were something I could do. "Worst thing," he began. He started kicking one foot against the other, pulling at a button on his torn white shirt. "Worst thing happen."

"Standard English, Theodore!"

He jumped like a scared mouse. "The worst thing happen to me is...are...when I...." He wiped a hand across his light brown pant leg. "Worst thing...."

Being humiliated in front of my friends, I thought.

"Theodore, you have provided us with an example of poor presentation, as well as inept—poor—English. Sit down. You will do yours tomorrow. Come prepared. If you have a mirror at home, practice in front of it until you are a pleasure to watch, as well as to hear."

Theodore fought back his hurt.

I wondered what kind of boy Theodore could blossom into with the right teacher. And what were students at Punahoa doing today? Looking at planets through the new telescope? I looked down the hallway to the little mahogany melodeon sitting beneath a window, with its smooth ivory keys. Punahou had raised enough for a shiny baby grand piano. Still, it was not where I wanted to go to school.

What was the worst thing that could happen to me? To be away from Keahi, but I could not say that in class. I thought of Tūtū, every day getting new bruises from bumping into things. What if I were blind? I thought of our recent lū`au, talk about annexation, our dying royal line, more and more Hawaiians getting the lepela, everybody wondering how much longer our kingdom could remain independent. It seemed like so many worst things were already happening. I heard Miss Spencer's voice.

"Ruth, you may go next." Hoaloha's Christian name.

Hoaloha raised herself slowly from her chair. She seemed so small that day. She turned and looked at me with frightened, swollen eyes. I froze—something was wrong. She wrung her hands. I wished I had arrived earlier so we could have talked.

"Worst thing could happen to me—" Her voice broke as she bunched her fingers and pushed them into her bottom lip. "Already happen." She banged the side of her knee against her desk, then again. I grasped the edge of my desk, wanting to jump up. Then a moan like a ghost came from where she stood. "Aauuuu-ahhhh." I felt it crawl up my back and across my arms. The boys squirmed.

"My tūtū...."

Mimo! I leaned forward. Hoaloha's shoulders began shaking and her voice cracked. She began to cough, wiping wet from her mouth onto her dress. I felt a rush of air leave my throat.

"She... turn...herself in."

No.

Wetness began to pour from Hoaloha's closing face. "She gone." Hoaloha choked on the words.

The room jerked—I tried to steady it. Miss Spencer looked over the rim of her glasses, down at Hoaloha.

"Ruth. Let us please remember the *purpose* of our exercise. It is not the inappropriate display of emotion, but rather to practice the use of proper English. Please start over, Ruth, and remember that precision is the hallmark of...Ruth? ...*Ruth?*"

Hoaloha collapsed into her seat and banged her head over and over on her desk. "*Auwē! Auwē!*" I stared in shock at Miss Spencer, then at Hoaloha. I wanted to run to Hoaloha, but my legs would not move. She covered her head with her arms, as if the roof were caving in. The sounds of wailing filled the space around Hoaloha, and then the room. "*Auwē! Auwē!*" The sound tore at the air. It pressed against the whitewash on the walls and the glass of the window, as if trying to get out. Everyone stopped moving; even Daniel Livingstone knew to say nothing.

Miss Spencer, now without words, stared at Hoaloha. I imagined Mimo's family at the dock, with darkness all around; Mimo being pulled from Hoaloha's arms by the deputy...his shiny badge...his pencil moving down the piece of paper, stopping to draw a line through her name. I tried to stop the image of Mimo on the deck of the tiny steamer, among shifting cattle and squawking chickens and flies everywhere. But I could not.

Hoaloha knew—she would never be wrapped in her tūtū's arms again.

Crash! I was jolted by a sound behind me, and I spun around. It was Keahi, jumping up as his chair crashed into the aisle. His chest was heaving. I had never seen him red in the face until then. He pointed a trembling finger toward the front of the room.

"You know *nothing* about this!" he almost shouted at Miss Spencer.

She drew back, her face pale.

"Do not speak," he hissed, "when you do not know!" An old saying on the islands.

Keahi burst down the aisle, past Miss Spencer and out of the classroom. I sat like a stone, trying to find some part of my body that could respond, looking at Hoaloha banging her head into the wetness on her desk...hearing her loud sobbing...watching through the corner of the window to where I knew Keahi would come out of the building. Then I saw him, leaning hard against a lehua tree. He slid down to the dirt, covered his head with his hands, and rocked. Then, over and over in an almost wild fury, he closed his fist and slammed it into his left shoulder. Hard.

I rushed forward to Hoaloha. All the Hawaiian students got up and left and went home, many with wet faces, walking right past Miss Spencer waving her arms and saying this would never happen in America. I held Hoaloha, crushed her against my chest. We rocked and rocked until the room was empty and we were both wet all down our fronts.

Tears poured down Mama's face when I told her. It happened so fast that Mama had not known. "How we going to tell Tūtū?" she cried, "and your papa."

Of course Papa had no way of knowing until he arrived home that afternoon from his trip to the Big Island. When Mama told him, Papa dropped his satchel to the floor. He walked across the lānai as if unaware of anything around him, past the barn, through the gate, to the far side of the pasture. He stopped among the waving grasses. Mama and I, holding each other, tearfully watched him from the lānai.

"Mountain moving inside a man," said Mama, "is a thing to see."

At supper, barely a bite was eaten. Tūtū stayed in her room. I told Papa I could not be in Miss Spencer's class, no matter how badly I was punished. He said nothing. Keahi wanted to change, too. So did John. And of course, Hoaloha.

The next day, we heard the news—it had travelled fast. Parents of every Hawaiian student, and many others, felt that Miss Spencer would do better teaching students in America. Mama and Papa agreed. The parents would raise the money themselves, they said, for her ticket on the next steamer to San Francisco. But Mr. Gibson handled the treasury, and he found the money.

I worried about Tūtū. I soothed her creased forehead, telling her that her hair was whiteness unfolding on the kukui tree. She rocked and cried and prayed to Jesus for the safekeeping of Mimo on Moloka`i.

She and Mimo had attended the first missionary school on King Street. "I remember," she said, patting her Bible, "we both learn Hawaiian alphabet same day, September 23. So proud! Not enough books, so we learn through chanting and singing. Then we teach others the same way, singing the lessons. We think missionaries *best* of all." She patted her palms toward the sky.

"Mimo and I make lauhala mats together, have babies and name them. We sing and make `ulī`ulī rattles for hula. We watch our men catch the shark for drum skin. But always we practice the alphabet, learning to read together. And we pray together too, like missionaries show us, and learn Bible verses."

Then the disaster came. The Smallpox Epidemic in 1853 was the first of four. It was the same epidemic that Papa lived through.

"We help each other," she said. "We watch them die. We lose our husbands. We sit up all night holding loved ones—brothers, sisters, aunties and uncles. Smallpox take them in the night. In morning, we count again. Thirteen die in our two families."

"Your mama and Kalina only two of my five keiki who survive. When epidemic over, half of us gone. We ask missionaries, 'Why does God let this happen to those who love Him?' Missionaries tell us, 'Give thanks to God.' So, we give thanks to God. But sometimes we wonder, who is this white God? What are these white diseases? We so healthy before!"

That night when the walls fell asleep, I had a dream. A rock was thrown into a still pond in the middle of my room. The ripples came closer and closer. Mama appeared and stood beside me as the ripples, now tears, washed over our feet. "Mama," I said, "Papa can make the ripples stop coming, can't he?" She shook her head. "Only a man," she said.

I woke up to the sound of footsteps, someone walking below my room. Back and forth, across the creaking parlor floor.

Papa.

Chapter 21

THE CROSSING

I sat alone on the terrace, watching the shade inch across the bricks, wondering how a fern knows to curl into a question mark. I looked toward the garden, remembering Hoaloha and me as children. We trailed behind Mimo, holding the young taro shoots as she leaned forward and stuck them in the mud.

I plodded through The Advertiser, our English newspaper. The first standard curriculum, it said, was to be formally adopted by schools in Hawai`i. *So we are more like America.* Another topic, always sparking a fight with Hawaiians, was the upcoming student vaccinations. As always, there were articles about the royalty and Queen Emma's illness—she was not getting better. Nothing was.

I looked up at the sound of the screen door opening, closing. Papa stepped onto the lānai.

"Mele." A tiny puff of air blew from his cheeks. He had closed his eyes.

I waited for his eyes to open. They did.

"I need to go see Mimo."

A section of the newspaper jerked in my hands.

He took a deep breath and pushed his hair back. His hand fell in a tired way at his side.

"To *Moloka`i?*"

"I owe it to Mimo."

"Papa, I know, but—"

To the settlement at Kalawao? To the place he said was a living hell? I remember waiting for him to say he felt dizzy. Like me.

"Mele," he finally said, "let's take a walk up the road."

Mostly in silence, we walked for miles. The tall grasses found our hands. Seeds fell from them as we stayed, like we always had, on the same side of the road. I had treasured these moments when I was younger, but we had not taken a walk together in a long time.

"When I was a boy of twelve," Papa finally said, "I came here with my parents. My mother became deathly ill on the trip over; she was already weak when the ship arrived during the height of the smallpox epidemic. My father was exhausted. He had helped to bring the ship through bad weather, plus caring for my mother." He tossed a hand in the air. "I'm afraid I was pretty useless."

I took his hand, something I had not done in years.

"Tūtū was right in what she told you. By the end of that first epidemic, thousands more Hawaiians had died, which represented almost half the native population. It shocked the islands. You already know that my parents died, too."

I nodded.

He let go of my hand and put his arm across my shoulder. I wrapped my arm around his waist.

"When Mimo's son died, who had been my age, she heard through Tūtū about a terribly depressed haole boy. His parents had died, and he had no other relatives. Tūtū knew this because your mama, who was ten, had found me sitting on a rock in the middle of Nu`uanu Stream, not knowing what to do. She told me I was too skinny—I would lose my mana, she said. I had no idea what mana was, but it was obviously something I shouldn't go around losing. So she took me home for supper. With Tūtū's help, Mimo hānai'd me and raised me with her children, at least those who survived the epidemic. I didn't realize at the time how difficult that must have been for Mimo. I didn't know my body had so many tears inside, but when they all came out, Mimo was there to hold me. I am ashamed to say that I was so absorbed in my loss that I did not realize Mimo had her own loss."

A tiny voice inside me. *Have you done that, Mele? Been so busy with your own pain that you forget the suffering of others?*

Papa picked up a chunk of broken rock and heaved it to the side of the road; wheels broke on such rocks, and horses could injure themselves. "Mimo cared for me until I was sixteen, when I left for school in Boston. I wrote and sent money when I could, but that can't repay the kindness she showed me."

Repay a kindness.

For an instant, I wanted to blurt out everything. "Then you understand," I wanted to say, "why I had to help Peter Kohala." I longed to tell him I knew what it was like, to want to give back when the memory of a kindness has stayed with you since you were a child, and still owns a place in your heart.

Suddenly, I felt awful. For Papa, repaying a kindness meant going to Moloka`i to see Mimo one last time.

For me, it meant betraying my father.

My chest sunk with guilt. Walking with my arm around Papa's waist suddenly felt like a lie. I pulled away and held my arms across my chest, holding in my failure to be the person he believed me to be.

"Papa," I said in a breathy voice. "Can we go back?"

The cane fields burned, yellowing the sky with smoke. Tūtū put curled fingers to her lips. I knew she was missing Mimo.

"Who will bury her bones when she is gone?" she asked through sudden tears. "Who will say the words, give the blessing?"

"Father Damien will," I said, but the words trailed off.

When my father returned from Kalawao, when he stepped over a pile of rope on the deck and onto the sloping gangplank of the *Mokoli`i*, he looked as if he had become old in a day. Only one visit to the settlement, and he already had the smell of sickness, the smell of rags because the patients were not provided adequate clothing. I knew Papa had been holding Mimo, rocking her. Or was it Mimo who held Papa?

I did not know what to say when Papa turned to me and reached for my hand and squeezed it. I looked down at the dust on his brown shoes, at his other hand limp at his side, at a streak of dried blood on his lower pant leg.

Where did the blood come from? *"Papa?"*

His voice was not distant, like when he gave a lecture. It sounded close.

"You cannot imagine," he said. His eyes were dull. "There wasn't a clean bandage in the place. The patients get almost no food. I had no idea, Mele. The kōkuas without disease...caring for their loved ones? The government says if they do not have the disease, they do not qualify for food rations."

He winced. "The kōkuas are so hungry that some are agreeing—even asking—to be inoculated with leprosy by Dr. Mouritz, in hopes they could at least get something to eat. Not surprisingly, the inoculations are not taking."

Try to get leprosy? So, you could get something to eat?

"But the Director of the Board," I protested, "I see it in the papers. He says the conditions are not as bad as people think!"

Papa looked away. "He does say that."

"Is he lying?"

He tightened his lips.

"...Papa?"

"Mele, it's not proper that I speak with you about this."

"It's not proper to starve people!"

All the way home, Papa wanted us sitting close to him. Mama and I wrapped around him in his silence.

The next day, Papa went to work without a word to any of us. Kalina told Mama that night that new shipment papers were drawn for over twenty of those with the disease. On the bottom of the papers, she said, was Papa's signature. Papa had signed the papers, she said, but in handwriting jerky and broken, and the t's were not crossed.

Papa had always crossed his t's.

My white, physician father. Mama was right—he was not God. He was only a man with his own kona wind, clinging to his cliff as desperately as I had clung to my own.

Chapter 22

NIGHTS IN TOWN

After his trip to Moloka`i, Papa started to miss supper sometimes. He came home late in the evening when the house was dark, the walls were quiet.

On one of these evenings, I sat in the kitchen waiting up for him. Everyone else was asleep. I reached for a piece of sugar cane, then put it down. Holoholo lay curled up in my lap. Her stomach was more rounded than usual; maybe she was going to have kittens. Plenty of tomcats had been around.

Everyone knew about the places in town where men went sometimes. I imagined sailors oozing along certain dark streets the way tomcats slink at night along shadows of the barn. I imagined sailors and businessmen, too, ducking into low buildings where murmuring curtains moved behind the light of red candles; where long gold tassels touched glasses of rum that lined the stained windowsills. Most people kept their eyes forward as they hurried past.

An early moon had silvered the clouds by the time Papa came home. I met him at the door.

"Mele, what are you doing up so late?" He quickly set down his satchel when he saw the way I was holding myself. "What's wrong?"

He led me out to the lānai where we always talked, sat me on the sofa next to him, and waited. The words were not coming, maybe because there was no good way to ask. Had I been so awful that he did not want to be around us anymore?

"Talk to me," he said gently.

"I'm sorry, Papa," I whispered. It was my fault. And now there was no way to fix it.

"Sorry for what?" He seemed confused and wiped away my tears with the back of his hand.

"What you do."

He leaned closer, trying to catch my words. Because of the differences between Mama and Papa about the those with the disease, Papa would abandon us. I would have to get a job, I thought. Working in the cane fields or selling eggs like Theodore's mother.

The Chinese lanterns moved with the breeze, causing the tiny lights to flicker. I wished they would go out, so the lānai would be dark and my face could be hidden.

"Mele, what are you talking about?"

I looked away. "That you go to town."

He drew back, surprised. "I go to town almost every day. You know that."

"I mean—"

His eyebrows pulled together. He looked lost for a moment.

"Oh," he said, reaching up to rub his forehead, 'now I understand. Mele, I feel terrible about this. I didn't realize. I had no idea you would ever think...well, that I was being unfaithful to your mother!"

"Aren't you?" By now I was imagining him in Boston… unpacking a trunk…pulling out photos of haole women wearing bright red lipstick, and lining them up across a dresser. Not a single photo of Mama or Tūtū or Pōki`i. Or me.

"Then why do you come home so late?"

"I've been studying reports. Some legislative things."

I wiped my sleeve across my eyes. "Why? You've never studied them before."

"I've wanted to investigate some Board of Health records, election information, legislative reports. About Moloka`i. And, if you pick a fight with me about this…" He squeezed my hands and gave a little smile, but I caught the warning. "Something seems out of sorts," he added.

"But why would elections have anything to do with Moloka`i?"

"The very question I've asked myself."

He stood up and put out the lanterns. But now I wanted light. Somewhere on his face there must be a clue, but I saw nothing.

Days later, Papa invited me for another walk up the valley. I quickly said yes. How does a daughter betray her father… while also guarding the moments she has him all to herself? I do not know.

I remembered walking up Nu`uanu Road with Papa when I was a child. If Papa reached for a blade of grass, I reached for the piece right next to it. If Papa stopped to listen to the night, I wanted to be the creature that made the sound. But on that night, when we came to a tall clump of grass growing next to the road, and Papa reached for a blade, I started to reach out but pulled my hand back. Such a small gesture, but it made me realize how torn I still was—wanting to please my father, knowing instead that I had to be the woman I was growing into.

"Papa, why did you marry Mama?" I asked.

Papa bent the long blade of grass. "Because I love her."

"Why do you love her?" Closer to my question.

His eyebrows jumped around.

"Don't think about it, Papa. Just answer, quick from your heart!"

I realized immediately, that was like asking Papa to fly. But I was wrong.

He smoothed the piece of grass. "Because she touches something deep inside me. A place that doesn't feel as alive without her."

My feet stopped. I stared at Papa in disbelief.

When Keahi's leg brushed mine, or when his finger drew a lazy line down my shoulder, I felt that way—more alive.

"But how do you know...?" Hoaloha said boys do not sit around asking themselves these questions, they just get hit by lightning and fall over.

"Oh, now I understand," said Papa, smiling. "Are you wondering how you feel about Keahi?"

"No...yes."

"Well, how *do* you feel about Keahi?"

"Yes!" Keahi and yes just sounded good together. But that was no reason, I scolded my brain, to say yes.

"Yes?" he said.

"No." That sounded more...haole.

"No?"

I could feel something start inside my throat—tears? I had loved Keahi since we were children. I felt as if something had been etched out of me a long time ago and set aside for Keahi. I moved closer to Papa, leaned against him, and wrapped my hands around his arm.

"I don't want to talk about it, Papa," I whispered. He made room on his side of the road, and we inched over.

He pressed his arm, with my hands clinging to it, close to his side. He told me about when he was young and first realized he loved Mama.

"One day I saw her at market. There she was, dashing wildly through the streets on a black horse with a long red waist scarf trailing out behind her." Papa chuckled. "And there I was, a skinny boy standing in a cloud of dust holding a silly rice cake. She was thirteen and I was fifteen, a year before I left for Boston."

Papa talked until we turned around on the road, then we were silent until we saw the dim light through the kitchen window. In my heart, I thanked him a dozen times for knowing something fragile was growing there, and that too many words could trample it.

When I walked up the porch and turned to look at Papa, his eyes were shiny in the moonlight. He, too, knew something between us had changed. A daughter had turned a page that a father was not quite ready to turn.

"Are you still my kekipi?" he asked.

My little rebel. I nodded, though realizing I could never again go back to my childhood. It was over.

Papa and I went inside, and more than the screen door closed behind us. I chewed my tears and swallowed them. I do not know what Papa did with his.

Chapter 23

PUPILS WILL BE EXAMINED

As the dry season approached, I fell into a happy rhythm of making biscuits and small gifts and leis for Peter Kohala, sending them with Kalina each time she went to Mānoa Valley to bandage his feet and control any infection as best she could.

About others being hidden, I never specifically asked. But I knew they, too, were receiving some of my gifts. Pears, bananas, and bandages continued to disappear. Mama made batches of poi larger than needed for our family, and I said nothing. I made more biscuits and sweets than needed, and she said nothing. We simply set them on the back porch, gave a quick squeeze to each other's hand, and waited for them to disappear.

For the first time in my life, I felt a part of something larger than myself—something that made meaningful the simple task of making biscuits and wrapping them with care so they stayed fresh and would not get crushed.

In the daytime, I did these things to follow my conscience. They were small actions, but they came from a place inside me that felt whole. In the early evenings, I took walks up the valley with my father, my arm wrapped in his. How did I walk out of one world and into another, without so much as a blink? I don't know.

In a man named Mr. Todd, students in my class gained not only a new teacher, but salvation from Miss Spencer. Even Theodore began to blossom. Mr. Todd encouraged my music and reminded me that our school had been gifted a treasure. In the hallway of Royal School sat a melodeon, a short stocky piano of mahogany veneer and massive tapering legs. It was brought to the islands around 1850 for a missionary who came with the Ninth Company, and, in the same way that good fortune blows from one hand to another, we somehow inherited it for our music program. It was nothing like the elegant baby grand piano at Punahou, but I loved it just the same.

One day after school I stayed late to play the melodeon. Keahi had to finish a job for Mr. Nott at the planing mill, so we planned to meet later near the bridge. I heard bare feet dashing along the hallway and recognized the sound—Hoaloha had returned to school to get a book she forgot. Over the weeks, she had slowly begun to heal, though I knew she missed Mimo terribly.

As we started down the hallway together, we heard voices coming from the principal's office.

"Shhh," said Hoaloha, "that sounds like Mr. Kenyon!"

"Who is he?" I whispered.

She made a face. "Teacher at English school; nobody to kill a chicken over!" I giggled quietly; when an honored guest arrived, it was often customary on the islands to kill a chicken for a special supper.

Mr. Mackintosh was trying to calm Mr. Kenyon. We stopped to listen.

"Mr. Kenyon! This is far from the first case, as you well know. But I do not set the policy. Therefore, I am in no position to say one way or the other what your duty is in the matter. You will need to take it up with the Board—please!"

"But Mr. Gleason is anxious about the subject. He insists I have a duty to report the name of all cases found in my school, with a view to their being taken up by the authorities."

Hoaloha and I looked at each other. We both knew there were students with the disease. We crept toward the voices.

"Well then," said Mr. Mackintosh, "perhaps you might simply write a letter to the Board. Surely they can opine on the matter."

"I shall!" said Mr. Kenyon. "And I shall suggest that if the Board wishes an examination of pupils, they undertake it themselves!"

We quickly backed away from their voices. An examination of pupils?

"They will require health certificates, too," I said. Most of us, like Pōki`i and me, were checked often by our parents for any sign of the disease. But with unreported cases, and families keeping it quiet for as long as possible, who from our school might be taken?

Hoaloha and I walked glumly down the street toward the bridge, neither of us saying much. She had a certain way of fidgeting when she was about to bring up a subject that turned me into a stingray. Anybody hurting Theodore was one subject. Daniel Livingstone was another.

"Daniel like me," said Hoaloha. "He asks me all the time to be his ipo." His girlfriend.

"No!" I grabbed her arm. "He's no good, Hoaloha. You stay away from him!"

She pulled away.

"You like him!" I said.

From the time Daniel came to Honolulu months ago, he had been interested in Hoaloha. I could feel her weakening.

"He is good to look at," she said.

I gave her another warning look.

She threw her hands up in frustration. "You have Keahi! Always you and Keahi. And John only wants to be friends!"

My best friend. What could I say to comfort her?

"I want someone to love, too," she said. A line of tears welled up in her eyes.

Even if that someone was Daniel Livingstone? I held her tight while she caved into me. Her loneliness was made worse by the loss of Mimo, I knew that. I felt horrible to know I had hurt her feelings, worse at the thought of my best friend being with a vicious boy nobody could trust. Then I had a thought that surprised me: I wondered if Daniel ever felt lonely, if he ever wanted someone to love.

Hoaloha and I had said goodbye after she was feeling better, and I was almost to the bridge at the base of the valley when I heard a familiar voice.

"Eh, Mele!" Keahi stood in the shade of a silvery ohi'a tree. In a cool afternoon breeze, his white shirt billowed. Long narrow pieces of wood, rolls of string, and folds of fabric stuck out from arms and pockets all over his body.

"You look like a stick man!" I teased. "For Tūtū's kite?"

He nodded. "Going to make it tonight! Mr. Nott gave me wood. Look! And lots of string. Tūtū will think she has floated up to heaven!" The piece of white cloth was painted in bright reds. "The Seventh Dragon," he said.

Part of his smile was about the kite, but there was something else, too.

We waded along a sandy part of the stream. Keahi bundled everything under one arm and reached for my hand. His eyes twinkled with pride.

"Mr. Nott asked me to work full time to learn cabinet work. He offered me a whole dollar a day!"

`Iolani Palace hired the Planing Mill for most of their jobs, including for the concerts. There would always be work.

"Keahi, what about school?" It made me nervous when Keahi talked about full time work. Papa agreed to let me marry a Hawaiian when Mama pointed out that he had married Mama. But still Papa was emphatic that my husband be educated. Sometimes schooling was an issue between Keahi and me.

His face changed. "Oh, Mele, you know I'm no good at school."

I straightened a piece of koa under his arm. "You can be!"

We climbed up the bank.

"I'd rather work with wood, with my hands."

He took my arm and turned me toward him. "Mele, this is a chance for me! In one year, I can make almost $600 if I do overtime. That is almost as much as haole teachers, and some of them do college!"

He squeezed my arm and playfully dropped his face to mine. "Mele, this is *good!*"

"Does Mr. Nott want you to quit school?"

Keahi looked at his feet. That meant he was thinking of quitting school. I dragged the whole story out of him. Mr. Nott had offered him a dollar a day to work full time now. It was good pay; the Chinese cane workers made pennies a day, and the work was awful. But Mr. Nott said he would pay more if Keahi finished school.

"How much more?" I asked.

"Fifteen cents more a day. But he says my grades have to be good."

Don't worry, Mr. Nott. His grades will be good.

"How much more is that in a month?" I asked. Keahi looked like I asked him to measure the drops in a waterfall.

"OK, I will stay in school." His face brightened. "Dr. Arning is always wanting more cages for his research. Mr. Nott says I can build all of them. I can save! Maybe build a little house, with white paint and green trim, like yours!" His hands were sweeping the air as he took a breath. "A white fence…and little lānai under nice mango tree." He slowed down. "And then maybe we get…"

Suddenly he seemed embarrassed. "Get…"

Say it!

Around our bare ankles, leaves tickled and teased. By the time they flitted over our toes and were lifted away, Keahi stared at me like he had tripped over a rainbow. Was this what boys acted like when hit by lightning? He swallowed and reached up to stroke his hair. The koa fell. He leaned to pick it up and dropped the string. He reached for the string and the sticks slid onto the grass. He stood with Tūtū's kite scattered on the ground in front of him, staring at me like he had just seen the Seventh Dragon.

Clouds carried me into the house and propped me up against the kitchen table, and made it look like I was still Mele. Mama looked up from her work and sighed.

"This is my daughter whose brain is carried off by love. She is no good to me now."

Chapter 24

THE TERRACE BRICKS CHANGE COLOR

We killed a chicken to celebrate. On the day the *Amy Turner* arrived, 139 days after leaving Boston, the trade winds were too strong to sail into harbor. The tug *Pele* was broken down, so Captain Newell and his crew, and Keahi's cousin Kalua with them, rowed in. They had anchored not far off Diamond Head.

I wondered what the American Consulate thought when a medical student named Vernon Briggs took Kalua to their offices, asking for the second time if Kalua could stay in America to attend school. They again denied the request. Kalua was too young, they said, to be traipsing around the world with salty crew on the high seas. A few weeks later, the *Amy Turner,* with Kalua on the ship, left for another long voyage back to Hawai`i.

Though I think Captain Newell was too fond of Kalua to be unkind, I am sure he warned him not to try to stow away again. I can imagine how politely Kalua smiled and nodded. I bet he saluted too! After stowing away two times, most people would give up and not try a third time. But Keahi and I knew Kalua would not stay in Hawai`i for long.

It was not that Kalua hated Hawai`i; it was that he loved the idea of America.

To hear Kalua and Keahi sing together again was wonderful, their voices high and sweet like most of the island boys. They sang together even as children while climbing the hills of Nu`uanu Valley. "We find good hiding places," Kalua said after one of their songs, "in elbow of the ravine." The trail started not far from my house, he said. It wound up and up into the hills, across a flat area to where an overgrown section dipped into the curve of a ravine hidden among the leaning trees—like an elbow. I half-listened.

"Tell me how you are related as cousins," I said, sending a challenging smile to both Kalua and Keahi. On the islands, people joke that almost everyone is related.

Kalua casually threw an arm toward the island of Kaua`i. "Oh, far cousin!"

"Yeah," said Keahi, tossing his arm in the opposite direction toward Maui. "Far, far cousin!" Suddenly they were all story, pointing this way and that, shouting out islands and names of every imaginable town. "Lāhainā!...Hilo!..."

"So," I said, "you are not cousins."

"No!" said Keahi, "we are *brothers*!" And off they went again, slapping backs and punching playfully. I think Kalua was the younger brother Keahi always wanted. I am not sure they were even related, but what did it matter?

Keahi urged Kalua to apply for work at the planing mill, but Kalua said he had other ideas. Keahi and I glanced nervously at each other. The *Amy Turner* was leaving in two weeks on its return trip to New York.

"Kalua, you stay here this time!" warned Keahi. "Go to Royal School with Mele and me!"

Kalua shook his head and smiled. He reached for his `ukulele, his voice already sweetening the air with "Aloha `Oe." During those evenings on the lānai, when Keahi pulled out his gourd whistle and Kalua strummed the `ukulele, the moments passed like crystals before a flame. Keahi was every moment the boy who brought magic to my dreams. When I looked at him, with his hair tossed back as he sang, I knew he would always keep me near an edge.

But the joy was not to last.

Days passed when I sat watching the terrace bricks change color in a wrong-seasoned rain, wondering why everyone was acting strange—especially Keahi. One minute he burst out in anger about something that would not ordinarily bother him; the next minute, he went numb.

A few days before, several of us had been in the schoolyard. Before anyone realized or could stop him, Daniel Livingstone forced a firecracker deep in the mouth of a gecko, lit the fuse, and dropped the poor creature. The gecko, a sign of good fortune, is believed to protect and watch over Hawaiians.

I turned at the sound—*tssst!*—and heard a muffled pop. I covered my ears and screamed at Daniel. Hoaloha pounded on Daniel's back while he bent over laughing. Theodore wrung his shirttail.

Keahi stood gazing down at red and green pieces lying in the dirt, then looked at Daniel.

"Hana Make," he simply said. There was no life in his voice. "You have given the gecko a gift."

"Keahi!" I shouted. How could he think such a thing? "Listen to what you are saying! What is wrong with you?"

He shrugged, walked away, and would not talk about it.

A few days later, Keahi almost had to drag Kalua to Mr. Mackintosh's office to talk about enrolling Kalua in school. After Keahi and I had talked about his quitting school, he was suddenly Mr. Finish School.

I waited outdoors near the verandah.

"Hey, hapa."

The voice made me turn cautiously. Whether calling me "half-breed" or chopping down a papaya tree, whether exploding a gecko for fun or destroying petroglyphs held sacred to the islanders, to know Daniel was to know he felt entitled to be cruel. The day he killed the gecko, loved on the islands for their sweet presence and good luck, Hoaloha had realized that, lonely or not, she wanted nothing to do with Daniel Livingstone.

I bristled. Was Daniel going to accuse me again of wishing I were all white, like him? Suddenly I did not care if he wanted someone to love.

"I think I saw your old grandma, "Toot Toot."

"Leave me alone!"

"Was that her at market with her chin hangin' down, all those brown marks on her face?"

"Stop it!"

"Kind of looks like another leper ready to ship out, wouldn't you say?"

Unknown to Daniel, Keahi had come around the corner behind him and heard every word. Daniel was spun around so fast he did not have time to react. Keahi's fist flew through the air. Daniel lay sprawled on his back, clutching his nose with both hands, screaming and slamming his boots into the dirt.

I froze at the sight of Keahi standing over Daniel. He stepped back and pointed as Daniel struggled to his feet and staggered before steadying himself. The grass where Daniel had fallen was red.

"You don't talk disrespect for Mele's tūtū. Or our lepers!"

"You *bastard*!" Daniel pulled a dirty sleeve across his bloodied face.

Keahi drew back his fist again. I grabbed his shirt.

"Keahi, NO!" His fists were like steel and could kill Daniel.

The principal and Kalua ran toward us. Mr. Mackintosh planted himself between Daniel and Keahi, facing Keahi.

"Keahi, what has gotten into you? You have *never* done anything like this!" Daniel shouted obscenities at Keahi over Mr. Mackintosh's shoulder. Mr. Mackintosh spun around. "Daniel, shut up!" Daniel's face was already swollen as dough. He slammed his mouth shut and glared at Mr. Mackintosh. He could not keep quiet for long.

"Wait'll I tell my Pa!"

"Daniel...he been looking for this for long time, Mr. Mackintosh." Keahi was breathing heavily, wiping his mouth with his fist still clenched.

Daniel was sent, swearing as he left, to Queen's Hospital. I shivered at his last words as he turned his horse and cupped his nose. Blood ran down his sleeve and onto the flanks of his horse.

"Just wait, island boy," came the muffled words. "Me and my pa...we'll find a way to get you."

When I told Tūtū what happened, she said nothing. She pressed the dog-eared corners of her Bible and whispered to herself. Then she shook her head slowly. I did not understand what was happening to Keahi. Every day, he seemed farther from the boy I used to know.

Chapter 25

THE GREEN PARROT

The *Amy Turner* had been in Honolulu for two weeks. At dawn, the bark would sail for China, returning immigrants who disliked the cane work and missed their families. From there, the ship would cross the Pacific Ocean toward the most dangerous part of the trip—Cape Horn, a place so treacherous it gobbled up ships as if they were sweet cakes. In February, after an eight-month voyage, they would arrive in New York.

More and more Chinese were leaving the islands. In their place, boatloads of workers came, including Japanese laborers new to the islands and willing to fill the empty places in the rows of cane.

"Come watch the crew load the *Amy Turner* tonight," urged Kalua. "She is going to sail in the morning."

We agreed to meet him at the docks. "Sure," said Keahi. "We will bring rope, too. Tie you down good!"

I wondered how Kalua would feel when the *Amy Turner* left for America without him. I wondered how I might feel to spend three years trying to reach a place that held magic for me, only to watch the ship sail away without me. But Captain Newell had warned Kalua. This time, with the crew watching for him, Kalua had to stay on the islands.

Keahi and I walked along the wharf, our eyes searching the crowd for the short build of Kalua. The air smelled of seaweed trapped in the harbor. Shiny ropes of green bobbed along the water and wrapped around pilings. Gangplanks were reflected in the night water.

We watched the sailors as they continued loading. Their tattooed muscles were beaded with sweat as they worked by the light of oil lamps hung from rigging. Everything loose—rigging, flags, oil lamps and dirty shirts—swayed in a breeze. Up the gangplank went the sailors, bending beneath an unending stream of cargo: heavy bags of white rice, repaired ship parts, crates of chickens, and steamer trunks. Two goats scampered up, frightened by their new home. One was swatted when it began chewing on the lacquer of a door; it leapt back and almost bolted over the railing. Fattened pigs shrieked and resisted with all their might as sailors tugged on ropes and pushed them from behind. "Move, bacon!" one shouted.

Keahi looked away and saw the movement first.

"Eh, Mele, look!"

I turned to see a drunk sailor staggering along the docks. On his shoulder sat a parrot. It was a flapping jungle of dark and light green, with bright yellow on its chest and thick neck. Its beak, shiny black and curving, reflected golden light in the evening sun. Its eyes held a promise of wildness, reminding me of why they are to be approached with care.

"So beautiful!" I said with admiration.

"I saw the same parrot at market. But the sailor—" Keahi shook his head. "He is no good."

I looked around for Kalua.

"You think maybe we get one someday?" Keahi laughed and began imitating a parrot. "Eh, Pōki`i—*squawk, squawk*—you no bodda Mele and Keahi, you hear? You go fish ulua, take loooong time." He winked at me and I slapped at his arm. He dodged away, laughing.

I knew how to tease him back in the same lazy English that Keahi often used. "Maybe I save myself for nice *haole* boy."

"Oh yeah, nice Punahou boy. Like kissing dead fish."

The parrot shook its whole body and glared at a child who threw a wad of paper toward it. I tugged at Keahi's shirt.

"Keahi, help me watch for feathers."

The sailor had skinny arms tattooed with roses and skulls. He reached up to pet the parrot, feeding it bits of stale bread. "Hey, pretty bird, how you doing? Hello, hello."

"He-llo, he-llo," came the words back.

At the sound of a foghorn, the parrot turned, ruffled its feathers, and creamy spots dropped to the dusty street. The parrot stretched its yellow neck and opened its mouth wide. Above the noise of the docks came a new voice, harsh and screeching.

"Kraah-kraaah. You ugly face!"

Several men laughed. Most did not.

Its screech became louder, almost a scream. "...Krah-krah-krah. Hawaiians stupid...stupid." It pecked at the air. I instinctively reached for Keahi's hand, feeling a knot in my stomach.

The laughing stopped. A Hawaiian man stepped suddenly forward. He was barefoot and wore a red bandana around his neck; his face was bright with anger at this insult.

The parrot screeched again, louder. "Stupid native, stupid native! Krah-krah-krah!"

The man wearing the red bandana took another step forward.

"Shut up!" he shouted at the parrot.

I drew back, grabbing at Keahi's arm.

"Shuddup! Shuddup!" mimicked the parrot back at the man. The senseless repetition angered more people in the crowd. The parrot flapped its wings, jabbed at the air with its beak, frantically dancing about on the sailor's shoulder. The sailor laughed. A foghorn blasted in the distance, making me jump. The drunken sailor raised his jug in the air and leaned his head back.

"Leper!" he shouted into the crowd.

"Leper!" screeched the parrot. Of course the parrot had no idea what would be aroused over these words.

"Leper...leper...leper," said the parrot. "Shuddup! Shuddup! Krah-krah-krah!"

Keahi's hand dug into mine. I felt a swelling rage. My own. Keahi's. Those around us. I felt a fury at the insolence of the sailor, at the unwelcome foreign ships filling our harbors as if they were their own, at the arrogance mirrored by the parrot.

The Hawaiian man lunged forward, the crowd parting. The docks and alcohol, most knew, were a recipe for trouble. He ripped the parrot from the sailor's shoulder, took giant steps toward the water, and hurled the squawking animal toward the gangplank.

Furious as I was, I gasped in shock. This was a sign of the frustration, the anger growing among the kanaka at the continual insults of foreigners.

The parrot shrieked, hit the rail of the gangplank, and bounced off. A broken wing flapped in the air. In one thrust of its body, the parrot flopped over and landed with barely a sound in the harbor below where we stood. The green mass of feathers bobbed face down. I stared as ripples of water moved away from the parrot. They reached the side of the *Amy Turner* and started back in a new shape toward the still, seaweed-covered body.

The sailor rushed to the edge of the water. His chest heaved as he stared down at the oil-covered feathers. He turned. A jug of rum dropped from his hand and landed in the dirt. The crowd stepped back as the sailor reached behind his waist. I slapped my hands to my ears as the terrible sound rang out. *Bang!* A Portuguese woman dropped her basket and screamed. Two Chinamen knocked over crates as they leapt sideways to the ground.

Keahi grabbed me and moved me behind him, backing both of us away. We turned and raced along a wooden building, down an alley, dodging bottles and trunks and barrels as we ran. Behind us, mixed with the sound of foghorns, were the shouts and cries. "Auwē! Auwē!" The kanikau, the great wailing.

I had turned back one last time, hoping to see Kalua's short build and to know he was safe. All I saw was chaos...smoke... and a boy running up a gangplank.

When we crossed School Street and could walk up the valley, Keahi went numb. Worst of all, he pulled away when I reached out to him. He had turned aside, his face burning with tears.

"Keahi." Though against his will, he let me slowly turn him back toward me.

I had no idea what I wanted to know.

"At the hospital," I finally said, "when Dr. Netten wanted to give you a physical examination." I waited for him to speak. Nothing came. "Have you not been well?"

A buggy rolled past. The sound of clopping hooves faded.

"I'm ok," he finally said. But there was no truth in his voice.

Never was I so relieved to come home. To see my green and white house sitting atop our little rise. To see light shining through the parlor window and Holoholo asleep on the porch. My gaze stopped at a corner of the screen door where Papa had started to repair a tear with a small piece of wire. On the railing were pieces of colored string Dr. Akita had given to Poki'i. All these things seemed so simple. But I could not fill myself enough with them.

What was happening to our island? What was happening to Keahi?

I lay on my bed, rolled on my side and rocked myself. Keahi and I were both upset at what happened at the docks, but why had he pulled away from me?

I felt the touch of a familiar hand. It stroked my forehead, wiped away my tears. Tūtū rubbed the palm of her hand along the arm of the koa chair.

"Things no good right now," she said when I told her what happened. "More and more the kanaka and haoles standing apart. Haoles talk about future, we talk about past." She pulled a sheet over my shoulders. "We caught in wave, Mele. Big wave."

I wondered what kind of wave Keahi was caught in.

The next morning, the *Amy Turner* threw off lines. Shouts filled the air and bottles were flung into the bay. Boys climbed the ship's chains and leaped into the water, shouting. The day the pretty barkentine backed out of its berth and turned to set sail for the South Seas and China and then New York, Kalua disappeared like a shiny stone tossed to the foaming sea. I had a strange feeling. It sat in the corner of my heart like a tiny rock. Kalua, it told me, would never return. I hoped he remembered to take his `ukulele.

Chapter 26

BELLY OF THE WHALE

Keahi began to be late for school. He no longer brushed against me as he walked past my desk. John Makahehi could not convince him to go fishing. His talk of being a carpenter ended. I felt helpless.

After staying late at school one day, I came around the corner of the verandah and saw Ali`i tied to a post. His head was down. His reins hung along his mane as if he had stood there, unmoving, all day.

In the shadows stood Keahi. When had he grown thin? I walked to him. His hair did not have the luster it had in the sun. His face had the same look as the day recently when Tūtū asked him to play a song on his gourd whistle. Half-way through the song, Keahi had quit. He had stood with the gourd whistle in his hand, looking toward the pali.

He leaned to one side, the way Daniel Livingstone does when he is looking for a fight.

"Mele." A hard voice. "You remember kanaka at dock? Who get shot by sailor?"

I nodded, wanting to ask if he would talk to Dr. Netten.

"Sailor, he get arrested for shooting kanaka, all right. But haole judge will think about what to do. Maybe nothing." His eyes matched his voice—ice. "What your *haole* papa think about that?"

His words stung. "You leave my father out of this."

But a barb had snagged him and already set. "Your papa only wants one thing. Get rid of lep—"

I pushed him away, feeling the slap of his words.

"What is it? *Tell me!*" I pleaded.

Keahi looked at his feet. When he raised his eyes, I saw again the boy I did not know.

And then my world changed.

His fingers moved to the top of his shirt. They trembled like those of an old man. He unbuttoned the top button…then the next…and the next. I swallowed, watching his hands. In one tug, he yanked his shirt away from his left shoulder.

I drew back. Every word I had ever known melted into this word: *No.* I could not stop shaking my head, was unable to take my eyes from the patch of redness on his shoulder.

"No, Keahi. Don't tell me what this is." Air rushed in and out of my lungs at the same time.

Bitter tears filled his eyes. "You know what it is, Mele. The ma`i Pākē has found Keahi, too."

Still I shook my head in disbelief. Not Keahi—he was too young, too strong.

"It can be *anything*!" I said. "Papa has said it himself. So often it is something else—not the disease at all!"

"I am *telling* you, Mele! I *know*."

He stood like a dying tree, everything falling downward.

"It is nothing," I pleaded.

"It is *everything*! You saw Peter Kohala; you know what it does. My life is *pau*."

In his look I saw his dreams ruined, his hope destroyed. Kalina was right: the haoles don't have to condemn us, we do it to ourselves. The only hope was to have him examined. But by whom? Not Papa! Whatever else happened, Papa could not find out.

"Let Kalina examine you," I said. "If she's not sure, we'll take you to Mānoa Valley...I'll come every day...In time the mark will go away, and you can come out. Please!"

There was no reasoning with him. The Board of Health did not even know of his symptoms, and already he had a hunted look. He was not even on Moloka`i, and already he was devoured by fear and despair.

"How long," I asked, "have you had this?"

His answer shocked me.

"Since I was a little keiki."

"That can't be!"

"It comes, it goes." His voice was raspy now. "But it always comes back."

A memory returned to me. As little children at the beach one day, Keahi and I were curled into Tūtū's lap, listening to waves lap at the shore. I had seen a red mark. Like this one. On his same shoulder, too, but lighter. When I reached out, Keahi had inched his shoulder away and dropped his eyes. Tūtū ran her fingers through his long black hair, lifted it, and quietly let his hair cover the mark.

Had Tūtū known all along? Was this why she prayed every night to Jesus, "Keep my Keahi safe, too."?

I never felt as empty as when I rode up Nu`uanu Avenue alone. Keahi had refused to even ride part way home with me. Miki clopped with her head down as we moved along the quiet dullness of gray-white fences with pickets closing in on gardens. We passed a woman throwing dead flowers in the corner of her yard. I stopped in front of the huge Afong house and watched their daughters running in circles on the verandah, each pretending to run away from the man they would marry. But all I wanted was to run toward Keahi. My mind flew from insisting that Keahi was wrong to the horror that he might be right.

Miki pulled toward the old path along the base of the ridge. At the grove of papaya trees, I stared at the stump full of axe marks, with the rain of fear pouring down my cheeks. I blinked, realizing what I knew all along: most at risk were Hawaiian males. Keahi had been in danger since birth.

How naïve of me, thinking I could walk out of my world and into the world of Peter Kohala, bearing a gift to a man ravished by something I never thought would touch my own life—not like this. I felt stupidly blind.

I rode on, not even leaning away as Miki brushed close to an `ōhi`a tree and branches scratched across my leg. I looked at a tear in my dress, felt nothing. The valley seemed empty, the air heavy. The folding ridges pressed against me like a ribcage—I was wandering in the belly of a whale.

If I felt this frightened, how did Keahi feel?

On the trunk of a tree was a green line. I watched the gecko, its sides pumping in and out with life. The gecko turned its head as if looking for danger. Then it rushed into a long dark hollow. Even the gecko has a place to hide, I thought. Even the fish finds a cool shelf in which to escape. Miki turned her head as if making sure I was still there, but I did not reach out to pet her.

I felt the first drop of slow rain, the kind of rain when you have time to look at the circle of lonely wetness on your hand before the next drop lands across the trail. It is said that such a rain denotes the presence of a god.

If a god was with me, I felt no such presence.

Miki turned toward the gully leading down to the stream; I hardly cared as her footing slipped among the scree. All around us, vines hung down from dark canopied trees. Stones were everywhere, holding everything down.

As we followed the stream, the water seemed to whisper the same words students at school had been thinking. Though most of us were checked at home, we leaned toward the mirror in the washroom, studied any unusual spot on our skin. We knew what the health authorities were looking for, and they were coming to Royal School the next day. Every student would be examined.

I closed my eyes. "Take me home, Miki."

Chapter 27

LIKE SMOKE IN THE NIGHT

When the school bell rang the next morning, I already knew that none of the bare feet walking past my desk would be Keahi's. He would not lean down to whisper in my ear, or brush his leg against mine, or tell me how birds sang at the sound of my name.

I turned to stare at his empty desk. One student was taken from Royal School, a boy I did not know well. Had Keahi come to school, it would have been two.

After school, I could not leave the classroom or be on Miki's back fast enough. Then I was galloping through the dusty streets. I was filled with bitterness toward my father, slapping at Miki as if her sweating flanks were his ugly policy. Up Nu`uanu Road and into the valley we burst, not like a girl galloping home, but like a warrior charging into battle. I swore nothing would stop me from finding Keahi. Sheriffs and deputies, the Department of Health, and my father too, could search the hills and the valleys; they could burn every cane field on the island, but they would never find him.

I reined Miki toward the hills, ready to urge her up every trail. Then I looked up. How many trails crossed the valley and threaded up the ridges? Dozens? I looked through new eyes at the valley stretching six miles up to the pali. I could wander for weeks or months; up and down the ravines, through the thickets, over streams, below pinnacles of rock, and still see no sign of him. *How do you find someone who does not want to be found?*

I made a circle of blame:

First, I blamed Jesus. Wasn't it his job to heal everything?

Then China. Wasn't it called ma`i Pākē—the Chinese disease?

Then I blamed Norway. Why hadn't the Norwegian researcher, Dr. Hansen, found a cure yet?

Then the Board of Health, the law, and our king for signing the law.

Then Papa.

Finally, when I ran out of things to blame, I blamed Keahi. How could he abandon me and not take me with him? I knew he had to hide from me because of Papa. But I still felt betrayed and pushed out of his life.

When I arrived home, I dropped Miki's reins in the dirt and stood. Whatever Mama saw on my face from the garden, she threw the hoe down and ran to me, pulled me toward her and together we sank to the dirt.

What I remember most were the hands on me: the coolness of Mama's hands and Tūtū's hands; Mama grabbing me, holding me away, saying words I shook my head at and refused to believe. Then hands again, pulling me close. When everything came out in one gush of agony, Mama rocked me. I did not even care that I was fifteen years old and far too old to be held in a lap.

I stood by my open window, watching the rain crawl up and down the valley. One moment I pleaded with Keahi, begging him to come back. Then "Run!" I shouted in my mind. One moment, I longed for the strength of Papa's arms around me. In the next, I wanted never to see him again.

Papa came home early that day. When Mama saw the buggy coming up the road, she turned to me.

"Go on. This for me to handle with your father."

I stood at the top of the stairs, listening as my swollen eyes and cheeks pressed against the wet doorframe. The last thing Mama said to Papa was this:

"Now your policy turn around and come back, come home to you. Now hurting *your* family, *your* daughter. You think about that. But I tell you, Reed Bennett. You lift one finger, you say *one* word to take that boy from Mele—from Tūtū and all of us—and I will leave you. These walls, they will fall down in silence."

My heart stopped when I heard the thundering sound of Papa bolting up the stairs two steps at a time. He threw open the door of my bedroom, breathing heavily, pale as a stone.

"Mele!—"

Every piece of my rage flew out of me. "He didn't even tell me he was leaving!" I screamed at Papa, pounded my fists on his chest. "You would send him away to *die*! You would send Mama, Tūtū, Pōki`i—all of us!"

"Mele!" He grabbed my arms.

"This house should have been a safe place for him! Not a place to run away from!"

"Mele, stop! *Stop*!" He gave me one hard shake, and I doubled over and threw myself across my bed. The only thing left inside, and it took me as completely as my tears and my rage at Papa, was exhaustion. Eventually, purple curtains of sleep began to lower around me. They pressed my eyelids down, wrapping my pain as if in folds of soft cotton. From the other side of the curtains came the sound of Papa's voice, then the touch of a hand on my face. Everything felt distant and unreal, as if pebbles dropped into a deep and sleeping pond on the other side of the island.

"...Should have been safe..." I whimpered to the curtains.

"You're right," the curtains whispered back, "it should have been."

For days, Papa and I did not know what to say to each other. He did not scold or punish me for being disrespectful and saying the horrible things I said. He just watched me. I built a wall of silence around my heart. When I looked at the world, I saw only life splintered away from itself, holes and deep gashes where hope had been torn away.

When I ate, I tasted nothing. In the evenings I talked to Miki in whispers, felt her mane turn damp as I buried my face there. At night, the last words coming through the walls of our house were always Tūtū's, asking Jesus to keep her Keahi safe, and saying an old prayer, "*E kaukolo aku ana au i ku'u akua, e kala mai i ku'u hewa 'iā'oe*," meaning "I am pleading to my god, to forgive my wrongs to you." The Protestants said Hawaiians who did not support the policy of exile were committing a sin against God, so Tūtū was pleading for forgiveness for wanting Keahi with us. I knew she was wringing the hem of her dress, digging the cross into her hands, not understanding why a loving Jesus would let such a thing happen. I could hear her calling on the name of Jesus, asking that he carry her prayer for Keahi along the thread of Truth to the Light, the High Self, that would present her prayer to God. I could hear her calling out to the ancestors, `aumākua, for strength, asking forgiveness for any hurt she might have committed that might prevent her prayer from being heard, then giving thanks for the hearing and fulfilling of this prayer. I had also heard these things when Mimo was taken to Moloka`i. More tears, until finally the walls went silent and I knew that Tūtū and I would both find sleep.

On the third evening after Keahi disappeared, Papa and I were alone on the lānai. He reached up to straighten the Chinese lanterns, even though they were not crooked. He ducked under a string of twinkling lights and stood up in a way that felt familiar. I remembered the day Keahi had come back from Maui and dipped his head under the string of lights and stood up with a smile on his face, and Mama had shrieked and dumped radishes all over the bricks in her excitement to see him. I burst into tears and threw myself into the arms of Papa. A silence, tight and knotted, held us both, for now I knew the meaning of a dream in which Mama told Tūtū, "Watch out if she ever have to choose between them."

For weeks, Papa and I spoke of Keahi in looks more than words. Mama and Tūtū led me through those days. I slept. I ate. I saw a rainbow fragment in the sky. I watched stars that used to appear so close. Now even they seemed to go away from me.

At times, Papa still came home late from work. But I asked no more questions.

Most of all, I watched the hills. That was where I knew Keahi would go, back to a place he knew as a child, where he could lift the branch of a shrub and look down to see my house.

When students asked why Keahi was no longer in school, John, Hoaloha and I simply said, "He went to Maui to help his uncle." Word began to spread, though Daniel Livingstone asked too many questions. This made me nervous. To test the rumor, I asked Keahi's aunty—I saw her at market—if she knew where Keahi was.

"Yes," she said, patting my hand to reassure me, "he has gone to Maui. His uncle needs help." I knew why she told me this: it was too dangerous for Keahi if people knew where he was. Even John had not been told. So I swallowed my hurt.

Everything was a sign. If between long slow drops of rain I saw round wetness on a leaf, I took that as a sign that Keahi would come back, and my life would be full again. If I saw a gecko with part of its tail missing, I took that as a sign that Keahi had been severed from the love of this white haole God. There were trestles of hope in the old stories Tūtū told me, of the pueo owl in Mānoa Valley who pleaded for justice. Then I crushed lifeless brown leaves and threw them to the ground. There was no justice.

Chapter 28

THE SEVENTH DRAGON

With Keahi gone, the rain seemed always wrong. When I wanted the rain that sits like a jewel on a fern, there came a rain that tears at the gullies, washing away my hope. When I wanted the rain that brings fragrance of the lehua, there came a skin-pelting rain. And when I wanted the rain that sounds like human footsteps coming toward me, there came no rain at all; only a mist that crept like a ghost among the trees and was gone.

What came with the rain was the mud, endless mud. Clumps lay dry and crusted on Miki's hooves the day Kalina told me that Father Damien was feeling new pain in his legs; a thick brown river ran down the road and pooled into a noose the day Hoaloha told me Keanu would be tried for murder in August. If convicted, he would hang.

Though Hoaloha said I refused to see the mountain before me, I still believed that Keahi was wrong. But he would need to come out of hiding to be examined, and once in the hands of the authorities, it would be too late. How could I blame him for what he had chosen? If he stayed hidden, I would lose him; if he turned himself in and had the disease, I would still lose him.

Only once did Tūtū waver in her belief that Keahi would one day be with us again. She had started to wash taro in the kitchen one evening. The next time I saw her, she was sitting in the parlor. Her closed Bible rested on the corner of a table. How does one age so much in such a short time?

I forced myself to read the newspapers, racing through *The Advertiser* in English, then struggling through *Ka Elele Poakolu*, ashamed that I was not fluent in Hawaiian. The content of the news was always the same: complaints in English newspapers of how the hula was destroying the moral fabric of Hawaiians and would send us straight to hell; complaints in Hawaiian newspapers that we were losing our independence and gaining only more debt. Everyone standing apart, pointing fingers but never at themselves.

The rainy season ended, the dry season came, the weeks went by. So did Tūtū's birthday. One morning I walked out onto the lānai to where Tūtū sat on the sofa.

"Come on, Tūtū." I nudged her playfully. "We're going to celebrate your birthday."

She looked like Theodore when he jerked to attention. "My birthday two weeks ago!"

"Come on," I said, taking her hand. "It's time to give you Keahi's gift."

Keahi and I had hidden the finished kite in the barn (as if she might find it!), so Tutu and I stopped there on our way to the pasture. The barn door gave a rusty squeak as I lifted the latch and glanced up. The kite hung from a nail on the rafters.

A breeze through the open door played along the tail, as if to nudge the dragon from a waiting slumber.

Part way across the pasture, we stopped. I laid out the kite and tail, attached the strings, and placed the spool in Tūtū's hands.

She let out a yelp of joy. "Is it dragon, like Keahi say?"

I squeezed her hands. "The Seventh Dragon!"

"With huge head...ferocious eyes?"

"Eyes that would terrify the bravest warrior!"

"Long licks of red tongue?"

"Spewing fire! Incinerating everything in its path!"

Tūtū stopped. She tilted her head. "*...Incinerate?*"

"Oh," I said. "...Burning."

"Incinerate!" she shouted. We both giggled.

I looked up to see clouds moving quickly across the sky. The breeze was already strong—maybe too strong. I pressed the spool of string into Tūtū's hand.

"Hold this tight, Tūtū." Across the remaining pasture I ran, carrying the kite and glancing at the ridges as I went. Keahi was up there, I was sure, in a place where he could look down and see my house. Did he watch me walk to the barn to brush Miki? See the oil lamp in my window at night? He could be hiding anywhere, but I hoped he might see the kite.

I waited for a burst of breeze. When it came, I lifted the kite as high as I could, moved back to take slack from the string, and called across the pasture, "Hold on! Pull hard!" She did. I let go. The kite lifted, fast. I ran back to Tūtū and yanked at the string, squinting up at the diamond of red and white rushing to the sky. Beyond it, clouds darkened—quickly, the way they can on an island.

Tūtū was like a child, giggles running up and down the length of the string. "This is better than my birthday!" she called.

"Keep tugging!" I reached to help control the kite. The harder she tugged at the string, the more the stubborn wind tried to yank the kite away. We had to keep the kite in the air, at least long enough for Keahi to see it and know we were thinking of him.

"Pull harder!" I shouted. "...Now let the string out!"

Instead, Tūtū let go of the spool. It bounced across the grasses, with me chasing after it. The kite dipped. I snatched up the spool and yanked hard, reeling in the string as fast as I could, running back to Tūtū and thrusting it back into her hands.

"Hold on, Tūtū! Tight!"

The wind reached down like a giant hand, dragging the kite up, up into the sky. There the little diamond went still, seeming to find a harbor where it could stay forever. I whispered, "Look up, Keahi, look up."

I glanced at dark clouds marching toward the pali and saw a sudden slackening of tension on the string. Tūtū felt it, and a tiny moan escaped her lips. My heart skipped as the string sagged and the kite dipped. *No*! In a gust of wind, the string tightened once more, and the kite surged. Tūtū tugged with all her might. The kite leaned on its side and shot toward the ridge. I yanked hard at the string several feet above the spool, trying to forestall what I feared was coming.

It was too late. The kite ricocheted off an invisible wall and burst upward in cartwheels of red and white. For a moment, the kite seemed to hold frantically onto the sky. Not moving.

Then it dove straight down.

The string sagged and floated limply to the ground like the end of a lonely day. At first Tūtū looked up, though I knew she could not see. She moved her head as if listening to the sky for a sign that the kite was still above us, but she knew her fingers had not lied. She let the spool of string slip from her hand; it fell among the browning grasses.

The kite had disappeared, crashing into a ravine part-way up the ridge—I would never find it. The taunting wind reached down and lifted our end of the broken string. "See?" it seemed to say. "Don't you know by now that the gods always have the last word?"

One night, not long after the kite was lost, I could see burning in the sky a cluster of stars, so close. An odd stillness settled over the valley. One cloud, then two, then the sky pulled on dark boots and a flash of light lit up the night. The screen door slapped shut again and again. Sheets of forlorn rain slammed like pebbles against the roof. Glass rattled in window frames. Even so, I felt a sense of peace. In a storm, even the hunting stops and everything returns to its place. Keahi was safe.

The next morning, I opened the curtain to an island scrubbed clean. It had the look of something new, everything moving. The trees swayed. The water in the taro patch rippled to a new level. Bamboo surged into the garden again. To the left of my window was a movement in the branches of the mango tree. Something red. I leaned to get a better look.

I raced downstairs and flew off the porch. Dangling from a branch outside my window, as if it knew exactly what would make me run around in circles like a crazy person, was the kite. I laughed, cried, and laughed again. I leaned into the mango tree and wrapped my arms around it, hoping that somewhere in his memory of holding the kite, Keahi might remember holding me, too.

That night when I lay in bed, I imagined myself a plover, gliding over the hills and gulches, looking for Keahi. He had risked his freedom to return the kite. What if Papa had seen him?

The kite brought new hope that I would find Keahi. I would convince him to go even farther away from Papa, somewhere in Mānoa Valley. Kalina and Liona would know a good place. These were the dreams of a girl who had not seen how money can poison a person's heart. They were the ideas of a girl not knowing that a cave in Mānoa Valley would soon be empty. And that next to a tin cup lying in the dirt would be a drawing of a peacock—tear-stained and frayed as if opened and folded a hundred times—fallen from a pocket.

Chapter 29

OWL HILL

Late in the dry season, when the brush stood up like brooms, two white men were seen riding into the hills of Mānoa Valley. They wore paniolo hats to shade their eyes. They cantered past Chinese workers standing knee-deep in rice paddies, trotted along the upper edges of thick banana plantations, and wound around Owl Hill. According to the old legend, the pueo, the owl who lived on the hill, was called upon to settle a painful moment. On hearing an accusation against an innocent person, the owl pleaded for justice. Compassion. Surely, offered the owl, would not all men wish for the same?

"Seen any lepers?" The strangers asked two laborers, nodding toward the upper slopes. The sun was to their backs. "We hear there's one up yonder."

The Hawaiian men looked up at the blue eyes of the strangers sitting high in their saddles and spitting at the land, and considered the rifles resting on saddle horns. Kalina knew this from the mother of the two workers and told me. The

Hawaiian men appraised the muddy rope leading back to a third horse shaking its empty saddle and pawing at the ground. The workers glanced at each other. They shifted from one foot to the other. They quietly shook their heads.

"No, no lepers here."

The white men looked at each other and back to the workers. The horse with the empty saddle shook flies from its ears.

"Two dollars if you seen 'em," said the older man.

The workers shrugged. One pointed toward the sea. "They all go Moloka`i."

A week later, I was in the barn searching for liniment to rub a sore muscle in Miki's leg. The tin reminded me of the mixture of noni herbs Kalina gave to Peter Kohala as a poultice for his sores. I felt like a brooding hen. Had he run out of herbs while Kalina was on Kaua`i for a few days? On her next trip to see Peter, Kalina would try to splint some of his fingers that were starting to curl. Miki nuzzled under my arm.

I heard fast talking and quickly wiped my hands on a rag. I coaxed Miki's head aside, stood on tiptoes and peered through the opening in her stall. Kalina was back from Kaua`i. She approached walking fast, her plum colored holokū whisked about her bare ankles as she walked. Liona was with her. My first frightened thoughts were of Keahi. I ran to meet them.

"And now too late!" Liona wailed, opening her hands to the sky and clasping them. "We should not have waited so long!"

This was not about Keahi.

"Mele, something has happened," started Kalina. They both talked fast.

"Should have moved him back to Wai`anae!" Liona shook her head, saying harsh things to herself. Her face was puffy.

"You know about the two men riding above Owl Hill," continued Kalina. She was out of breath. "Dr. Netten told me."

"What?"

"Someone found Peter's hiding place. They cornered him in his cave."

I dropped the rag.

"Shot him in the leg, so he couldn't get away. Brought him out on a third horse with his hands tied around the saddle horn and turned him in. The sheriff told Dr. Netten." She paused to catch her breath. "I was at the clinic in Kaua`i with your father, and just heard."

"*Shot* Peter?" *As if he could run away on feet he could barely feel!*

"Who?" I asked.

Liona sighed deeply. "On all the islands."

"Moka!" I shouted. *"They are nothing but moka!"*

I remembered Peter's pride in the shirt I made for him. How he stroked the piece of silk in the collar. How he held it up and let the sun come shining through the white cotton. Now I fought away the image of bloodstains on it.

"For the bounty," Liona said, bitterly.

To shoot a helpless man, already weak and despairing from disease. For *money*! Through my shaking hands covering my ears came the words.

"He'll go next Shipment Day."

Across the watery grave of his daughter.

Kalina and Liona left to go tell Peter's remaining family in Wai`anae. I lay on my side in the hay, pouring my pain into the dry straw. I raged at the missionaries for coming to our islands; it was they who insisted that separation of the lepers was God's will. "You mean *your will!"*

All through supper, the food in my calabash sat untouched. When Papa went to the lānai, I followed him like a hunter with a loaded gun.

"Papa." My voice must have sounded like it had gone through a grinder. "You knew about what happened to Peter Kohala."

He gave me a sharp look. "I heard. Don't lean on me about this, Mele."

"Who was he hurting, to be in the hills? What harm was he doing?"

"I don't approve of what the bounty hunters did; there's no excuse to shoot a harmless man. But he's got to be—"

"How much more isolated can you be than hiding in a cave in Mānoa Valley?"

He bristled. "I do *not* have authority to release patients confirmed as lepers."

"Don't you mean *prisoners*? Are they free to leave Moloka`i? To come home to their families? You could change it, Papa. Make it so Keahi and Peter could—"

"Mele, I am *not God*."

"What if it were me instead of Peter Kohala? Would you throw me away? 'My daughter, the leper.'"

I never saw Papa change so fast. Like the slap of a sail.

"Do you think I don't feel anything about this? Do you think I don't know it puts a family through hell?"

"It's tearing families apart!"

"Mele, if this isn't stopped there won't *be* any families!" He paced and tried to steady his voice. "Mele, I know this is ugly. I know you must hate me for what I am doing." He pressed his fingers to his temples. He stopped pacing. "In not much longer than Tūtū's lifetime, ninety percent of the Hawaiians have died." His voice quivered. "*Ninety per cent*!"

He wrapped his hands around mine, pressing them as his face welled up and his eyes brimmed with wetness.

"Mele." His voice turned to a raspy whisper. He spoke slowly, letting every word fall in a way that even an angry girl might hear. "Mele, listen to me. This disease could kill the rest of the Hawaiians. In *one*... generation." His voice broke. "In *your* generation. If this disease is not brought under control, you and Keahi...could be among the last generation of Hawaiians."

For once, I did not want to be part of the adult world. It held too much truth.

Papa's hands fell away from mine. He turned and walked down the hill into the windless night until all I could see was a curve of white cotton lit by moonlight. The whiteness stopped next to the taro patch, folded into itself, and shook.

Then Mama was standing next to me.

"A man naming his sorrow," she said. "Something about your Papa you need to know. What he told Mimo and your Tūtū the day he left for Boston. He would come back to fight the diseases, he said, that killed so many in our families. Mimo laughed. 'A boy full of ideas.' But your papa hugged them both. 'And when I come back,' he said, 'I'm going to marry Nahoa. Tell her that.' He slung a duffle bag over this shoulder and away he went to America."

Now I watched as the moon lay across his shoulders and his back. Mama's eyes glistened as she talked about Papa.

"Nine years," she said.

"But he was gone for so long."

She nodded but kept her eyes on Papa. "Man who holds a woman in his heart for nine years. Half-way around the world, too. Is man worth having. Your Papa and me, we have big differences. But don't you forget." She pointed toward him. "That man came back for two things: marry your mama and help fight diseases. Of all men on the Board of Health, if one has a conscience, it is your papa. You wait and see."

Then she was gone, and screen door closed. I was left standing alone in the dark with Mama's last words:

"Not all things visible, Mele Bennett. Maybe you think about that."

Chapter 30

THE STRANGER

During the months Keahi was gone, I tried to remember above all that he was safe. But the day Peter Kohala was captured, I knew Keahi, too, could be found.

Early one evening I set out, hoping to find and warn him. How many trails were there in the six miles of Nu`uanu Valley? Fifty? A hundred? How many ridges and gulches? How many ravines? How many places where Keahi could hide, wide open to blue sky but hidden from everything else, and never be found? In less than a year, a trail could grow over.

I haltered Miki. We rode up the valley, then turned toward a trail less than a mile from my house. The trail started up into the lower hills, then turned back toward the ridges above my house. It was from this trail that I sometimes heard gunshot—hunters looking for boar...or perhaps a wild goat.

All afternoon, sheets of slanting rain had beat down. The upper trails would be treacherous, so we would not get far.

Miki's hooves sloshed in and out of mud as we started up the lower and wider part of the trail. Mountain creeper grew in abundance, fronds curled into the browns that Mama used for dyes. The delicious smell of nectar was everywhere, on the panicles of grape myrtle and in the calyxed hibiscus, waiting for the birds. In these valleys thousands of small colorful birds had once lived. Some, like the black and yellow-feathered `ō`ō, had feathers used in the tall kahili stands that adorned the palace and accompanied royal funerals. The sun was low, the trees casting angled shadows across the trail.

Where the trail began to narrow and become too slippery for Miki, I noticed an unfamiliar horse tied to a tree. On its frayed saddle were loops of sun-bleached ramie. Hoofprints in the mud showed a missing horseshoe. I already sensed what sort of man it had for an owner.

For a moment, I hesitated. I searched the brush with my eyes but in my determination to find Keahi, I set aside caution. I tethered Miki to a low branch, out of sight from the other horse. She munched on a green apple as I continued by foot, staying to the drier side of the trail. The center was reddish-brown; mud in some places, hard as clay in others.

Long sliding boot marks appeared in the mud. Kāwili manu, I thought at first—a bird catcher setting traps. But no, I realized, a Hawaiian would be barefoot.

Again I set aside caution and went on. The trail braided along the spine of a ridge, then forked. I knew this trail. Keahi and Kalua had spoken of it, too. Like most, it would split again and again as it wound along ridges and down gulches and along more ridges. Eventually, after you felt dizzy from twists and turns and watching your feet, you would look up to realize: the trail was gone. Things disappeared like that on the islands. Trails into undergrowth, songs into the night air. *Boys into their fear.*

I turned to look back across the wide valley. Keahi could be anywhere. But I believed with all my heart that he would hide here, part way up the ridge, where he could look down and see my house. After all, hadn't Tūtū's kite crashed into a ravine not far from here? As I climbed, the trail narrowed and became more slippery, especially at the switchbacks.

A sound came from not far away—the snap of twigs. Rounding the next bend and coming down the trail was a white man. The horse I saw would be his. Full of regret that I had glanced at him, I passed quickly. One look at a man like that and you know you want to be somewhere else. Hoaloha called them landed seaweed: the ragged loose ones put off foreign ships by captains glad to be rid of them. The islands had to absorb them. People came to the islands for many reasons. Not all were riff raff or here to evade the law. Still, I was glad he would be gone by the time I came back down the trail.

From the thicket somewhere below came a startled chirping. I paused. A quickness, red and small, zig-zagged through the shaking brush, then up and away. The `i`iwi bird.

I glanced nervously behind me and hurried my pace. At a bend in the trail, another bird cried out. Then a branch snapped. The bird's cry was too far down the trail for me to have been the cause of its fear. Perhaps it had triggered a bird snare.

"Lookin' for someone?"

I spun around, stumbling and almost falling as I grabbed at hau branches.

The man I had passed on the trail!

"Who are you?" I scrambled backwards until I was against a wall of brush. Within heartbeats, my chest was a drum.

"I'd say that ain't your business," he said. Between laughs, he rolled his tongue along cracked lips, touching crusted saliva in the corners. Even from across the trail I knew his breath stank. A scar, wide and bumpy, pried open the whiskers along his jaw.

I tried to get around him. With a stride of his long legs he blocked the way. I stepped back, feeling knots in my throat.

"Who are *you*?" he said. A voice that knew chewing tobacco.

I did not answer. My eyes flashed across the features of his face. His cold blue eyes were more frightening than the rifle in his hand.

"What you doing up here?" he asked, looking around. "Nothing here but wild boar." He patted his rifle. "Maybe a goat or two."

I let my breath out but still said nothing.

He studied me. "Unless..." The longer he looked at me, the more his eyes narrowed. "Yeah."

Papa! Come get me!

He looked up and down the trail, then at me. Thinking, calculating. As if he were searching for a missing piece of a puzzle.

"I hear the health authorities went around," he said, "checking students for the ma`i Pākē."

He studied me. I felt my throat tighten.

"Day they came, a kid didn't show up. Flat out disappeared."

I could feel tiny spasms in my legs. I bit my lip and felt the metallic taste of blood.

"Official story is he went to Maui." He shook his head and grinned. "But I don't think so."

He watched me for a reaction. I tried not to swallow again.

"I figure this kid's hiding out," he said.

He swung the barrel of his rifle in an arc above me, taking in half the ridge. "Maybe up here somewhere." He pointed to me. "Maybe somewhere...you'd know about."

I shook my head fast, trying not to blink. "I don't know who you're talking about." Even I could hear the lie.

His voice took on an edge. He pulled at an ear. "Well, I think maybe you do."

I glanced again down the trail, calculating the space between us.

He followed the path of my eyes. "You ain't thinking of leaving, are you? 'Cause if this here was a game of chess, I'd say you was just checkmated."

My shoulders would not stay still.

"You're not supposed to go breathing all choppy like that. Just tells me you're scared to death." He gave a small snort.

Sweat began to trickle down my back.

"And I already got the power here, now don't I?" He shifted on the trail. "Tell you what," he finally said cheerfully. He shaded his eyes and scanned the hills. "We'll make us a deal. You tell me where the kid's hiding..." He raised the rifle as if to track a bird through the sky, then lowered it and looked over the barrel at me. "...And I'll split it with you, fifty-fifty."

Like we were thieves striking a bargain.

"Best I can offer," he said, "cost of ammunition and all. A wild boar's only worth a couple bucks. But a leper! Girl like you could buy a nice dress with five bucks."

Was this the man who shot Peter Kohala?

I was taught compassion, but at that moment I could feel nothing but a snarl.

He could not miss my disgust. He looked down the trail as he spoke.

"You know, there's *ways* to get a girl to talk. 'Specially a little thing like you." His mouth curled into a slow smile. He laughed, deep and low and quiet. Never until now had a laugh made me quiver under my dress.

His gaze came back to me.

"I see you get what I mean," he said.

Not taking his eyes from mine, he held the rifle out to his side, hesitated, smiled, and let it drop to the grass. His eyes were full of filth and greed as they went down my body. I clutched at my dress. And felt naked.

"No. *Please* no—" When my voice cracked, my strength crumbled too.

His eyes held me like a snagged fish writhing on a hook. He smiled arrogantly, leaned down, and slowly reached a hand around to the back of his boot. I staggered backward into the shaking branches as he brought the knife around, fought to regain my footing as I almost fell. The curved blade glistened, shiny and terrible in the sun. I clawed behind me, feeling frantically for a path through the shrubs.

"Now don't go getting panicky on me. Makes me nervous. And when I get nervous, my hand slips. And when a hand slips with a knife in it, well." He slashed the air inches from my chest. "Things happen."

Screams lay buried in the bottom of my throat. I begged my feet to run but could not find them. Colors blended. The trees turned to wavy lines. I was being held under water by hands I could not see. Through the thickness of the water came the sound of low laughter. Only my eyelids could still move. He could have carved his initials into my arm and I would have watched. Detached. Numb. Intrigued by the curving lines.

From a long way off, I heard Mama whisper, "Find your power." *Mama!*

He licked his thumb and ran it along the slow curve of the blade. The movement pulled me, too, along the sleepy edge toward the point. I felt dragged in circles smaller and tighter, coaxed into tunnels that tugged me toward darkness. He touched the tip of the silver blade against the pad of his thumb and gave the blade the slightest twist. A drop of red formed. I felt the warmth of wet terror running down my shaking leg and past my ankle, and into the earth.

I was the `ō`ō—he was Kāwili manu. Some birds lift on tatters of the wind; they swoop and dip in the freedom of the valley. Some come to this, the snare. From somewhere, far inside a winding tunnel, his words climbed toward me.

"Not too late. Though I'd kind of hate to see you change your mind, now that I think of it."

Perhaps it was as simple as the breaking of silence, or the sound of a twig snapping beneath his foot. But in the time needed for the hei snare to spring and capture the `ō`ō, my fear turned into something else. Whatever that was, it grabbed at life. A wild piece of me sprung from the depths of the wet I had poured into the living earth. Out flapped a single black crow bearing my fire, returning to me what the knife had taken from me. My power came like a wild river.

"NO!" The word blasted toward him. "Don't you *DARE*! You *touch* me and he will shred you to pieces!" I felt that I could shred this man myself. I screamed at him. For me. For Keahi. For Peter Kohala. For anyone else on whom this man had turned his ugliness.

"Well, that ain't no pretty picture. And what makes you think he still *has* hands?" He smirked. "Ain't that the first thing to fall off when you're a—"

"You are moka—trash!"

"You little bitch! I'll teach you!"

He threw down the knife and lunged at me. Between us was mud packed hard and slick.

He went up with arms and legs twisting in the air and came down like a chopped tree. *Hhhungh!* He curled on his side and grabbed at his leg, yelling. He had landed with his thigh on the point of a jagged broken root and writhed in pain. I jumped past him to where his rifle and knife lay in the grass. With all my strength, I flung them over the shrubs and into the gulch below. He tried to get up, slipped and fell again.

With sounds of yelling and swearing behind me, I slipped and grabbed at brush as I raced down the trail. At the first curve, I glanced back. He was still lying in the middle of the trail and covered with mud, grasping his leg and swearing. When I reached Miki, I untied the other horse, removed his bridle, and gave him a slap on his flank that sent him bolting down the trail. I threw the bridle as far as I could into the brush. By the time the man would be able to drag his injured leg down the root-covered trail, his horse would be gone.

The banister moaned as I crept upstairs. Mama, Papa, and Pōki`i were at Aunty Kalina's. Tūtū was fast asleep. I washed my body over and over, trying to wash away the look, the laugh, the filth. In my bed, I turned over and over in the darkness, shaking away each visitation of his face. When I fought away his scar, his laugh returned. When his laugh was silenced, the knife appeared, carving into my memory a promise that it would never fully release me.

I had not helped Keahi at all—if anything, I had made things worse. And now there was no way to warn him that he was in danger. No way to beg him to hide somewhere else.

As much as I wanted to feel supportive arms around me, how could I tell Mama or Papa what had happened? I was desperate to be considered an adult, not a girl who had no sense.

Before today, the stranger was hunting only wild boar in the hills above my house. Now he would seek vengeance. What if he learned who I was? Who Keahi was? If he were to corner me on the trail again, and if another bounty hunter was with him—I spent much of the night throwing up.

Chapter 31

NIGHT VISITOR

The thought of a fresh new school year, or a fresh new anything, came as a blessing. I hoped the distraction of school would help me to heal—from the capture of Peter Kohala, from the terror I still felt when I thought of meeting the man on the trail, from the empty space left in my life where Keahi used to be.

On the first day of the new school year we learned that Theodore's chickens, all six of them, had been stolen. They had disappeared the previous day through a suspicious hole in the fence. Theodore was devastated. We all knew that Theodore's chickens meant everything to his education.

This was the kind of moment in which Hoaloha sparkled with generosity, the kind of moment that reminded me of the treasure she was. She promptly borrowed a handkerchief from Mr. Todd, tied a knot in each corner, and passed the handkerchief among students waiting on the verandah for school to begin. In the center of the handkerchief she placed a note that said, "Chickens for Theodore. Mahalo!" Students dug into their pockets. Brown and white hands dropped in pennies, nickels. John Makahehi put in a quarter, and Hoaloha and I together donated seventy cents. She counted the change…two dollars and thirteen cents.

"Theodore deserves more than junk chickens!" she snorted.

At lunchtime, there she was, passing the handkerchief around again. By the end of afternoon recess, she was nicknamed Minister of Finances, Theodore was presented with enough money to buy six healthy laying hens, and he was bashfully twisting his shirt in gratitude and thanks.

On the second day of the new school year, a five-dollar bill fell out of the pocket of Daniel Livingstone. Hoaloha picked it up.

"Five dollars!" She stared at the money in her palm.

Daniel snatched it away. "Keep your hands off my money."

Hoaloha and I looked at each other.

"Lotta money," said Hoaloha. She looked at Daniel with accusing eyes. It was probably more money than Theodore's family saw in a month.

"What you lookin' so big-eyed for?" Daniel said to me.

"Where did you get that?" I demanded.

"Well now, ain't you the little hapa-haole boss?"

"Daniel, you steal Theodore's chickens?" challenged Hoaloha.

Daniel laughed. "Well s'cuse me if I look insulted, but I got better things to do than steal a bunch of scrawny chickens."

"You give that money back to Theodore!"

"Well." Daniel gave her a cocky smile. "I never seen a girl clamp down her face like that before. Sure is scary."

He turned and walked away.

"Every one of Theodore's chickens missing!" Hoaloha sizzled. "And poof—Daniel Livingstone has five dollars!" She slapped once at the air with her fist.

"Come on," I said, pulling her arm, "we'll tell Mr. Mackintosh."

Mr. Mackintosh was sympathetic and even added half a dollar to the fund. But he said there was likely no way to prove Daniel had stolen the chickens. As we left, he sighed. "I'm sorry about this," he said, "but between you and me, I think you're spot on in your assessment of this. Certainly not beyond the likes of...." He trailed off, perhaps thinking better of finishing his thoughts.

A few nights later, it seemed as if even the full moon was hurting. Sometimes on an island the moon appears harsh. Talons of moonlight tear at the skin of the earth, and the roughed-up land bleeds yellow. Maybe this is what drew me to stand barefoot at my window weeks after my encounter on the trail.

In the darkness, something shifted. I looked again. It was not part of the moonlight. My eyes fixed on the movement. Then it stopped. I held the curtain, feeling my breath across my fingers. A pueo's *hoo-hoo* came from a nearby tree. I imagined the owl, too, watching a form that reached into the moonlight. The figure, or maybe the shadow of a figure, moved again. Leaves in the mango tree outside my window rustled my fear. The dark line of an arm went into a curve; something along its bend felt familiar. A memory shivered in my chest.

I closed the curtain quickly, carefully inched it open again and squinted into the tangled darkness. I felt the movement of air behind me, slightly warm. A hand, sliding down my back! I spun in the darkness and slammed myself against the wall, clawing at the curtain, expecting to see a crusted mouth.

"Pōki`i! What are you *doing*? Don't sneak up like that!" He blinked and backed away as I blew into his face all the frightened air I'd held in my chest.

"I heard things," came his small voice. His bedroom was next to mine, also with a view of the barn. He rubbed a finger nervously along his face. "Downstairs."

By the time I soothed Pōki`i and turned again to look through the curtain, everything was still. Branches shaped like broken arms hung down from the tree next to the barn; there was no sign of a visitor. The shadowy form I saw and the sounds Pōki`i heard had only been etched into our minds by the talons of moonlight. There was nothing after all.

"Why you so quiet?" Mama asked the next morning.

When I did not answer, she frowned. "What, my daughter can only run her finger along rim of a calabash?"

"Mama?" My voice was a whisper.

She came to the table and sat down. With a look, she told Pōki`i to go outside. Tūtū began rocking, humming quietly.

"Do you think Keahi will forget all about me?"

Mama's shoulders dropped as she let out the sigh she saved up for big questions. She took my hands.

"Mele, Mele, Mele." She shook her head, as if trying to shake out all the things that did not matter to make room for what did. She pulled both of my hands to her. With strong, large thumbs she pressed into the middle of my palms, rubbing away from the center. Both of my parents had done this since I was a child, seeming to know how soothing it was. "You want him to?"

Did I? Would I be relieved if I had never known Keahi?

"No."

"This is a good thing for you to know. You two!" She took my cheeks in her hands. "Always been Mele and Keahi." She wiped my tears with her thumbs. "That is what you must hold in your mind—those memories."

"But he's *gone!*" I licked wet salt from my lips.

Mama lifted my chin and gently scolded me. "No. No room for self-pity. You must remember who has the bigger pain in this. Keahi, not you."

There it was. The same whisper. *Have you been so attentive to your own pain that you forget others have suffered too?*

She pressed her lips together.

"Hardest part of life is part we can't know, Mele."

She hugged me and turned me toward where my books were sitting on the kitchen table. "Go on, or you will be late for school."

When I unlatched the barn door, I noticed something unusual—the smell of plumeria. Miki stood with her head down. Her mane was bumpy, as if fluffed up. I dropped the latch and stepped back, one hand trying to contain a smile. Miki raised her head as if to say, "Here I have stood, bringing you this gift. Where have you been for so long?"

Hanging around Miki's neck was a mass of white plumeria flowers strung together in a double lei. Woven into the strands of Miki's mane, neat as stitches, was a small object. A corner of it reflected a bit of light. My fingers flew as I unraveled the soft strands.

Soon I held a small red tin, old and rusted and full of dents. The lid resisted as I pried upward with my thumb. With my fingers in a close row along one side, I rocked the lid back and forth while I lifted, hearing rust against rust. With one final tug, the red lid popped off and flew into the hay. Inside was a folded piece of butcher paper. I wiggled it loose and lifted it out. I tingled as I unwrapped the paper and saw Keahi's gourd whistle. I clutched it to my chest and dropped to the hay beside Miki. Slowly, deliciously, I unfolded the letter.

Aloha Mele,

It's me. Everything going okay for you? I have found a good place to hide, where I can stay dry most of the time. My aunty and uncle are helping me. I made a pillow of leaves for sleeping, and I have a blanket too. Sometimes I hear guns and wonder if it is safe here. Maybe Mānoa is better. Maybe I will find the cave where you told me Peter Kohala is hiding and stay with him, where I can be sure nobody will find me.

There are some things happening. I have help, but I cannot say. Not yet. Keep my gourd whistle to know I think of you. I miss you all. But you must not try to find me. It is better this way.

Aloha nui,

Keahi.

PS. Tell Tūtū I think of her every day.

My joy was crushed when I came to the words, "Maybe I will find the cave where Peter Kohala is hiding." He would have no way of knowing.

Chapter 32

WORD FROM KALUA

There were nights when Papa continued to come home late. "In due time," he said when I asked what he had learned. There was no further word from Keahi.

"Tūtū," I said one morning in the parlor, "I'm going to write a letter to Keahi. I'll put it in the same tin, in Miki's stall, and hope he finds it." I had told her, Mama, Kalina and Hoaloha, extracting promises of secrecy about the gourd whistle and Keahi's letter.

"Would you like to say something to Keahi?" I asked. "He would like that."

She drew her head aside. A breeze pulled at the parlor curtain. "Tell him, you still our Keahi, no matter what."

By the time I had poured out my heart and torn up the paper, told him of Peter Kohala's capture and smeared tears all over another sheet, I realized this was not a grand idea. How silly to think Keahi would come back to the barn—more foolish yet to imagine he would rustle around in the darkness, prying open the lid of every tin on every shelf, hoping to find a letter inside. I found the box of matches from the kitchen, took the letters to the nearest gravel, and burned them.

As I watched the paper turn to ashes, there had been words I could not bear to write. I had laid his gourd whistle on the verandah at school during lunchtime, to fish a pencil from my pocket. It was not until after school that I realized. Hoaloha and John and I looked everywhere. We pulled back vines, lifted fragrant branches; we dug in the dirt along the front of the verandah; walked up and down the aisle of our classroom. Theodore helped, too. Nothing.

Keahi had entrusted his gourd whistle to me, and I had lost it. I felt horrible.

A few weeks later, I flopped down at Papa's desk in the parlor with a brown envelope in my hands. The letter from Kalua had been written months before, in India ink. I cherished receiving this as another connection with Keahi—an anchor that grounded me.

"AmyTurner"
Pacific Ocean
August 12, 1884

Aloha Mele and Keahi,

An American boy Chad is helping me to write this. Good practice for my English! I am on the Amy Turner again, on our way to China. When Captain Newell found me, he scolded me but not too bad, and said I should obey the consul and stay in Hawaiʻi. Then he gave me a big bowl of rice and fish and told me to wash up. He smiled and made me Cabin Boy again.

I am sorry I did not say good-bye. There was shouting and gunshot and the sailors ran to the railings to see. I ran up the gangplank...

That was Kalua I saw!

...and hid around a corner, then crawled on my stomach under one of the life boats. I heard people running away. The crew told me later. I hope you are safe!

We will be in Boston next year, but we sail to Hong Kong first. To take the Chinamen home. There are 314 Chinamen, five women and three little children on board. All the fore and aft bunks are full, people everywhere!

We had two goats on board, both of them not with a good brain. One would not stop eating the paint off the lazaret, and we buried her at sea. The other broke its leg jumping from the quarterdeck to the main deck. The sea again.

My English I learn mostly from the sailors. But their talk is full of things that ought not be said. Captain Newell helps me to know what is proper.

This is what it is like here. In a day we use 120 gallons of water to boil rice, and 36 gallons for tea. The Chinamen squat on the deck to eat, holding little blue bowls full of rice.

Today we saw Luzon, one of the Philippine Islands. It was foggy all morning. So steam was got up in the engine and the whistle blew every forty seconds. So loud it jumps you out of your skin!

At night, in the foc'sal, I sing or play my harmonica. From the sailors I am learning "Marching Through Georgia" (somewhere in America) and "Shoo Fly."

There are no smells of pīkake flowers here, only of oil and smoke. Sometimes I get to play checkers with Charlie, the Mate. When he gets my king in a corner he says, "Your King is pau." Chinamen say it, too. That Hawai`i is pau. This is my only fear: not that our ship *will sink, but that I will be in Boston and hear that the American flag flies over our palace.*

I miss all of you. I think of where Keahi and I used to hide when we were keiki. Do you remember? In the elbow of the gulch, on the pali side of the rock that looks like the mo`o lizard?

Mo`o Rock. Up the ridge from my house!

Remember when you told me about the haole boy who got mad and chopped down the papaya tree? Just because he could not climb it? Same thing here. A haole sailor got mad and threw the checker game overboard. Just because he lost! So Charlie and I made a new game using extra nuts and bolts the carpenter let us use. Charlie says "nuts" also means crazy. So when we choose sides of the checkerboard, I always ask if I can be bolts.

Aloha nui!

Kalua

Written by Chad Hetherington

I was thrilled to receive this letter from Kalua, and even happier to learn about the secret hiding place. The Mo`o, Lizard Rock. Was that where Keahi was? I reached for Papa's writing tablet, tucked my legs to my chest, and closed my eyes. Starting near where I had encountered the stranger on the trail, I imagined which gulches would lead into the deep ravine, which one might have an elbow of a gulch on the pali side of the rock that looks like a lizard. But there were so many ravines and gulches! I drew it in the air first, following with the pencil along the trail, around bends in the trail, up along the short ridge to the gulch.

I opened my eyes and quickly sketched on paper, drawing as fast as I could with my face close to the paper. The curves in the trail, the ravine, another ravine, the elbow.

"Mele, what are you doing?"

I jerked my face up and slapped the tablet closed. He looked huge standing in the doorway of the parlor.

"Papa!" I felt my face go bright as sin.

At supper, Mama gave me a scolding look. "What, my daughter is raised with manners and one day begins eating like a horse?"

"Sorry, Mama." I swallowed my bread more slowly. I glanced down the hill. An oil lamp burned brightly in the window of Kalina's house.

After supper, I ran down the hill. It would place Keahi in danger if I tried to find him, but at least I knew where he was! I threw open the screen door, out of breath and excited to tell Kalina.

Bent over the kitchen table, holding onto each other, were Kalina and Liona.

When they saw me, nothing stopped—not the banging of Liona's fists on the table, not the rocking, not the wailing, not the tears.

"Auwē, Auwē!"

I knew before they said it.

Chapter 33

TEARS OF HEAVEN

Of course Father Damien would be the one to dig the shallow grave, maybe on a rise or in the shade of a pandanus tree. Wearing his dusty cloak and smelling of tenderness and tobacco, he would wedge rocks out of the earth and toss them aside; he would kick clods of dirt until they broke apart, then scoop them up and reach for the shovel to make a place in which to lay Peter Kohala. The whole time, the cross hanging around his neck would fall forward, swinging from side to side as if trying to find the middle ground between right and wrong. I thought of Nā waimaka o ka lani, the tears of heaven pouring down the day Peter Kohala went into the sleep that lasts through the seasons. Nobody knew how many times Father Damien had done this—a thousand times? Two thousand? Who was left to count?

For three years Peter Kohala had been hidden; first in the hills, sometimes in the cane fields, then in his cave in verdant Mānoa Valley, always moved with care by Liona and Kalina or his family. But once severed from ties with his family, he lost the will to live.

I wondered if it was raining the night Peter Kohala died, and if the stars were still. I dared to hope that wild boars missed his shallow grave as in moonlight they rooted among the rocks.

How long could Keahi last in the hills? *How long could I last?*

It must have been dawn somewhere on the island when I took two mountain apples and walked across the paddock and toward the pasture over the knoll, wanting to be alone. I did not want to feed the apples to Miki, but to someone else's horse—a horse I did not know and did not love. A flash of color lit on a fence post, and a tiny honeycreeper tilted its head as if it had nothing to do but watch me stand there. I tried to call back the surge of power that rose in me the day I escaped from the stranger on the trail. If that power anchored anywhere to my memory, I could not find it.

A gray dappled stallion plodded toward me through the dried grass. He turned his head sideways, slid it between the strings of wire, and nuzzled my hand for an apple. I pulled back, tossed the apples to the ground in front of him, and walked away. I did not want to feel his soft nose on my hand.

I did not want to feel anything.

Some days I read the newspapers, other days I folded them and pushed them down into the crack of the sofa in the parlor. Dr. Arning reported a discouraging lack of progress in his inoculation studies. Keanu was convicted of murder and would be hanged. I no longer shivered at the thought.

For weeks John Makahehi and Uncle Elia and other fishermen had seen the red akule swimming in the harbors. When this happens, the whole island holds its breath. Would once again the presence of the red akule foretell the coming death of an ali`i, royalty? No, we thought at first, this could not be—not so soon after the death of Princess Likelike. But who could say? The royal family was dwindling as quickly as hopes that the kingdom could be saved from the long fingers of America. Of course, the haoles waved aside talk of the red akule as nonsense. Tūtū smiled at this; she found a way to sew a loose seam between the old ways and the new ways. "Jesus always right," she said, "but red akule never wrong!"

One evening, Mama and I sat in the kitchen. She gave me an impatient frown. "All evening you have been there, slumping across the table like waiting for pali to fall down. You think mangos are ready to pick?"

I folded a napkin, unfolded it, folded it again.

Mama stood up. "Time to pick mangos."

Couldn't Mama see that I did not want to do anything?

"All the more reason." She pushed open the screen door.

Tūtū sat in the shade of the lānai, stroking her Bible and singing "Amazing Grace" in Hawaiian. Usually her voice was full of mana, but today it was flat. I followed Mama along the front of the house to the mango tree.

From across the stream came the evening croaking of a mud hen, another bad omen. With a small ladder in place, I climbed toward a branch of the mango tree.

"Mama, do they know yet if Father Damien has the disease?" Papa had heard at work that Father Damien was having more pain in his legs; now he could hardly feel his feet. I remembered watching as Kalina had cut dead tissue away from Peter Kohala's foot—he had not flinched.

Mama opened an empty rice bag for carrying the mangos. "He has it," she said.

I did not even know what to feel anymore.

"Mama, aren't you afraid of getting it?" I pulled down a branch and dropped a mango into the rice bag. Her shoulder lifted a little. "Nothing about it scares you?" Surely, I thought, she must be a little afraid.

"Just a bad disease." She brushed a spider web off the top of a mango stem. "Only thing scares me...is be taken from all of you." She looked down the valley toward town. "Your Papa, too."

I climbed down and turned to pick up the ladder. Mama reached out and gently pulled me back. She stroked along my cheek with the back of her hand. She brushed her fingertips across my forehead, as if painting a picture she had always held in her mind.

"So full of thinking, just like your papa. Go on." She shooed me toward the house. I folded the ladder and turned back to the porch, trying to understand how life works. How can a good man like Father Damien give his life to serve others... and get leprosy in return? How does Daniel Livingstone have a five-dollar bill fall from his pocket...while Theodore's family struggles for pennies? And now the red akule in our harbors.

I was a leaf trying to know the mind of the wind.

On the same day I learned that Father Damien had leprosy, I learned about one of Dr. Arning's experiments with the leprosy bacillus, and it gave me chicken skin.

Keanu had been convicted of murder and condemned to hang. But a deal was proposed. The experiment was Dr. Arning's idea. When he could not successfully infect any of his test animals with the lepela—to try to learn more about how the disease was transmitted—he suggested to the Board of Health that they offer the courts a trade: spare Keanu from a hanging if Keanu gave himself as a live subject to inoculation with the bacillus. At least, Dr. Arning said, Keanu would have a chance to do something with his life that might benefit others. After a series of three inoculations, Dr. Arning proposed,

Keanu would be transferred to Kalawao on Moloka`i. To live among the lepers until he died.

The courts approved, shocking the island. I do not know how the offer was relayed to Keanu. I imagined him sitting alone in his rancid jail cell with his head down and his shoulders bent. I imagined beads of sweat on his face as he weighed in the silence of his cell what some said only a crazy man would agree to. The whole town seemed to gasp at his decision: Keanu agreed to trade a sure hanging for a deadly disease.

On a day when the līpoa seaweed of Waikīkī was so fragrant one could smell it from the shore, on a day when children leaped off verandahs and ran giggling through hibiscus, Keanu sat down in Dr. Arnings's laboratory, took a deep breath, and bared his forearm.

Even Dr. Arning was unsure what would happen. He said years could pass before the results were known. Keanu was an opportunity to see if the bacillus would "take" on a human subject, but he was not the first. Papa told me that others had subjected themselves to this experiment in Europe. As had some kōkuas on Moloka`i.

I sat at the kitchen table, watching a dragonfly land on the screen and flit off into the night—such a free and reckless life they had. The screen door banged once, and I jumped. It banged again, reminding me that we were close to the season of sudden storms and rough seas, the season when reef fish are caught offshore and squid fill with dark ink the water all around them.

Chapter 34

THE ELBOW OF THE GULCH – MO`O ROCK

I knew the day would come. Like Peter Kohala, Keahi could not hide forever. As I look back on that afternoon, it seems anchored in my father's voice. I had been working in our taro patch all afternoon, reaching down to swirl my hands through the pond, listening to the church bells, then looking up at drops of rain falling from a clear blue sky. It was the kind of sky that changes quickly. One moment you are standing beneath a bowl of blue, then everything around you cracks. The sky comes apart. Even the geckos run for cover. In moments, the red earth jumps and your toes squish as you try to pull them from the sucking mud.

But it was the sight of dust rising from the lower part of our road that sent me out of the garden. I splashed to the edge of the pond, lifted my dress, climbed hurriedly over the short wall of lava rock, and ran to meet Papa at the barn. By the time I rounded the corner and passed Miki's stall, Papa was reaching for the bridle above the star on Hoku's forehead.

Papa removed the bridle slowly, deliberately. He was not smiling—or looking at me.

I came to a stop. What came out of me was not even a whole voice. Something in me already knew.

"P-Papa....?"

He reached to the fencepost next to Hoku, lifted off the halter, and turned it over and over in his hands. His jaw was moving, but no words were coming out.

I felt as if every piece of gravel on our road had found its way into my throat. "Tell me!"

Papa pushed Hoku's ears beneath the halter like he was trying to push away the truth. Finally, he found the words.

"It's Keahi." His jaw tightened.

"*Papa*?" Before me burst an image of the cliffs of Moloka`i and the dark peninsula below.

"He's at Mo`o Rock," he said. I did not think to ask how Papa knew. I stood staring at the man I had once thought could do no wrong. He would find a way, I had once believed, to save the Hawaiians. But on that day and knowing Keahi had been found, I believed Papa had betrayed us all.

He shook his head. "You mustn't go!" he warned.

As fast as I turned, he grabbed my arm. "I forbid you!" he commanded.

I twisted loose, ran across the barnyard, down the hill and past the taro patch to Kalina's house, shouting as I yanked open the screen door and burst in to where Kalina sat peeling sweet potatoes.

"They've found him!"

Hope drained from Kalina's face. "The sheriff?"

Who found him? "I—I don't know!"

"Is he—?"

"I don't *know!*" I shouted.

"Damn them!" she yelled. "First Peter Kohala, and now—!" A bowl of sweet potatoes flew from her lap as she jumped up and rushed out behind me, leaving the screen door to slam with a hollow *bang.*

We raced, me leading the way and Kalina following, starting toward the main trail. I saw two riders on the far side of the next low hill, so we turned, cutting across the pasture toward the lower part of a shortcut to the trail. I did not care that I tore my dress on the fence, or that hard drops of rain started hitting at my face. Farther and farther behind us, and then below us, I could hear shouts from Papa and the sound of birds flapping from the brush. But Papa calling my name did no good; a Board of Health doctor in a suit cannot run as fast as a barefoot girl in love.

As I led and Kalina tried to keep up with me, we went deeper in the hills. Red dirt kicked up. It lay along my eyelashes and lips and tasted gritty. The rain turned the trail to rusty mud and shiny roots. Where the path was steep, we slipped and slid backwards, grabbing at branches and each other's cut hands. I pulled Kalina up and over rocks that began to fill the trail. The sky turned dark. The trail widened and narrowed, as if breathing gulps, then letting go.

"Mele." Kalina stopped; she stood panting near a rock, wiping her hand across her forehead. "You must be ready for whatever we find. Are you ready?"

I nodded, but fear chewed at the bottom of my stomach.

Above us, the sky gathered like a new bruise while dark lines of rain slanted down both sides of Nu`uanu Valley.

I watched the ridge weeping ahead of us. Above us were all the colors of wet green I had ever known. Gecko green, cane green, the green of pili grass. But mostly, dark green. The dark green of dripping forests, of changing light that pulled at my imagination when Papa read stories of faraway places when I was young. When a boy like Keahi was only a dream that girls wear on the inside of their heads.

We crossed a freshet seeping out of the hillside, then a dip of the valley came into view. Below us, my house sat like a little white box among the mango trees and cascades of flowers, the house and barn and garden—like a little dream.

While he was gone, I tried not to wrap all my dreams around him. But how could I not? That would be like asking the shore not to thirst for the rising sea; the salt not to need the air that would carry it across the islands and deposit it into every living thing. That was like asking the hills to ignore the morning fog, the land shells not to make the sound of the washing surf. Not love Keahi? You might as well hurl a torch over a cliff and ask it to not light up the night sky.

Would it matter to me, not in my child-wishing heart, but in my coming-into-woman heart, if he had the lepela? Would it? *This is not like when you were a child, Mele, and could reach behind your back and cross your fingers.*

Rain pounded down. It came in sheets of piercing gray that slammed into my arms and face and drowned my tears. The dark clouds burst open. My soaking dress clung to my body. I raced up the winding path toward Lizard Rock, stumbled over large roots writhing in the trail. Red mud splashed across my bare legs.

At a bend in the trail Kalina grabbed at my arm to stop me. We were both out of breath.

"Mele," she said, almost gasping for air, "are you sure you are ready?"

I turned and ran up the trail. A small ravine was now to our left, carving out a valley all its own.

I stopped on the trail and stared at a rock in the switchback ahead. It was shaped like a lizard—the mo`o. Clouds rushed across the sky, the rain suddenly ceased, and the sun began its daily struggle for space in the sky. I turned to look up at the last bend in the trail.

I imagined the circle of redness on Keahi's shoulder the day before he disappeared. Each time the mark came, he must have prayed he was only dreaming; each time it left, he must have held his breath. How could we have known that one day he would be like others on all the islands? Hiding—running to save what he could for as long as he could.

The path wound around blistered roots, twisting deeper, pleading for a piece of sun. Then the trail was gone, disappearing as suddenly as Keahi had, into the shadowed treetops of a patchy ravine.

We had reached Lizard Rock. I turned to look.

In a small clearing stood an old and spreading lehua tree. Its trunk rose through streaks of sunlight and shade, its branches touching down. In the grass nearby lay a soaked blanket. In the slanting shadows—with cobwebs clinging to his hair and barefoot as the last day I saw him—stood Keahi. A familiar blue shirt hung from his shoulders. His rolled-up trousers were torn and covered with damp red earth. His eyes showed months of watchful sleeping.

And he was beautiful.

I could feel myself laughing, crying, pleading from one gulp of hope to another. If Tūtū could have seen Keahi after all those months when we thought he was gone forever, she would have cried, "Oh, Sweet Jesus—an angel!"

At first, he drew back in fear, his eyes begging me for a promise of safety. He was full of the smell of the islands as he stepped over the gray and holding roots. He took a breath, and then, as if forgetting what one cannot endure to remember, he let me wrap around him.

He pressed a soaked red bandana against his cheek. I felt certain that it hid a new mark. As if he had no power to stop me, or even to stop himself, he let me pull his hand gently away. Perhaps it was better that he could not lift his eyes to see the look on my face at what I saw. It was not the new patch of discolored skin that made me press my hand to my lips—but the end of his dream. For a moment I saw what Keahi must have seen every day he was in hiding—an image of the great white stallion, screeching to a halt at the bottom of a ravine as a single lasso stole its freedom forever.

My fingers were shaking against my lips, then against the outline of Keahi's.

"Eh, Mele." Keahi dipped his face to mine. "Why these tears which are wetting your face?"

I imagined my father signing in bold strokes the shipping papers that would take Keahi from me forever—and telling me it was for the sake of us all.

Perhaps it was the sound of shifting feet that made me turn. When I did, I saw at the edge of the clearing a man I had known and trusted for my whole life. Now my heart sank to see him. Dr. Netten had been our family doctor and Keahi's since we were children. He had saved Tūtū's life. He had been present at Keahi's birth and had loved him like a son for sixteen years. But Dr. Netten was no longer just a family doctor. Now he was also a government doctor for the Board of Health, like my father. *Now he was a doctor who had the power to send Keahi to Moloka`i.*

Keahi's eyes flickered with something which in anyone else I might have called hope. But his hands went limp.

"They tell you?" Keahi asked.

The path shifted beneath me. I swallowed hard, looking from Dr. Netten to Keahi, then back to Dr. Netten. He could read the question in my eyes.

"We don't know for sure yet, Mele." Dr. Netten looked at Keahi and Kalina, then at me. I was already shaking my head. "But your father and I—."

I spun to Keahi, then back to Dr. Netten.

"My father?" I stepped back in a sudden panic.

I looked at the blue shirt Keahi was wearing—Papa's; the brown trousers rolled up above his bare feet—*also Papa's!*

A noise down the trail made me turn to look and see my father. He was panting, stepping over the last of roots and rocks between us. Before I could find another thought, he was next to me.

Chapter 35

IN THE LAST SUNLIGHT

At first I barely noticed the new sound from down the trail. Only a branch in the wind, I told myself. But with it came another sound—a laugh, low and familiar.

I knew before I saw him, recalled with shame the sensation of wetness running down my legs and along the inside of my ankles.

Dr. Netten, now next to us, reached for Keahi and moved him back. Papa took hold of my arms and inched me back. "No," I heard myself whimper. I closed my eyes in some futile prayer.

The steel barrel of a Winchester shimmered in the last sunlight.

"Now ain't this a nice little gathering." A voice dripping with satisfaction.

The man I encountered on the trail looked straight at me. His eyes dropped to my chest as he ran his tongue once across his lower lip and smiled. My chest sunk as I slipped against my will into a state of hypnotic fear. I felt Papa take a step forward, but he stopped as the Winchester shifted in the man's arm. The man drew a dirty hand across his mouth. He smiled, and the scar rearranged itself across his jaw.

"Couldn't have planned it better myself," he chuckled.

He stroked his rifle and appraised Keahi. But he addressed Papa.

"I reckon you know who I am," he said.

"I do," said Papa. His voice was level. He spread his feet just a bit, the way a man does when he wants his body to lay down words of its own. "Which is why you just need to turn around and head back down that trail. There is nothing for you here."

"Well, that ain't the kind of generosity I come to expect from the islands, now is it?" The man looked at me in a way that made me feel naked again. "Besides," he said with a grin, looking back at Papa, "we been waiting awhile for this."

We?

"How did you know where he was?" asked Papa.

"I was out hunting wild boar couple of weeks ago. Saw you heading up this direction carrying a satchel in the evening. Seems kind of odd, don't it? A doctor carrying a satchel up a muddy trail? But today, seeing this big crowd running up here like there's a fire? Just plain luck, I guess."

"You need to leave," said Papa. "Dr. Netten and I speak as physicians for the Honolulu Board of Health. This situation is well under our authority. I can have you arrested."

The man ignored Papa's words. "Didn't take much to figure it out, now did it? Lucky for us, unlucky for the kid here." He pointed toward Keahi.

"Us?" Dr. Netten's voice.

The man turned and hollered down the trail.

"Son! Get your ass up here!"

There was a rustle of leaves. Then, from behind a shrub, a boy stepped onto the trail and turned to face us.

I felt sick to see his cold blue eyes, the blue of shallow water. His lip curled in a cocky half smile, the anxious rifle pulling at the crook of his arm. I should have known—we *all* should have known!

"Well, Pa," said Daniel, looking straight at Keahi, "looks like we got ourselves a fine specimen of a damned leper."

A moan slipped from Keahi as I felt his arms twitch. Daniel took a slow step back and to the side. His father stayed in place.

Papa stepped decisively forward. His voice was cold. "I've told you once, Livingstone. You and Daniel need to go on home. Dr. Netten and I will handle this."

Dr. Netten, smaller in build than Papa, stepped forward and nodded once as Daniel's father shifted his weight on the trail. Keahi and I wrapped tighter around each other; Kalina stepped closer to my side. I could feel the drumming fear in Keahi's chest, his short, frightened breath against my hair.

"Well now, I don't think so," said Daniel's father. "Ten dollars is a lot of money. Now ain't that right, Son?" He glanced over his shoulder at Daniel.

"Sure is." Daniel glided two fingers along the barrel of his rifle, never taking his hateful eyes from Keahi. "Guess we can split this ten, Pa. Like we did for the one up Owl Hill."

Peter Kohala! I have no words to say what I felt in that moment. Every rotten thing Daniel Livingstone had ever done crossed my mind; but none matched the realization that the five-dollar bill falling from his pocket was not from stealing Theodore's chickens—it was traded for Peter Kohala's life. All those days in school...I had been sitting next to Daniel, while he—

"We knew roughly where the kid was," said Daniel's father, "but we couldn't find him in this mess of trails." He nodded toward the ridge with an annoyed look. "Mighty kind of you all to lead us right to the spot."

He shifted his weight evenly to both feet. "And now," he said, trying to sound like a professor, "it's time to dispense with in-tro-ductions and get on with the business at hand." A dirty finger opened and closed around the trigger of his rifle. The light changed, and a darkness raced along metal as the barrel rose in a slow arc toward Keahi. I felt like I could choke.

Daniel's father gave Papa a sinister smile. "Step aside, Bennett."

"Don't!" urged Papa. The slow and careful level was gone from his voice. "I've told you twice, Livingstone. You are *not* taking Keahi." He took a breath and his voice drew a boundary. "No matter what."

"Well, we're goin' to, *Doctor,*" said Daniel's father sarcastically. "The kid's a fugitive. He's breaking the law and we're entitled to take him in, dead or alive."

Daniel stepped off the trail to better footing. The barrel of his rifle slowly came up. "Be a darned shame," he said with half a smile, "if he were to resist."

"Daniel," said Keahi, "don't do this. I am telling you!"

"Shut up, island boy." Daniel cocked his rifle.

"Don't be a fool," said Papa, starting forward. Just as Papa raised his arms, Daniel's father cocked the trigger of his rifle. I shrieked. Papa lunged in front of Keahi and me, facing Daniel's father and shielding us with his body and outstretched arms. Keahi tried to push me away. I clung to him fiercely.

"Out of the way!" demanded Daniel's father, jerking the rifle to his shoulder and taking aim. "You don't humiliate my son!" he shouted at Keahi.

"Boyce! For God's sake!" shouted Papa.

Dr. Netten grabbed me. I was yanked away hard. I felt Keahi leave my hands. The last thing I remember before I fell was the sight of Daniel lunging forward and tripping on a large root across the trail, with the barrel of his rifle pointed at Keahi. Everything blurred.

Crack! The noise came like a snap of lightning.

Daniel, crazed with realization, dropped the rifle. He stumbled forward and almost fell. He caught himself and lunged forward. "Oh my god!" He sunk to his knees beside a pool of red in the middle of the trail, shaking him, shouting at him, and then shaking him again.

"Pa!" he shouted, *"don't do this to me!"*

Dr. Netten dropped to his knees, pressing his fingers deep into the side of the wet crimson throat. Papa knelt. He dropped his face to his hands, murmuring.

He looked across the body of Daniel's father.

"Daniel," he said, "you've killed your own pa. And he was all you had."

Chapter 36

THESE WALLS WILL NOT FALL DOWN

Two days later, Daniel Livingstone buried his father in a remote corner of O`ahu Cemetery. Someone stuck a small white cross in the freshly turned dirt. His father's rifle lay in the bottom of a trunk at the jail, with the initials "E. L." carved crudely into the handle. Daniel's rifle was confiscated for evidence. At the hearing, Papa spoke on Daniel's behalf and confirmed that the death was an accident. I suppose Papa had his reasons for not mentioning that it was Keahi who Daniel was intent on shooting. He asked the judge to take Daniel's age into account. The judge winced at Daniel, said he did not take to boys killing their fathers, and slammed down the gavel.

Among other things, Daniel was required to repair—to whatever extent possible—damage to the petroglyphs on the bridge; he was to start with his own carved initials. He was to learn three hundred words of Hawaiian as well as fifty phrases showing respect for our culture, one of which would be—and Papa said the judge spoke it with conviction—"Ua mau ke ea o ka `āina i ka pono." *The life of the land is perpetuated in righteousness.* He was to plant ten seedling papaya trees on the grounds of the arboretum and care for them until they were established.

That evening, Papa and Dr. Netten and I talked in the parlor. Keahi was with his aunt and uncle. The next day, Keahi would be taken to Dr. Arning for a final diagnosis. As confident as Papa tried to appear, I knew that he, too, was nervous.

"It's too bad the law placed me in the position it did," Dr. Netten told me, "but I was prepared to stand behind my choice; so was your father. When Keahi's uncle told me where Keahi was and asked me to go examine him, I couldn't say no; you know Keahi's like a son to me. His condition was elusive, the way this disease can be. I needed a second opinion, so I asked your father. He knew the risk to his position on the Board—we both did. He said yes anyway."

Papa, risking his job to help Keahi? This stunned me.

"Why didn't you tell me you knew where Keahi was? And that you were helping him?"

"For one thing," said Papa, "I needed to think about your safety. The sheriff told me Livingstone could be looking for Keahi—Daniel had probably suspected why Keahi quit coming to school and told his father. If you knew where Keahi was, there was the chance you would try to see him, putting both of you in danger."

I started to take offense, then considered what I had done the moment I learned where Keahi was. I ran to find him, placing us all in danger.

"Helping Keahi was dangerous enough without implicating my own daughter. Keahi and Dr. Netten and I all agreed: we would keep this quiet for everyone's sake. Keahi didn't even want John Makahehi to know, so John wouldn't have to lie to you."

Before I could protest, he went on.

"For another reason, too." He turned to face me squarely. "Not seeing you was Keahi's choice."

"But...!"

Papa put up a hand to stop me. "That's what he wanted, Mele. Keahi felt that your seeing each other again would be too hard, on both of you. Remember, he has no idea where this is taking him. Agree with him or not, it is what he wanted. You need to respect that. Keahi has a lot on his shoulders right now. This isn't over yet." Papa had said many times that misdiagnosis in either direction was not uncommon, and the cost was too high for mistakes.

"I don't know what has been harder to watch," Papa continued, "you peeling splinters from the kitchen table or Keahi staring at his feet, saying your name, asking me over and over to tell him what you wore that day, describing how you looked as you bridled Miki, if you had mentioned the tin yet."

The tin? My face asked the question.

"It was me who brought Keahi's letter and his gourd whistle to the barn that night." For the first time that day, Papa smiled.

"The lei for Miki?"

Papa nodded. "All Keahi's idea."

"The shadow? Was you?" So Pōki`i did hear something. And the way the tin was woven neatly into Miki's mane—as neat as surgery stitches.

He nodded.

I was spinning. "And the kite?"

"Keahi saw you and Tūtū in the pasture. He watched as the kite crashed into the kiawe trees below Mo`o Rock. That was the hardest moment of all, he said, holding himself back from rushing down to you. He and I pulled the kite out of the kiawe branches, me holding onto his legs and him reaching up to grab the kite. He repaired it with branches we stripped with my pen knife."

I stared at Papa. All this time when he came home late, long after it seemed he should have completed his research; all this time I thought I had to choose between Papa and Keahi. It never occurred to me that for the whole time, I had them both. I had built a small picture frame around Papa. Now I realized he had stepped out of it and into a frame larger than I had been able to imagine. I had not accounted for the vastness of the space we hold inside.

Papa looked at me intently. "There's something else you don't know. When Peter Kohala was brought to Branch Hospital by the sheriff, Dr. Netten said there was a note in his pocket. From you."

I felt my face flush. But there was Papa; not angry, just telling the story.

"Peter was delirious from losing so much blood, but he kept talking about the shirt you made for him." He shook his head, almost smiling. "He was more worried about that shirt than the darn hole in his leg."

My voice came out wide-eyed and breathy. "You knew."

He nodded.

I felt almost dizzy from everything unfolding at once and so fast. For all these months, despite our bitter differences and as painful as it must have been for him, Papa had been watching me define the size and shape of my own conscience. And he had allowed me this. He had allowed me to enlarge, even as I was not returning the gesture. Here I was, so full of myself, so harsh in my judgment of him, while he was embodying the generosity I thought the providence of Hawaiians.

"It started with Mimo," he said. "I saw everything through different eyes. Then Keahi, and I knew I could never see it the same way again. I still believe careful hygiene and separation are the best ways to control the disease, but there's got to be a more humane way."

After his visit to see Mimo, he said, he began to wonder if the lepers were being dealt with fairly after all. He began doing research during his long evenings in town, and he found something disturbing. It changed his thinking even more.

"Elections," he said. "Hawaiians have the majority voting block; without the Hawaiian vote, officials have difficulty staying in office. So, during election year, officials want to keep the Hawaiians happy. I studied statistics on shipments of lepers to Moloka`i over a period of years. I noticed something. Every fourth year, during an election year when officials wanted the Hawaiian vote, the enforcement of the policy of exile became lax, and the number of cases sent to Moloka`i went down. I'm embarrassed to say that I never noted this in my daily work."

Slowly realizing, I stared at him.

"But after elections," he went on, "when officials were safely in office—"

"—The policy tightened up again," I said, "and more lepers were sent."

'Political pawns,' wasn't that the term Kalina talked about? Using a deadly illness to manipulate votes?

Papa ran his hand through his hair. "I hated to think what that might mean. If the disease is really that contagious, the number of lepers sent should be handled in an evenhanded manner, one month to the next, one year to the next. The number exiled shouldn't be going up and down like a wild wave with something as fickle as elections."

So, this was the research he was doing in town.

"I had to consider," Papa said, "that the disease might not be so contagious after all. That's what Arning's research has been suggesting all along. I realized the Director had not been exactly forthright with our medical staff. We believed what we were told when...well, maybe we should not have. Even the royalty in England are urging us to discontinue the policy of exile. There are countries far ahead of us on this curve." He looked discouraged. "Given the powers that be, I'm not sure we will ever catch up."

"And then, Keahi?"

"Yes. By the time Dr. Netten asked me to examine Keahi, I was well on my way to reaching these conclusions."

I stared at him, blinking. *And all this time.*

Mama brought pears, nuts, and rice cakes. She touched Papa's shoulder. Even someone with their eyes slammed shut could have felt the spark between them, the same love that held a boy's heart from half-way around the world. Had Mama suspected—after all, clothes do not just disappear!—that Papa was helping Keahi? She knew. Of course she did.

Papa reached for a slice of pear.

"It was maddening," he said, "trying to make a diagnosis with incomplete information. First we thought Keahi had the disease, then we didn't, then we weren't sure. We watched him for over a month. The waiting drove all three of us to the edge. There were times when Keahi exploded in frustration, then collapsed in tears. I felt helpless, Dr. Netten felt helpless, and Keahi was too afraid to come out of hiding to have a final diagnosis. I can't say I blame him for not knowing if he could trust me."

How, I wondered, did Keahi find the trust and courage to place his life in the hands of Papa, the very person who could destroy him?

"He would come with us only on one condition," Papa said, "and we all need to honor that. If he has the disease, we will not report him. We will set him free to go back into the hills. Dr. Arning has agreed as well."

I was not prepared for this possibility, but if Keahi wanted his freedom, I would give him that. If he wanted to be alone,

I would respect his choice. But I cannot say how I arrived at this. Something had been growing me up. Maybe I realized that there was more to this world than what Mele Bennett wanted.

But Papa was right, the hardest part was yet to come. Dr. Arning's final diagnosis.

Chapter 37

HOWEVER...

Fishermen were hoisting their nets under a lumpy sky the next morning as Keahi, Papa and I went to the shed that served as Dr. Arning's laboratory at one end of Branch Hospital.

I had never met anyone like him. To the extent that Father Damien was a barrel of a man anchored in the grit of earth, Dr. Arning was a man obsessed with tidiness and propriety. Even his glasses seemed to obey the command of sitting properly on his nose. He was short and slight; his hair and eyes were brown, but his extravagant mustache was blonde. You just knew this man abhorred wrinkles in shirts, allowed no buttons to go missing from his vest, and would rather be trampled than be found smiling. His long thin fingers held stories of soap and water as much as Father Damien's fingers held stories of hammers and nails. If either swore, I knew which one.

Dr. Arning stiffly ushered us into a room. He told us he would return shortly with results of his tests on Keahi. He had taken cultures the previous day.

We waited.

The door swung open and a slight smell of chemicals followed Dr. Arning into the room. Papa, Keahi and I stood up.

Dr. Arning was not smiling.

"I've secured cultures from the patch on Keahi's shoulder," he said, "and also from his face, allowing me to reach a conclusion."

Tell us! I wanted to shout. Keahi put his hands in his pockets, took them out, put them back in. I could hear his breathing.

Dr. Arning wiped his hands and neatly folded a beige cloth, smoothing an unruly corner.

"The patch visible on Keahi is a benevolent surface skin condition, recurrent and unpredictable in frequency and length of duration, but treatable with simple applications of chrysophanic acid when it does occur. A bit different from the skin condition you hoped for, Dr. Bennett, but similar. I see it often. But it's understandable why Keahi was so sure it was leprosy, and why it took you and Dr. Netten so long to arrive at your conclusion that it was hopefully otherwise. The symptoms are, as you know, strikingly similar to leprosy."

Keahi's shoulders started to release their tension.

Dr. Arning took a breath. "However—"

Papa reached for Keahi and me, pulling us to him in a tight embrace. "I told you," he whispered to Keahi, shaking him as if a rattle. Other words I did not hear went across the top of his breath to Keahi. Papa clutched at us both, holding us in his shaking arms. All that came from Keahi was wrung out air. I knew he had cried himself almost dry. He groped for my hand as if a frantic child. His shoulders, where he had held his agony and fear, could not stay still. He began to shake.

The question occurred to Papa and me at the same time. I could feel it in a jolt of his chest. He spun around to face Dr. Arning.

"However, *what*?"

A crease came to Dr. Arning's forehead. "Can you come back tomorrow?"

"No...what? Why tomorrow?" asked Papa.

Dr. Arning hesitated. "I said 'conclusion' because that was indeed one conclusion. But there are two. I want to duplicate another test; it will take a while."

"We'll wait!" insisted Papa. He stood several inches taller than Dr. Arning.

We waited, sat, stood up, walked in small circles, sat again.

I tried to distract Papa and Keahi by pointing out the work Keahi had done for Dr. Arning. It was everywhere. In one corner, grasping the sides of a cage, was a monkey. In other cages sat rabbits, guinea-pigs, rats, hogs, and pigeons. I noted the monkey was still alive and healthy. I did not know whether to be happy for the monkey or discouraged at the lack of a cure for the disease. One moment Keahi was showing pride in his carpentry skill; in the next moment, he was perspiring with fear.

My father was agitated and pacing by the time Dr. Arning finally opened the door and invited us to be seated again.

"No," Papa said curtly, "we'll stand."

Dr. Arning reached to pull a curtain. He opened his file on Keahi, made a note, and fiddled with a button on his vest. He was avoiding something. Keahi and I looked at each other. When Tūtū was in the hospital, my hand was hiding in Keahi's. Now his was hiding in mine.

"It's an unusual case, but I do see them," hedged Dr. Arning.

Even my father seemed puzzled. And annoyed. "For God's sake, Arning, just *say* it! What did you find?"

"There are several cases where people are confirmed as lepers at one point in time," said Dr. Arning, "but later show no signs of the disease. Or they show no signs at all. Sometimes it resurfaces years later, sometimes it never returns. Yet there is validity to the saying, 'Once a leper, always a leper.'"

Keahi and I looked at each other, not understanding. Papa turned slightly pale. Something had just happened, something between the words, but Keahi and I both missed it.

"Can't you see this is killing him?" Papa almost shouted. "Get to it, Doctor!"

Keahi and I looked from my father to Dr. Arning and back to my father.

"Tell me," said Keahi.

"All right," said Dr. Arning. He turned to address my father. "Though it was not in the patch on his shoulder or on his face, I can say with certainty that Keahi does carry the bacillus in his body. He is a leper."

Keahi's chest jerked. A rush of air carried a moan, like the sound of someone in the grip of a bad dream. We sank back into the chairs, numb.

"Right now, it's inactive," said Dr. Arning. "He has likely carried the bacillus most of his life. In some cases, like Keahi's, the bacillus does this—it just sits there."

Papa leaned on his hand, rubbing his forehead. Keahi took a gulp of air. My fingers dug into his arm.

Dr. Arning looked straight at Keahi.

"I can tell you that it's not active now. It probably never has been. But I can't tell you that it won't become active when you walk out that door. It could surface today or tomorrow. Or in ten years. Or never."

Despite all the tears that had poured down my cheeks in the last year, I sat there with a dry face, everything inside me feeling parched of life-giving moisture. I felt like an empty husk.

"This can go either direction," said Dr. Arning. "I don't know if that's good news, or bad news."

"Will the research on Keanu tell anything about Keahi's case?" I asked.

"Likely not," said Dr. Arning. "My studies with Keanu relate to how the disease is transferred, not how it manifests."

He looked back to Keahi. "All Hawaiians are at risk; you more because you're male. But on the other hand, if the disease were going to become active in your case, it should have done so long before now. In its own way, I'd say that's reason for celebration."

Keahi did not look like someone ready to celebrate.

"What about Mele?" he asked. His voice was almost inaudible.

"She has inherited a substantial level of immunity from her father. He and I have talked about it, and I agree with him. Given her white blood, I think she's quite safe."

"Can she get it…from me?" asked Keahi.

"I believe hygiene is important in any event. But no, very doubtful. I found in you the tuberculoid form. The bacteria are sparse, so not easily transmittable—if at all. You must understand though, that we are never able to make guarantees with this disease. I believe, though research has yet to prove me correct, that this form is far less contagious even than the lepromatous form; again, if even that form is transmittable. As you may know, my thoughts on this are not well accepted by most of the Board of Health, but that is the form that usually attacks Hawaiians. As a race, you haven't had time to develop immunity; the disease is relatively new to the islands and took hold with frightening speed."

"How long will it take?" I knew Keahi was swallowing gulps of fear. "For Hawaiians to build up immunity?"

"Conceivably several generations." He closed the file and handed it to Papa.

Keahi and I looked at each other with the same thought: *But we don't have several generations. We only have now.*

"Keahi," said Dr. Arning, "I've agreed not to report this case as a professional courtesy to Mele's father, whom I respect. And I shall keep my word. I will still be needing cages to further my work here, though I admit the Board and I do not see eye to eye on much. Frankly, I suspect they would be happy to see me walk up the gangplank of the next ship to England. Still, I should hope you will want to continue in the construction of those cages for as long as I am here. You have done a more than adequate job on them; in due time, you should make a fine carpenter."

Some tension fell away as Dr. Arning squeezed Keahi's shoulder.

"I recognize this is a challenge, not knowing," said Dr. Arning. "I don't know whether to tell you to live as if it will become active tomorrow—or as if it will remain dormant. I'm afraid you'll need to make this up as you go along."

Keahi turned to Papa. "You promised. You won't tell the Board. It the ma`i Pākē goes active, you'll let me go back into the hills."

"I couldn't tell the Board anyway," said Papa. "Not now."

I stopped practically crushing Keahi's arm. "What do you mean?" I asked.

"I'm not on the Board of Health anymore."

Keahi and I looked at him blankly.

"I resigned. Submitted my letter to Mr. Gibson this morning."

Questions swirled in my mind. Why?

"I've been looking at Ni'ihau's unwritten agreement with the Board. The island seems to be having some success: patients can be separated for treatment, but still see their families."

Was this the same man who jabbed his finger into the front seat of the buggy while vowing to send "every last leper" to Moloka`i? It was not.

"It will be a battle, given the adverse feelings of the legislature. But Kalina and I hope we can make that happen on other islands. It's worth a try. We would need to be rehired by the Board, but on our terms."

Kalina resigned, too?

"The patients deserve to be heard," said Papa.

The *patients...deserve....* When I heard these words, I could not explain why I cried and laughed at the same time, telling Papa through slippery wet fingers that I loved him big as the moon.

Chapter 38

A KNOCK AT THE DOOR

A few days later, on an evening when the lights of town were just beginning to wink their way up the valley, Keahi and Tūtū and I were in the kitchen. We heard three quiet raps on the door casing. Usually people just walked in. Keahi looked through the screen door and hesitated. He reached to open it and stepped back, leaving his hands out of his pockets. Tūtū asked who was at the door. I knew she could hear boots being pulled off and dropped to the porch, the sound of stocking feet stepping into the kitchen. The boots were polished, the socks were clean.

"I'm Daniel Livingstone," he said to Tūtū. It was the first time I heard no arrogance in his voice. His hair was washed. His clothes were clean.

Tūtū's eyes widened. Mine were already wide.

Keahi's narrowed.

I waited in the silence, almost wishing Tūtū would start humming. She did not, leaving the silence to grow even louder.

Finally, Daniel turned to Keahi.

"The judge gave me three days," he said, "to undo the wrongs I did—much as I can anyway. Then he'll decide what to do with me."

Daniel reached into the front pocket of his trousers and pulled out a small object.

"Seems like this is the place to start," he said.

Keahi took a breath and lifted from Daniel's open hand the tiny gourd whistle. I did not lose it after all—Daniel had stolen it. Keahi closed his palm around the whistle, opened his hand, and looked at it again. For ten years he had carried the little whistle, protected it, honored it. Now it had come back to him.

Keahi watched Daniel, waiting.

Daniel studied the kitchen floor as if one of the planks might offer the right words—or any words. "Guess I've been up to no good since I been here," he said. "Fact is, I know I have."

Keahi had separated his feet and stood flat. After all, this was a boy who a week ago was ready to shoot him dead.

"What you going do about it?" he asked Daniel.

"I don't know all the pieces yet," said Daniel, still looking at the floor. "But somethin'."

He turned and pushed open the screen door, leaned down and worked his feet back into his boots.

"Daniel," said Keahi.

Daniel turned. The screen door was between them.

"I want to ask you a question."

Daniel nodded.

"Why did you and your pa come to the islands?"

It was hard to know how Daniel felt about being asked this. When he answered, he did not look like a boy proud of his father. At the same time, he seemed relieved to be able to say the words. I knew such a feeling...the way a secret can weigh us down....the way truth can free us once spoken.

"He killed a man in San Francisco. Last year. A knife fight in a bar. The law was after him so he grabbed me, got two tickets on the *Mariposa*, and we came to Honolulu. Promised me we'd start over."

"That's where he got the scar," I said. "From the knife fight."

He nodded.

"Did your father have a job?" I asked.

He laughed—the kind of laugh that hides the pain inside. "I'd been supporting us since I was fourteen, working for the phone company in San Francisco."

Daniel? Had a job?

"So," started Keahi, "would you have shot me? Up on the trail?"

Daniel gave a small snort and looked across the lānai. "I did a lot to try to please my pa; guess some of it pleased me, too. And look where it got me."

We watched him dip under the string of Chinese Lanterns, walk across the wavy bricks of our lānai and down the hill. The sun was papaya juice smeared from the hills of Wai`anae all the way to the harbor. All over town, streetlights were winking like stories wanting to be told—even Daniel's.

Sometimes I was almost sure I could hear Tūtū smiling, and it was happening now.

"You watch," she said, opening her Bible. "There be *mountain* moving inside that boy!"

"How you know, Tūtū?" asked Keahi.

"Say so *right here*." She picked up her Bible and dramatically opened it. Upside down.

Keahi and I looked at each other, grinning.

She tapped her finger along a few lines of text. "No pile of rock in which something cannot root!"

Papa and the judge reached an agreement. Once Daniel had met his responsibilities, Papa was willing to pay his way back to San Francisco so Daniel could get his old job back. That is, if those were Daniel's wishes. He said yes.

Papa did not extract a single promise from Daniel. He only told him, "Carve out a life that makes sense to you, Daniel."

The morning the *Mariposa* was scheduled to depart, Hoaloha went to the docks to wave Daniel good-bye.

He said he would write to her.

She shrugged and said, "What, you think I'd read a letter from some haole boy?"

Daniel grinned, walked up the gangplank, and was off to America.

Although Keahi came out of the hills months ago, he is not quite himself yet. We know we live a mix of honey and its sticky wax. We know we needed to have our souls turned upside down and shaken out good, to make room for what is coming next. I tell him that he is even closer to life than before. "There is a gift in this, Keahi," I say, "but we must grab hold of life with both hands. Feet too!"

"I talk to bacillus," he says, "tell it take looong nap!"

And then, and this is the miracle, he laughs. I know his laugh hides a question. But we are learning to live with what cannot be known, and each day we seem to find enough strength and joy.

"I want us to get married," Keahi said a few days ago. "I will work for Mr. Nott and stay in school. Your Papa says you need to finish nursing school. Then we can live at your house, he says, long as we want!"

Keahi shyly dipped his face to mine and smiled.

"Eh Mele, you going to say yes to Keahi?"

I did not say yes right away. A dozen thoughts flew through my mind. I remembered once feeling as if my childhood was tangled in a fishnet on our tiny island of O`ahu, while my adulthood was soaring above a giant continent on the other side of an ocean I would never be able to navigate. But here we were, growing each other up, both of us navigating that ocean, finding our way. For the first time, everything that had happened over the past year made sense. Maybe there is a rightness in things, after all, I tell Keahi. Maybe the rightness is there all along, lying on the bottom and waiting for the water to settle, so it can be seen.

When I did say yes to Keahi, I said yes to more than marrying him. I said yes to believing that good would come from everything that happened to Father Damien, and that his work would continue after he was gone; I said yes to seeing that the lives of Jacob Maila and Peter Kohala and Mimo became specks of light that illuminated for Papa and for me the paths we each needed to take. Without that pain, would either of us have realized the need for change?

I had asked for a moment that would define me. I know now that life works the other way around, too. At one moment we are being defined, and in the next moment we are defining. Keahi and I will endure this, though we will be changed by it, too. I hold in my mind this vision: a firebrand hurled over the pali cliffs, lighting up the night sky. The firebrand defines the darkness—but the darkness, too, will have its say.

Our house no longer changes colors. Most of the time, whether the sky is clear or rain is pounding against the roof, our house is light brown. I like this color—it suits me.

*****

Thank you for reading **Running from Moloka`i**. If you have enjoyed it, would you please take a moment to leave a review on Amazon?

Reviews send a good story out into the world and give it wings. They help other readers wondering, "Is this a story I'd like to read?" And they let *you* play an important role in the forward positive energy of a story. Thank you!

Thank you! ... In Hawaiian, Mahalo!

ABOUT THE AUTHOR

Jill's sensitivity to marginalized groups began as a little child in the warmth of her grandpa's sunroom. As a minister, he read Bible stories to her. She remembers asking, "Grandpa, why were people so mean to the lepers?" She still ponders variants of that question and of his answer. Characteristics of marginalized groups may differ, but fear, lack of understanding, and lack of compassion, do not. Her goal is to write stories that will allow the exploration of meaningful themes on the part of her characters and if so desired, on the part or her reader. **Running from Moloka`i** and **Saving Jeremiah** (release date spring 2021) share similar themes: following the path of characters as their hearts open and as a vision for their lives is enlarged. This is Jill's path as a writer.

What has most impacted Jill's writing style? Attending film school. "Be a camera." A setting has its own personality, but there is also the wisdom of letting the reader experience the character's inner world of thoughts, feelings and vulnerabilities. How else can we feel a connection with them? She was deeply influenced by Nabakov's masterful gift of revealing a character's inner world by projecting it onto something in the character's outer world, or physical environment.

Though the Pacific Northwest is Jill's forever home, she left a chunk of her heart in Hawai`i. Writing allows Jill to gather her interests and graduate studies in Psychology, Education, Natural Healing and Philosophy.

Jill lived in Hawai`i for several years. On Oahu, she was a mediator for conflict resolution at the Neighborhood Justice Center in Honolulu. She was invited by the Dept. of Health to conduct mediation training for the medical staff at Kalaupapa in hopes of smoothing bridges between the medical staff and the patients. After her visit to Kalaupapa, Jill began research that became the basis for her first novel, **Running from Moloka`i.** The story won two awards for fiction—one award as YA, and the other in both YA and Adult categories.

Fun facts about the author:

1. She enjoys building streams and ponds.
2. She loves pickleball.

3. As a child, she once offered a divine trade: God could have her parents...in exchange for a horse. Preferably Rastus, pastured at the Elkhorn Lodge in Estes Park, CO., where she grew up. [Spoiler: it probably will not work for you, either.]

Next release: **Saving Jeremiah**, release spring, 2021. *They say Alaska has no heart—but that is not true.*

Next project: The further adventures of Kalua (Keahi's "cousin"). Watch for **Kalua's Dream**. See more of Kalua below.

Visit the author at www.jill-anderson.com

Join her mailing list at the "Contact" page
to stay informed about future book releases.

CHARACTERS

<u>Fictional</u>

Mele Bennett
Keahi
Dr. Reed Bennett
Nahoa Bennett
Poki`i
Tūtū
Aunty Kalina
Liona
Peter Kohala aka. Manu
Hoaloha
John Makahehi
Daniel Livingstone
Boyce Livingstone
Miss Spencer
Theodore
Dr. Akita
Dr. Netten
Mule Train Driver
Sailor

<u>Historical Figures</u>

Father Damien
Keanu
Dr. Arning
Dr. Mouritz
Kalua
Capt. Newell
Mr. Mackintosh
Mr. Kenyon

END NOTES

KALUA, 1884

K **alua** is an intriguing historical figure. His life story is amazing, inspiring, and unknown on the islands. An American visitor to the islands named Vernon Briggs wrote of Kalua in his book, **Experiences of a Medical Student**

In Hawaii, 1881. Briggs, aged 17, had come to Hawaii on a three-mast barkentine called the *Amy Turner.* His family sent him for a year in hopes Vernon would recuperate from an illness. The barkentine is at the heart of Kalua's story. The ship sailed only one route: back and forth between New York and Honolulu. Regardless of the direction it was going, the *Amy Turner* needed to sail around the dangerous Cape Horn (long before the Panama Canal was built). A two-week layover took place at the end of each voyage. Then the ship turned around and set sail for the other port. Back and forth. From Honolulu to New York was a longer voyage (eight months) along a meandering route that reached out and snagged China.

Kalua was eleven years old when he met Vernon Briggs. But he was old enough to have a big dream for his life: he was going to reach America, attend school in Boston, and come back to Hawaii where he would become (you might as well dream big!) the next king. When Vernon Briggs left the islands roughly a year after his arrival, to return to New York, Kalua begged him to take Kalua with him. Of course Briggs could not do that. Kalua waited a year and a half for the *Amy Turner* to come back to Honolulu. At the end of the ship's layover, Kalua snuck on board and stowed away, bound for America and in search of Briggs. He was caught part way into the voyage. As soon as the ship reached New York, Kalua was promptly sent back to Hawaii on the *Amy Turner's* return trip. He stowed away again, was caught again (you can't hide in a bin of onions for eight months!) and was again returned to Hawaii. Kalua was too young, the U.S. Consulate said, to be traipsing around the world with salty sailors.

This went on for over four years.

Kalua won everyone's heart, and he must have worn down their resistance, too, because eventually the U.S. Consulate agreed to let him stay. Now sixteen years old, Kalua—thrilled to pieces—finally enrolled in school in Andover, Mass.

Kalua pursued his dream with focus and unfaltering devotion. For a young boy, those qualities are amazing. Some say that our destiny is in our willpower; others say it is in the stars. In Kalua's case, maybe the stars overtook his willpower because after six years of unwavering vision of what his life would be, his dream ended within seconds. He never saw the end of his first school year in America. For the story of his journeys and his short, inspired life, watch for **Kalua's Dream** (tentative title) by Jill P. Anderson.

Updates will be posted to www.jill-anderson.com.

Dr. Eduard Arning in 1884, about the time he began his experiment on Keanu.

When **Dr. Arning** refused to turn over his research to the government—he felt it would be unprofessional to publish work not yet completed—he was fired. He returned to Europe in 1885, having failed to reach his goal; until he could grow the leprosy bacilli in a culture, there was no hope of discovering a cure. (Later researchers showed that Dr. Arning's work was destined to fail: the bacilli cannot be grown in a culture.) Though Dr. Arning tried to infect numerous mammals, he lacked access to the one creature vulnerable to the disease: armadillos, whose body temperature of 93 degrees mimics the ideal growth conditions of human skin.

Just as Dr. Arning suspected, leprosy is not easy to contract—actually, it is difficult to become afflicted. Only about 5% of the general population can acquire it. Just like a finicky seed, leprosy requires peculiar conditions and a unique environment before it can "strike," or take hold. Unfortunately, Hawaiians (and the climate) provided a receptive environment. Fortunately, medications can now halt the disease. Years ago, Sony took on "the worldwide eradication of leprosy" as a major financial/charity commitment, though the results fell short of the company's lofty goal. Sony provided financing for widespread distribution of medications, but with a lack of education (about the disease) in place beforehand, stigma and fear prevented many with the disease from coming forward.

Father Damien was diagnosed with leprosy in 1885 and died of the disease four years later at Kalaupapa, on Moloka`i. For years, he suspected he had the disease. Odd as it might seem, he had asked for this in prayer, so that he was more connected to those he cared for. Historians tell us he was joyous when he contracted the disease. In the last days until his death (at the age of 49), he was cared for by Mother Marianne, who had joined him at the settlement to continue his work. Father Damien was buried at Kalaupapa. Much later—against the fervent wishes of those at the settlement—his remains were exhumed and returned to his native land of Belgium at the insistence of powers there. In 2009 (120 years after his death in 1889), he was canonized and granted sainthood.

Keanu was spared from hanging because he agreed to become a human subject, to see if leprosy could be transferred from one person to another. After Dr. Arning inoculated him with the bacillus, Keanu's life changed. At first, not seemingly a lot. Dr. Arning went to Oahu Prison regularly and took samples from the inoculation site on Keahu's forearm. The bacilli slowly disappeared, with no sign that the disease was developing.

A few years after Dr. Arning left the islands, Keanu began to show signs of the disease. He was transferred from Oahu Prison to the settlement on Moloka`i. He was not a very congenial patient. A small jail cell, 6 x 9 feet (the lawless days at the settlement were over), became his new home. He lived in this cramped space for four years until his death. This took place over eight years after Dr. Arning inoculated him with the bacillus. Though Keanu died of leprosy, a question arose: where did he acquire the disease? Eight years seemed too long of an incubation period. After investigations, more facts came out. Keanu's jailer on Oahu had the disease; Keanu's nephew, cousin, brother-in-law, and son all had leprosy—it was rampant in his family. As a young man, Keanu had lived with these relatives. It was concluded that Keanu had become infected prior to his inoculation by Dr. Arning.

Treatment Centers on Each Island:

The arrangement on the island of **Ni`ihau** (to keep those afflicted at home and treat them locally) was considered successful. The foreign-controlled legislature, however, was averse to expanding the plan to other islands.

What became of the settlement at Kalaupapa?

The year 1969 (thanks to dapsone treatments effective in controlling the disease since the 1940's) was a momentous year at the settlement. The residents at Kalaupapa were free to go. Or, if they wished, they could remain and be cared for by the state for as long as they wished. For many residents, Kalaupapa had long ago become their home—they had spent most of their lives on this tiny peninsula, cut off from the world. Often the other residents at Kalaupapa felt more like family than their own birth families, who had frequently moved on with their own lives. In some cases, patients were welcomed home; in some cases, they were encouraged to continue in a separate life. At an earlier point in history, the law had declared the lepers to be legally dead; years later, the law admits it was wrong and those with the disease are declared free to go live their lives as they wish. It is hard to imagine what this could do to a psyche, both individually and as a culture.

The peninsula is now (since 1980) the **Kalaupapa National Historic Park**. It was dedicated to serving and protecting the few remaining residents and to preserving the history of what happened there. This designation hopes to somehow mitigate a stain on history created by the inhumane treatment of those exiled to Kalaupapa. It is also a testament to the strength and versatility of the human spirit.

BIBLIOGRAPHY AND RESOURCES

Books:

Best, Gary Dean and Mary Lani, ed., Glimpses of Hawaiian Daily Life and Culture 1778-1898, publisher information unavailable.

Bird, Isabella L., Six Months in the Sandwich Islands, Charles E. Tuttle Co., Rutland, Vermont, 1974.

Bookwalter, John Wesley, Canyon and Crater: Or, Scenes in California and the Sandwich Islands, Springfield, Ohio, Republic Printing Co., 1874. (Glimpses....)

Brassey, A Voyage in the 'Sunbeam,' Our Home on the Ocean for Eleven Months, London: Longmans, Green & Co., 1879). (Glimpses...)

Breitha, Olivia, Olivia: My Life of Exile in Kalaupapa, Arizona Memorial Museum Association, Honolulu, Hawaii, 1988.

Briggs, Vernon L., Experiences of a Medical Student in Hawaii, 1881,

_________, Around Cape Horn to Honolulu on the Bark "Amy Turner," 1880, Charles E. Lauriat Co., Boston, 1926.

Brocker, Jim, The Lands of Father Damien, James Brocker, 1998.

Buckingham, Dorothea N., My Name is Loa, Island Heritage, Aiea, Hawaii, 1999.

Bushnell, O.A., Molokai, University of Hawaii Press, Honolulu, Hawaii, 1963.

________, The Gifts of Civilization: Germs and Genocide in Hawaii, University of Hawaii Press, Honolulu, Hawaii, 1993.

Conrad, Agness C. (compiler), Hawaiian Registered Vessels 1800-1900.

Coon, Titus, Life in Hawaii, New York: Randolph & Company, 1882. (Coan, a missionary, wrote of his life in Hawaii from 1835-1881). (Glimpses...)

Crawford, David L. Hawaii's Crop Parade, Advertiser Publishing Co., Honolulu, Hawaii, 1937.

Cumming, C.F. Gordon, Fire Fountains, London: Blackwood & Sons, 1883. (Glimpses...)

Daws, Gavan, Holy Man: Father Damien of Molokai, Univ. Hawaii Press, 1973.

Daws, Gavan, Shoals of Time, A History of the Hawaiian Islands, UH Press, 1968

Dougherty, Michael, To Steal a Kingdom, Island Style Press, Waimanalo, Hawaii, 1992.

Farrow, John, Damien the Leper, Doubleday, 1937.

Gugelyk, Ted and Bloombaum, Milton, The Separating Sickness, Interviews with Exiled Leprosy Patients at Kalaupapa, Hawaii, The Separating Sickness Foundation, 1979

Hiroa, Te Rangi, Arts and Crafts of Hawaii: Games and Recreation, Bishop Museum Press, Honolulu, Hawaii, 1957.

Kawaharada, Dennis, Storied Landscapes:Hawaiian Literature & Place, Kalamaku Press, 1999

Kepler, Angela Kay, Trees of Hawaii, University of Hawaii Press, Honolulu, Hawaii, 1990.

________, Hawaiian Heritage Plants, University of Hawaii Press, 1998.

Law, Anwei V. Skinsnes and Wisniewski, Richard, Kalaupapa and the Legacy of Father Damien, Pacific Basin Enterprises, Honolulu, Hawaii, 1988.

Loomis, Albertine, Grapes of Canaan: Hawaii 1820, The True Story of Hawaii's Missionaries, Hawaiian Mission Children's Society, Honolulu, Hawaii, 1951.

Michener, James A., Hawaii, Random House, New York, 1959.

Mifflin, Thomas (compiler), Hawaiian Inter Island Vessels, published1982.

Mouritz, Arthur, M.D., The Path of the Destroyer, further publisher information not available.

Nicholson, Capt. H. Whalley, From Sword to Share: Or A Fortune in Five Years at Hawaii, London: W.H. Allen & Cko., 1889. (re: his visits to Hawaii in 1870's) (Glimpses...)

Nordhoff, Charles, Northern California, Oregon, and the Sandwich Islands, Berkeley: Ten Speed Press, 1974. (in Glimpses....)

Pukui, Mary Kawena, Olelo No'eau: Hawaiian Proverbs & Poetical Sayings, Bishop Museum Press, Honolulu, Hawaii, 1983.

Pukui, Mary Kawena and Elbert, Samuel H., Hawaiian Dictionary, University of Hawaii Press, Honolulu, Hawaii, 1957.

Root, Eileen M., Hawaiian Names, Press Pacifica, Kailua, Hawaii, 1987.

Schutz, Albert J., The Voices of Eden: A History of Hawaiian Language Studies, University of Hawaii Press, Honolulu, Hawaii, 1994.

Taylor, Clarice B., Hawaiian Almanac, Mutual Publishing, Honolulu, Hawaii, 1995.

Von Tempski, Armine, Born in Paradise, Ox Bow Press, Woodbridge, Connecticut, 1940.

W.S. Merwin, The Folding Cliffs: A Narrative of 19th-Century Hawaii, Alfred A. Knopf, New York, 1998.

Wisniewski, Richard A., The Rise and Fall of the Hawaiian Kingdom, Pacific Basin Enterprises, Honolulu, Hawaii 1979.

Articles:

Bloombaum, Milton and Gugelyk, Ted, "Voluntary Confinement Among Lepers," Journal of Health and Social Behavior, Vol. 11, No. 1, March, 1970, pp 16.20.

Bushnell, O.A., "Dr. Arning, the First Microbiologist in Hawaii," Hawaiian Journal of History, Vol. 1, 1967.

Chapin, Helen, "Newspapers of Hawaii 1834 to 1903," The Hawaiian Journal of History, Volume 18, 1984.

Frazier, Francis N., "The True Story of Kalauiko'olau, or Ko'olau the Leper," The Hawaiian Journal of History, Vol. 21, 1987, pp1-41.

Frazier, Francis N., "The 'Battle of Kalalau,' as Reported in the Newspaper *Kuokoa*," The Hawaiian Journal of History, Vol. 23, 1989.

Gugelyk, Ted, "Self-Isolated Leprosy Patients," Pacific Health, Vol. 3, 1970, pp 8-11.

Miscellaneous Documents:

"Leprosy" Report of the President of the Board of Health to the Legislative Assembly of 1886, Daily Bulletin Steam Printing Office, Honolulu, Hawaii, 1886.

Personal Letters:

Selected Letters Written to the Honolulu Board of Education between 1883 and 1885:

DD. Baldwin report dated January 29, 1883

A.L. Rafferty, dated February 3, 1883

Alex Mackintosh dated September 27, 1883

Staff of Royal School and Fort Street School dated October 1, 1883

Staff at Fort Street School dated Jan 28, 1884

Thomas P. Unea dated April 4, 1884

G. Carson Kenyon dated May 14, 1884

Staff at Fort Street School, dated June 28, 1884
Salary Schedule for Schools (approximately 1888)

Personal Interviews:

Bernard Punikai`a, Honolulu, Hawaii, February 2000. Mr. Punakai`a, a Hansen's Disease patient, was the Chairman of the Kalaupapa Patients' Council. He has addressed the United Nations promoting efforts to enhance the respect for and dignity of those with the disease.

Ted Gugelyk, Honolulu, Hawaii, February 2000. Mr. Gugelyk is author of The Separating Sickness.

Francis Chapin, Honolulu, Hawaii, February 2000. Mrs. Chapin was past-editor of the Hawaiian Journal of History and professor at the University of Hawaii.

Personal Knowledge:

The author resided on Oahu for three years. She visited the settlement on Kalaupapa, invited by the Honolulu Board of Health to conduct a joint workshop with the Social Worker to train medical staff in conflict resolution, hoping to address some of the friction between patients and medical staff.

For more information, please visit the author's web site.
www.jill-anderson.com

Made in the USA
Coppell, TX
07 May 2021

55176836R00154